The Stone Girl

Harder They Fall

Private Investigator Crime Thriller Series Book 2

Solomon Carter

Great Leap

One

Chris Geller and his boys reclined at the back of the glamorous Ice Bar, a well-known venue tucked behind London's Leicester Square. The big open-plan venue was halfway between a glitzy bar and a nightclub, the ambience infused with a chemical enhanced excitement. All around, eyes roamed the abundance of flesh on the dance floor. Flashing lights were everywhere, pulsating in time with the pounding dance music. Dan Bradley continued his slow stalk around the edge of the crowds, pleased that he still recognised a couple of the DJ's tunes. They had been sounds he used to train to at the boxing club and had even danced to now and then. But he soon realised the tunes weren't really the same as the ones he knew. They had the same singers, the same catchy floor-filling riffs, but then there were a few new added spices to make them cool for the new generation. A new baseline here or a piano synth added there. Dan frowned. He always preferred the originals, and he wasn't enjoying the lightshow either. The blinding, colour-changing lights were messing with his concentration – and his rehearsed plan of what to say to Chris Geller when he finally reached the man. Dan knew he had only a small window of opportunity and it mattered a great deal that he got a result tonight. Some awful, violent scumbag was after his old people – *his* old-time boxing tribe – which meant they were picking on *the wrong people*. In the old days, an attack against Malachy's boys would have been insane. A suicide mission, pure and simple. But what had happened to Carl Proberty showed Dan that everything had changed. Malachy's old boxers weren't so tough anymore. They were tired and flabby. They had grown apart, had no common cause, no reason to stand together. Life had taken its meandering course, and the years had pushed them apart. Which meant they were vulnerable. Ready to be picked off like flies trying to escape through a closed window. Part of it was natural, he knew that. The natural course of life was that a man had his fighting days, then settled into the belt-loosening comfort of middle age. Nothing else but the family unit mattered. Comfort. Security. The past was done with. And in normal times, that would have been fine. But Malachy's old boys hadn't been so lucky. The normal course of life had been invaded by a man with a grudge, or a serious problem, or who had lost his mind. And he was hitting them when they were weak and defenceless. But Dan wasn't ready to become a victim, and he hadn't yet surrendered to age or family. And he intended to find the scumbag who was hitting his people and bring this thing to an end. But first he needed to know who the sick bastard was, and what exactly he wanted. Why was he targeting Malachy's old boys? Even in his weakened state, Dan was up for the fight and seeking out one of Malachy's most successful fighters of recent years. Chris 'The Slick' Geller. The 'Slick' nick name came from a pun on his name – 'Slick' as in hair gel. It was a bad pun, but the man had shamelessly worn the name for ten years and more in the grand circus of the boxing ring. Geller had even taken to wearing his hair short and shiny to match his moniker. Geller was a mixed-race fighter who lived the life of a US hip-hop star, though with a London accent. Tonight, Geller looked the part – and then some. Dan stalked on, uninvited and unexpected. He didn't know how his appearance was going to go down – *but it was still going to go down*. Dan sipped from his over-priced pint of Kronenbourg, passing short-skirted girls who drank peach Bellinis while shaking their hips to the beat. He blinked and let the views pass by. In the corner, the DJ whooped and shouted from behind the decks, and Dan tried to block it all out. Only Geller mattered.

Geller was in sight, seated on a leather chesterfield at the back of the club, grinning at the ladies on the dance floor while he talked to his friends. His gang were hidden and safely obscured in the shadows, only occasionally illuminated by the flashing dance floor lightshow. Geller's jewellery blinked every time the lights hit him, and Dan counted the faces in his entourage. He counted five, plus maybe a couple of others getting drinks at the bar. Seven in total. And he guessed they probably all boxed too. As in boxed to help Geller with his training. Which meant they were fighting fit and probably hadn't had their guts shot away by a psycho and stitched back together in the last six weeks. Smiling, Dan guessed that they'd edge it in a brawl. He needed to tread carefully. As the thought crossed his mind, Geller's eyes met his. *The matador and the bull.* Dan watched the lusty smile drop from Geller's face, slow as a feather, heavy as a brick.

Dan nodded in greeting and made his advance, circling around the busy bar tables. The other eyes around Geller latched on to him within seconds. The watched him, and Dan saw their body language change. It wasn't all chillax now. It was stiff and showy, arms folding, muscles bunched. The pack were getting ready for whatever came next. Dan looked at them as he came near, sipping his beer as a gesture of the cool and collected man about town. *Still chill. You don't frighten me.* But it was all bluster. Since the night of the bullet, plenty had frightened Dan. But what frightened him most of all, beyond anything else, was the monster's slow drive-by past Eva in Devon. He had played it over and over in his head, blocking out all the what-ifs as best he could. As he reached the edge of Geller's private circle, the slow-motion image of the drive-by came back to him again, happening just like the first time. The car. Eva's eyes. The eyes of the man inside the black car fixing on his. If Dan needed any motivation to push on, he had it all right there. He breathed long and slowly to ensure he seemed calm and forced the replay out of his mind. Dan recognised only one Geller's entourage. The big guy, Terry Tubbs. Tubbs by name, Tubbs by nature. But Tubbs packed a punch too. The man had never lived up to his full potential, and a gut like his showed he was lazy. But Dan remembered the raw power in his long arms. He had seen the man knock down sparring partners like pins at a tenpin bowling alley. Fifteen years was a long time, but Terry Tubbs was still a mean looking lump of gristle and lard.

"Terry," said Dan, shouting over the music.

"Bradley," said Tubbs, with no nostalgia or friendliness anywhere in sight.

Tubbs stared at him. Dan shook it off and looked past the unknowns of the gang. He didn't care about them.

Terry Tubbs stepped closer, like a bouncer getting ready to deal with a growing problem. Dan looked both men in the eye. Tubbs was a clear foot taller than him. He peered down his flat nose at Dan.

"Message received, Terry. But you can calm down. I didn't do anything to Carl."

"No? But I heard you were there, man," said Chris Geller, calm and cool.

"What?" said Dan.

"Heard it on the grapevine. You know."

"What grapevine? Who the hell told you that?"

The eyes from the black BMW flashed into his mind. The eyes above the tinted window. The drive-by.

"Like I said, the grapevine."

"Then I think you've got some very bad grapes on that vine. The police don't know I was there. No one's called me, and I found him, Chris. I found Carl hanging from the ceiling in his bedroom. And I saw one of Malachy's old red bag gloves was there on the floor. The guy had hung him up to hit like a punchbag."

Chris Geller's eyes flicked between Dan's as he sipped his brandy. He was looking for the truth. It seemed as if he found it.

"That's bad karma, man," said Geller.

"Proberty was running scared. This killer had been targeting him for three years, pushing him to the edge, ruining his life, driving him near insane. I saw the results first hand and Carl told me the rest himself. Proberty was a broken man. And he's not the only one."

Dan sipped his beer for a moment's silence. A pause to let his words sink in.

"You're spoiling the vibe, Bradley," said Chris. "I'm here for a good time."

Dan nodded. "I get that. But I knew there was no other way you'd see me. Not in this world."

"Yeah. There is that," said Geller, in agreement. "Last time. What do you want from me? The party's calling."

"The truth, that's all I want. Have you been targeted yet?" said Dan.

"Depends. Are you the one doing the targeting?" said Geller, cool as ice.

"I told you already, Chris. I didn't top Carl. The same guy, whoever he is, shot a bullet through my guts six weeks back."

Geller looked at Dan's face afresh, then down towards his gut. Dan nodded, and pulled his T-shirt up to reveal the healing wound. It looked ugly, a raw pink line. It was healing badly.

"The way it feels, he may as well have stuck a hand blender in there too. It still hurts all the time. But I'm healing fast. And it helps me never forget what I'm going to do to this guy when I find him."

"Sorry for your trouble, Bradley," said Geller.

"I didn't come here for sympathy, Chris. Have you been hit? Has anybody targeted you in any way?" said Dan. Geller shook his head. "Then are you aware of anyone watching you, following you, or plotting against you?"

"Only you here tonight, Bradley. Only you."

Dan shook his head. "Seriously?"

"I'm the Unified Cruiserweight World Champion. Are people watching me? Yes, you bet they are. Good and bad. Are people plotting against me? Yes. My boxing rivals, Joey Suarez, Fredo Podorov, Leonard Donovan and their management teams. And yes. Then there are the freaks, the haters, the jealous ones. The psychos. The oddballs. Yes, they're out there. And that's part and parcel of being famous. But we're ready for that. For all of that."

Terry Tubbs took the hint and stepped even closer into Dan's space.

"This isn't like that, Chris. Malachy's old boxers are being targeted by someone. I don't know what it is. A grudge. A vendetta, maybe. I don't know. But he's killed Proberty already. If you aren't being targeted, then you'd best be ready. He'll get to you too."

"Like I said. You're spoiling the vibe. And I'm always ready. Have a good night, Bradley. *Elsewhere.*"

Chris Geller turned his back and walked slowly towards his chesterfield, and the wall of muscle closed in. This time, they seized Dan's arms.

"Be careful," called Geller. "Don't be mean to him. Once upon a time, we were friends."

"Nice," said Dan. "But my friendships don't have expiry dates, Chris," said Dan snatching his arms away from Tubbs and the others. They gave him hard stares and Dan gave them right back. "And I didn't come here to spoil your vibe, Slick. I came here to see if you could help. Or see if I could help you."

"And now you know that the answer to both those questions is, no," called Geller, who was now hidden from view on his chesterfield perch. "Like I told you. You best look after yourself instead. Besides, I left Malachy's stable a long, long time ago. I was aiming for the big time. Malachy was strictly local."

"Yeah. And you made it," said Dan, calling through the human barricade. "But you're not invincible, Slick. No one is. Best remember that in the ring, and outside it too. You hear anything, or you need my help, call me," said Dan.

He turned away before they laid their hands on him again, sipped his beer once, and turned back to look at Terry Tubbs.

"This isn't about him being famous, Terry. I couldn't care less about that shit."

"Whatever. Just leave now and stop making an arse of yourself."

"Nice to see you too, Terry. But remember what I said. If you hear anything, call."

"Go before we bust your stitches."

"Funny. As far as I can remember, Terry, you were strong as an ox."

"Stronger," said Terry.

"But you're as slow as a double-decker bus. I'd be back in Southend before those hands ever reached me."

"Don't tempt me."

"Peace," said Dan, making a V sign with his fingers. He set his pint down and turned away. Keen to get away from the poison of Geller's bloated ego and the flashing lights which were making his head hurt. As soon as he got outside, Dan wiped his brow and looked around. He kept looking. He took a full twenty seconds to make sure there were no Black BMWs in sight. No sharp eyes watching from the dark. And then he set off on the long walk back to Fenchurch Street, hoping Geller's insults would wash away before he got home. But as thick as Dan's skin had become, a few of the barbs had still hit home.

On the train back to Southend, Dan studied his pale image in the dark glass. He looked at his leather jacket and shrugged it back into shape.

"Geller just hasn't got any taste," he muttered with a smile. But when saw the reflection of his own dark, hollow eyes, Dan's smile dropped away.

***

Dan had asked Eva not to wait up. But he was still disappointed to see she had done as he'd asked. It was almost one in the morning when he reached the pavement outside the old shop which was their office. The big metal shutters were down over the windows and the office was pitch black inside. Upstairs, the blinds and curtains were shut tight with no sign of life.

He'd been brooding on the attitude of Chris Geller and
Terry Tubbs the whole way home. No matter how hard he'd
tried to think of other things, the mood stayed like bad food
which he couldn't quite bring himself to swallow. "Pride
comes before a fall," muttered Dan. But he knew even those
words were beneath him. He didn't wish Geller harm. He
didn't like him much either, but all he wanted was to find the
scumbag who was hitting Malachy's old boys and stop him
cold. Every move he made seemed to confirm that he would
have to do it on his own. Boxers were a selfish breed and
Chris Geller had turned into the epitome of the worst.
The London trip had been a waste of time and train fare
money. Now he'd have to think who else to try. The list of
Malachy's ex-boxers was a long one, and most of the biggest
names were already ticked. Dan wondered if the bastard was
watching him while he hunted – waiting for him to give up
until he emerged to strike again. The thought brought a nip
of cold to the skin of Dan's neck, and livened his eyes to the
street. The warm spring weather was bringing the local
crazies and late-night junkies back to life. He watched a
couple of scarecrow types shuffling along at the far end of
the street, no more than silhouettes in the darkness. Nothing
to worry about.

Then he heard a noise much closer. A cough. A sound of
feet scuffing on the concrete. Something falling and rolling
along the deck. It was a bottle – the sound was as clear as a
bell. Dan stopped breathing as the hair pricked up on the
back of his neck. He pictured the small collection of empty
wine bottles which Eva had left in the yard just outside their
back door, ready for taking to the bottle bank. A grim feeling
of certainty came over him. *Someone was in their backyard.*

Dan took his hands from his pockets, pulled his collar high about his neck then set off around the corner, past their office and into the side street. The lights upstairs stayed off. Eva hadn't heard anything. As Dan turned the corner, he looked at their tall wooden gate, which was set into the high brick wall of their backyard. The wall and gate were bathed in light from a nearby street lamp. Most of the time the gate was locked, but Dan rarely bothered to check it. Eva was the one who took care of things like that. He walked to the gate and put his hand around the metal ring handle. He paused, took a breath and yanked at the gate. The wood shunted against the frame, but it didn't give. Eva had remembered to lock it. Dan sighed in relief and let go.

It was nerves. He was on edge, that's all. The noise could have come from a nearby garden or house, or even from the next street along. Dan turned away, pulling the shutter keys from his jacket, ready to open the front door.

A fresh loud skitter of a glass bottle came from behind the gate and inside the yard wall. There was no mistaking it this time. Someone was in their backyard. Wide-eyed, Dan turned back to the gate. He noticed a dirty piece of timber sticking out from behind the wall. He passed the gate quietly, listening to the rapid breathing and muttered swear words on the other side. Dan reached the corner and picked up the piece of timber and turned it over in his hands. He leaned the wood quietly against the wall and traced a hand over the surface. Sand and mud were ingrained in the wood and had dried on... *there. He found it.* A faint trace of a shoe print. The bastard had used some street junk to help scale their wall. Dan took out his phone and dialled Eva's mobile number. He let the call ring four times, then he cut the call dead before Eva answered and punched out a quick text.

"WAKE UP BUT STAY INSIDE. STRANGER IN BACKYARD. I'LL DEAL WITH IT."

A new light hit the street out on the main road at the front as Eva switched on the light. But there was still no telling if she would do as she was asked. These days it seemed she was as worried about him as he was about her. Dan pressed a testing boot down on the wood and pushed down hard. The wood chafed against the brick and mortar before it bit in. Dan put his weight on the wood, leapt up, and grabbed the top of the wall. The wood held, but now he was exposed by his noise. He pulled himself up with an effort and gritted his teeth. His shoulder strength had slackened since his injury. He had only been back at the gym the last few weeks, and every weight he lifted, every mile he jogged, seemed ten times harder than before. He thought of Eva and he pulled hard. His arms burned, his shoulders complained, and his stomach seared with pain. But he didn't give in. Dan pulled his body up and swung his leg over the top of the wall then dropped down into the yard with a bounce which sent a shock of pain through his shins and jarred his teeth.

He faced the figure hunched by the back door. He'd caught the man staring into the darkness of their back kitchen. The huddled figure froze, like a creature hoping it hasn't been seen. It wasn't the monster. It wasn't the man who'd killed Proberty, Dan was sure about that. That man had the physical stature of a warrior and the head of a brute. This figure was slim and slight. But it didn't mean he wasn't dangerous. And it didn't mean they weren't working together. The sound of Dan's landing had the man turning around, but Dan denied him any time to acclimatise. Any chance to right himself. Dan stormed towards him, his face all fury and gritted teeth, all his pent-up anger and bitterness ready to explode in the stranger's direction. Dan seized the man's jacket and a hideously floral cologne filled his nostrils. A pricey cologne, no mistake, but an ugly one too. Dan pulled the man away from his door and lifted him up in the dark.

"Who are you?!" Dan shouted into the man's face. "What do you want here? Tell me and tell me now!"

Dan had clenched a fist and was ready to drill it deep into the man's gut, when a new light came on directly above them. He saw the frightened look in the man's glassy eyes, then froze as his stomach lurched. He recognised those eyes, but they were badly out of place and time. Disconcerted, confused, Dan dropped the man against the back wall.

"Dan!" said the rasping voice. "Thank God that it's you! I thought some local ruffian had broken in and was about to take advantage of me. God knows this place is even worse than last time I came here. Do you have any idea of how rough Southend looks after where I've been…?"

Damn it. The rasping voice… the amateur dramatics… it shouldn't have been, but it was… the light from the back kitchen flicked on, and Eva appeared behind the glass, looking tired but very much alert, her bed-hair hanging wild about her head. She had dressed hastily in yesterday's blouse and skirt; the buttons were fastened out of place.

"Eva. I told you I would deal with it!" said Dan.

Eva unbolted the door and swung it open. "And when did I ever agree to taking your orders?" she said. They both looked down at the figure huddled against their wall.

Exposed in the light spilling from the back door was a man in a fine-cut tan suit, and a pale orange shirt. But the smart clothes could do nothing for his wrinkled face. The face of old Jonathan Parker was almost as tan as his clothes, and his steely hair was slicked back with shiny oil. But the lines on his forehead and face were as deeply entrenched as ever. He looked up at them both with a half-smile, and appeal in his watery eyes.

"It's so good to see you both."

"Jonathan…?" said Eva, looking up at Dan.

"Parker," said Dan, in confirmation and disgust. It was Jonathan Parker – JP – the brother of Devon Parker, the man who'd led them both into the investigations business before the decline and fall of his later years. JP, the man who had already led them through merry hell the last time they saw him. But back then JP had walked away into the sunset as a happy old man, much richer and about to embark on his new adventure.

"That's the name, don't wear it out, as they say," he said, aiming for jollity to soften the welcome. "Now are you going to help me up, or do you want to keep me at your feet like this. It doesn't feel very dignified, I can assure you."

Dan tutted, shook his head and pulled the man up to his feet. "I don't recall dignity being at the top of your wish list," said Dan.

Parker winced, but Dan wasn't going to feel sorry for him. "What the hell are you doing here, in my backyard. I almost beat seven shades out of you. I thought you were… someone else…" said Dan, not wanting to go into detail.

"Yes, you did seem a little alarmed there… what brought all that on? And… Dan? Are you well? I think you look a bit off colour if you don't mind me saying?"

"Mind you saying? JP! It's one in the morning, it's a week night and you've just broken into my backyard. Now you're offering me a critique on my appearance? Why would I mind any of that?"

"Bit testy tonight, isn't he?" said Parker, eyeing Eva.

Eva's eyebrows dropped low over her eyes. She folded her arms.

"What are you doing here, Jonathan?"

"Well don't roll out the red carpet, or anything, will you? I just came to see you, that's all. But I ended up here a bit earlier than expected, so I thought I'd wait out here, in your backyard. I really didn't plan to disturb you until morning."

"You were going to stay out here, all night?" said Dan, with the doubt plain in his voice. Jonathan nodded. "Yes. As you say, dignity and all that. I still know how to rough it, if I have to."

Dan recalled the pitiful South London hovel he'd once found Jonathan Parker barely surviving in. Yes, JP had been through the mill. But his clothes said times were still good. "You're crazy," said Dan. "And if you're here it means that you're after something."

"Um… this doesn't seem a good time, does it?" said JP, scratching his bony chin. "Maybe I shouldn't have come."

"Yeah. Maybe you shouldn't," said Dan.

"Dan!" said Eva. Dan looked at her and found her eyes imploring him to be kind.

Parker twisted his shirt collar and picked up a trilby from the floor. It was the same colour as his tan suit. The old man ignored Dan's enquiring look and nodded at the collection of green bottles knocked over by his feet.

"And I see you haven't lost your liking for a spot of white wine, Eva…" said the old man, with a wry smile. Eva's eyes hardened once more. The old man had hit a tender target. Eva's seriousness and focus were part of her make-up. Her fondness for white wine had been the counterbalance and a relaxation. She liked it too much, she knew that. They all did. But Dan had all but given up pushing her on it. Eva stiffened.

"What is it that you want, Jonathan?" said Eva. She softened her tone, surprised at her own voice. "Come on. It's late."

"I see. If you must be so brusque, then I'll admit it. I do need your help for something. And don't look so glum and defensive. At least this time I can pay you for your help."

Dan remained sceptical. "Seriously? That's why you broke in? You want to hire us? What for?"

Parker shrugged his bony shoulders and looked away.

"It's a personal matter. If you don't mind, I'll tell you all about it in the morning. I'm very tired. It's been something of a long day," said Parker with a theatrical yawn. He stepped past Eva into their back kitchen.

"And it looks like it's just gotten even longer," muttered Dan.

"Now where can I sleep?" said Parker.

"I thought you were happy out in the yard?" said Dan.

The old man turned and looked over his shoulder.

"You could always try Quality Lodge in town. But seeing as you're so flush, why would you settle for that?"

"Why indeed?" said Parker. "When I've got such good friends in you? I mean, I know you're feeling grumpy, but you are practically family."

"Parker…" said Dan in a loud groan. Dan was about to launch into a rebuke, when a window creaked open in the street behind them. A large old man leaned his head out of the upstairs window of one of the neighbouring terraced houses and peered down at them in the yard below.

"Will you all just shut up?! It's the middle of the bloody night, in case you didn't know!"

Dan glared at the man, but Eva responded just in time to prevent another flare up.

"Yes, of course. You're quite right. It's very late. Don't worry. You won't hear another peep out of any of us."

"I should hope so too," said the old man, tutting, before he withdrew and clunked his window shut.

"Jonathan, you can sleep in the upstairs front room," said Eva walking back into the office.

"*Eva!*" said Dan.

"No arguments. He sleeps on the sofa. We can sort out all the rest in the morning." Passing close by his face, Eva paused to look JP in the eye.

"But there are two rules," she said.

"Rules, eh?" said Jonathan.

"Yes, that's right. Two of them. No more clever observational comments or insights," said Eva. "And no thieving."

"I'm shocked. I'm aggrieved," said Parker.

"And please do be quiet," said Eva. She yawned and headed for the door up to their apartment.

"That was three rules by the way."

Eva arched an eyebrow. She stomped away up the stairs and left them to it. Dan and Jonathan stared at one another in silence before Dan finally said. "Go on then. You win. Up you go into the front room. Like she said, we'll talk in the morning."

"Um. Yes. To the sofa, eh?" said Parker. "Don't we get a little nightcap around here beforehand?"

"Nightcap? No, we don't. Now come on," Dan opened the door and steered the old man up the stairs before he locked the doors and turned out the lights. For the first time in a long time, Dan forgot all about the man in the black BMW as Parker filled his mind with a new kind of tension. But then came Dan's dreams. And those dreams weren't kind at all.

Two

With the living room out of bounds, due to their very unwelcome guest, when the morning came Dan didn't waste much time upstairs in the apartment. He took his slice of toast and mug of coffee downstairs to the office and pitched up behind his desk. When he was two bites of buttery goodness into his breakfast, the door creaked open behind him, and Dan scrunched up his eyes and stopped chewing. He looked back and found Eva standing in the doorway of the stairs to the upstairs apartment. Her red hair was damp and darkened from the shower, but she already looked jaded.

"I guess you couldn't take it either," said Dan.

"Why doesn't that man ever learn? And where did he buy that aftershave? It smells like a Victorian toilet cleaner."

Dan smiled. "Yeah. And it probably cost him a bomb. Just like that suit he's wearing. It's so bad it must have cost a fortune."

"And his snoring," said Eva, stepping into the office. "I didn't know it was possible for a man to make such a racket. He kept me awake the rest of the night. What is he doing here, Dan?" She turned away into the kitchenette before getting her answer. Her need for coffee was far more pressing.

"I don't know any more than you do. But he says he wants to hire us. So, I guess that must be a good thing. We're not exactly snowed under with paying work right now."

"No. But I prefer cases that really exist and pay on time," said Eva.

"Clients that pay on time? Those are pretty rare, Eva."

"Rare but not extinct," called Eva. "The Croyde Crew money is already in the bank. I checked. Letitia was good as her word."

"But she's a celeb. She has a reputation to think of, especially now with her whole project in the balance. What does Jonathan have? Apart from very bad taste?"

"We'll find out, I suppose. But last night was the last time he ever stays here. He can afford a hotel, so he can stay in one."

"It's not me you need to preach to. I was all ready to kick him onto the street last night, until you felt sorry for him. It's part of his act."

"Yes, and now you want us to take on his imaginary case., said Eva.

"I'm interested, Eva. He came here for a reason. And he has money, and he owes us. If we must put up with him, we might as well earn some money out of it."

"Yes. You've got a point there," said Eva, with a sigh. She ducked back into the kitchen to attend to the coffee machine. "And you haven't yet told me about your little mission to London. What happened at Leicester Square? You went to meet Chris The Slick. How did it go?"

"Not good. It was like I'd walked into a 'who's got the biggest dick?' contest. Not my scene at all. Chris Geller had a squad of boxer boys around him like his very own gangster mob. But it's all fake. Those meatheads are just in it for the glory."

"But that's a world boxing champion for you," said Eva.

"I've seen him interviewed on TV. I could have told you his ego was bigger than Mount Kilimanjaro before you went. So, didn't he talk to you about Malachy? Or about the others being targeted?"

"He only wanted to pretend I was his enemy, or that I was some fanboy coming to worship him. As if! On another night with no gunshot issues, I would have liked to have tested him out. It was a bad time, Eva. He tried to make me feel small."

"And from the sound of it, he succeeded."

"No. He made me angry, that's all. I wanted to see if he could help prevent any more guys getting hit. I want to nail this scum. And I would have helped Geller too, if he'd been hit. No matter how much money or how many belts he has, none of it matters to me. But Chris Geller thinks he's invincible. I did learn one thing, though. He let slip that he knew I'd found Carl Proberty dead in his house. I think he knew I'd been there. Which was almost like insider information. *You know* I was there and *I know* I was there. But the police don't. If they heard or had found prints I would have been hauled in by now."

"Then you must have done a reasonable clean up job on your way out…" said Eva, hoping.

"No. I was lucky. So, what does that tell you?"

"That your Mr Punchinello shooter has links to Geller…?" said Eva, straining to guess.

"Sounds that way. But I don't think Geller understands that. He was too busy sipping his Courvoisier and talking crap to bother with engaging his brain."

Eva nodded in thought. The floorboards thudded and creaked above them. Eva looked up at the ceiling before she looked at Dan.

"Coffee," she said sharply, before retreating into the kitchen.

"I'll take another one too…" said Dan.

Dan looked at the office clock from the corner of his eye. It was ten to eight. Soon, the kid would be in to start work, then before he knew it, JP would get in his face and spoil his day. Dan decided to treat himself to a spot of online news before the day did its worst. He clicked open the UK news site and scanned the headlines. The Croyde Crew case had been stage-managed well so far. The news about the chemical agent had been announced, and the government had changed its tone from the clumsy war-drumming of the Salisbury mess. But there were still some loose cannon egos from Westminster chipping off about the Ruskies, blaming them for every crime in sight. Dan was no fan of the Russian government, that was for sure, but if these jerks didn't stop sabre rattling, there were going to be all kinds of problems. Before Dan could scan the rest of the article, his phone buzzed in his jeans pocket. Dan groaned, fearing it was Jonathan calling him from upstairs about how to work the television. Then he saw the unknown caller ID on screen and thought again.

"Dan Bradley," he said, putting the phone to his ear, his early morning voice croaky and dry.

"Dan Bradley?" said the caller.

"Yes," he said. It was a woman's voice and she sounded nervous. "Can I help you at all?"

"Yes… I hope so. I think so. Do you remember Greg Saunders?"

Dan blinked. His mind composed an image of a young man with a broken nose dancing like a kid on Christmas day. In his memory, Greg Saunders had just won the East of England Light Featherweight ABA title. That night was almost twenty years ago. But it still felt like last week.

"Of course, I remember Greggy boy," said Dan. "Wait a minute… is that Alison?"

Before she replied, Dan already knew the answer. Alison had been Greg Saunders' girlfriend. And by now she was surely his wife. But then Dan's face dropped in sudden understanding. He stiffened and sat up in his office chair, his smile gone.

"Alison?" he said. "Has anything happened?"

"It's difficult, Dan. Greg really wouldn't want me to say anything. But I must. Greg's been in a spot of debt with some people for a while now. It was my fault. I was stupid. I got us into a bit of trouble with the pawn brokers and the catalogues… and a few other things. Old habits and all that. Back in the old days my little habits didn't matter, Dan."

"Greg never said anything about it," said Dan, flatly.

"No. He was good like that. It was my problem and he looked after it. Greg was earning from the fights, and then there was the door work… and his money stayed steady. But I got carried away."

The woman was now talking so fast Dan could hardly keep up. Her voice trembled and tremored as she spoke. He supposed it was the confessional aspect of her call. But he knew there was something else.

"Alison… honestly, it's okay. Just tell me what happened?"

"The debt people paid us a visit yesterday. Or at least I thought it was them. I made Greg answer the door because I was scared of them. I always have been. And the debt collectors always get a bit intimidated when they see someone of Greg's stature opening the door. It sometimes buys us a little extra time. But then I heard him arguing at the door, and so I guessed they'd had enough. I hid upstairs. Then I heard a loud shout. I waited a second or two, then I ran downstairs and found Greg lying inside the hallway with our youngest crying next to him. It was awful, Dan. I thought he was dead… and it was my fault." The woman sobbed.

Dan grimaced.

"Where is he now, Alison?"

"He's in Basildon hospital. He's unconscious. They're keeping him sedated to make sure there's no swelling on the brain, but I'm terrified, Dan. I keep thinking it's my fault. I saddled us with all that debt, and now this happened. I pushed everything too far. It feels like karma."

Dan narrowed his eyes.

"Alison… who told you to call me?"

"Ed Malachy of course. Greg's been in touch with the old man ever since he was a boy. I called Ed about it, a shoulder to cry on and all that, and Ed told me you'd want to know straight away."

Dan nodded, and a thin smile crept across his face. Malachy had said he didn't want Dan stirring the pot and getting hurt, but Malachy knew him better than that. The old man must have known Dan would never quit the pursuit. That's why he'd got Alison to call.

"Did you see the guy who attacked Greg?" said Dan.

"No. I was hiding upstairs while Greg dealt with it. Like a true coward."

"Did you see anything at all?"

"No. I'm sorry."

"Don't be sorry, Alison. And Greg... what's the prognosis?"

"He'll live. But we don't know how he'll be when he comes out of it. The doctors won't give me any comfort at all."

Dan gritted his teeth. Yet another senseless attack on one of Malachy's old boys, and another dead end without a hint of a clue. Without a witness there was almost nothing he could do.

"...until when they wake him up."

A spark of hope lit Dan's eyes. "When are they going to wake him?"

"Not long now. This afternoon, so they tell me. I'm so nervous, Dan, I'm shaking."

"I need to be there, Alison. If he can talk I need to hear what he saw. Do you mind if I come along.? I know it's asking a lot, but..."

"No, I don't mind at all. From what Ed Malachy told me about what you're doing, I think Greg would want you to be there."

"Thank you, Alison. What time should I come?" said Dan.

"One o'clock, that's what they said. I can't wait to see him myself... thank you, Dan. Whoever did this... I don't know how they can live with themselves."

"Neither do I," said Dan. "And Alison – I don't think this is anything to do with your debts. This is something else altogether."

"What do you mean?" said Alison.

"I'll see you at one, okay. Be strong, Alison."

A fresh mug of coffee landed on Dan's desk right beside the first. Steam curled up from the dark shining surface with the promise of a much-needed energy boost.

Eva looked at Dan, her worries for him etched on her pretty face. She leaned a hip against his desk.

"It's happened again, hasn't it?"

Dan nodded. "I'm beginning to lose count. This time they hit Greg Saunders."

"Greg who?"

"Exactly. Nice guy, Greg. Safe hands, Greg. Greg who was too nice to box. He was so nice he used to apologise after hitting you in the face. He pulled his punches. There was no way he was going to make it in the big wide world, but he managed to get through a few professional fights before he quit the game. Why the hell would anyone want to hurt Greg? From what I just heard the last fifteen years haven't exactly been easy on the guy. He had nothing worth taking."

"Then what was his story?" said Eva.

"His wife got him into debt and it sounds like Greg had been drifting for a long while too. Not much money around the house, from what I gather. And then this scumbag hits him and hurts him bad."

"How bad?" said Eva.

"Hospitalised bad. He's unconscious at Basildon Hospital. They're going to wake him this afternoon."

"But can you even be sure it's the same guy that hit him? It could be someone he owes money to?"

Dan shook his head. "Debt collection agencies don't work like that. Not real ones anyway. And the sharks wouldn't do that. They'd break a bone or inflict pain. But Greg was knocked unconscious on his doorstep. His wife found him lying in the hall with their kid crying over his body."

"That's cold…"

Dan blew out a long breath. "This guy is a psycho, Eva. But I think something is changing."

"What?" said Eva.

"He's beginning to show his face. He knocked Greg Saunders out cold afterwards, granted. But he still showed his face. So, if Greg can remember him – and better still, if Greg knows him – maybe I can finally fix this thing and get on with my life."

Eva considered Dan's words. He was making it sound too easy. But she decided to hold back on giving him a warning. Dan knew all too well what he was up against. He had a bullet scar on his gut to remind him.

They both heard the slow footsteps coming down the stairs from their apartment and tensed as the door opened to reveal JP fully suited and booted and still clutching his trilby in his hands. He looked like a nineteen-forties gangster in a garish zoot suit. His tanned, wrinkled face would have dated him a similar vintage. Parker hadn't aged well. His wrinkles read like a map of the life choices he'd made. Parker paused in the doorway as he met their accusing eyes. The old man cleared his throat.

"Ah. Coffee. That'd be a good start…" he said. "And what passes for breakfast around here?"

"There's a café on the corner down the street. They do all kinds of food," said Eva.

"Do they now?" said Jonathan. "And is this how you treat all your clients?"

"Most of our clients don't ask if bed and breakfast is included," said Dan, reclining and folding his arms behind his head. "So, come on. Out with it. What is the deal here, Jonathan?"

"Can I have a coffee first?" said Parker.

"No," said Dan. "First, you speak. I want to hear it then I have some other business to attend to. Urgent matters. So, come on. Out with it.

"Does it really have to be like this?" said Parker. "I'm an old friend, after all."

"Jonathan," said Eva. "If you want us to work for you, we need to know."

"Very well. But you'll see, it's rather sensitive."

"It always is. Especially with you."

Parker stuck a finger behind his shirt collar and tugged at it. Dan and Eva waited.

"It's about a woman."

Eva rolled her eyes. Dan sighed out loud. "Here we go."

"A rather young woman at that."

"Uh oh," said Dan. "What is it? Let me guess. She's taken Sugar Daddy to the cleaners?"

"Nope. I'm no fool, Dan. I avoided that kind of scenario a little while back. By the skin of my teeth as well, mind you. No. This girl is very special. And she's as sharp as they come."

"I'll bet," said Dan.

"Happy now?" said Parker.

"Ecstatic," said Dan. "But you still haven't told us anything worth hearing."

"But I've started the ball rolling. Now I need that coffee before I tell you anything else."

"What's happened with this young woman, Jonathan?" said Eva.

"Coffee," said Jonathan wandering towards the kitchen with a finger raised in the air.

"Jonathan, we need to know much more than that," said Eva.

"I'm not sure I can stomach anymore," said Dan.

"Oh, I'll tell you much more. And if I'm hiring you, I'm going to need you to meet her."

"What? But isn't she the purpose of the case?"

"She is indeed. But she's not the target, if that's what you mean. No. But she is something special. You'll have to meet her to see that," Parker smiled. "I'll tell you everything you need to know when you meet her. I can't wait to see what you think."

"Neither can I," said Dan, with an air of cynicism.

Eva hid the look on her face behind her big coffee mug. It was somewhere on the crossroads between disgust, disapproval, and mild bemusement.

***

Dan found that Basildon Hospital had been improved since the bad old days. The austere concrete edifice of the new town's hospital was much the same as he remembered. But inside, it reminded Dan much more of the clean London behemoths Dan had visited across the last few years. Not only did it smell clean, but it looked clean too. Even so, these were small comforts and did nothing to dispel his anxiety at the thought of seeing another fallen comrade. He followed the signs for the ITU and eventually came upon a large, pale blue ward, full of nurses buzzing around between different beds like worker bees. The ambience smelt of disinfectant, chemical wipes, and somewhere beneath it all was a faint whiff of faeces. Dan did his best to ignore the odours and looked around for a woman he would recognise as Alison Saunders. He didn't see anyone and paused awkwardly in the centre of the ward. A nurse eyed him with suspicion and started to approach. Just then a large woman waved a heavy arm at him from the back of the ward.

"Alison?" said Dan, with a hint of shock.

"Yes," she called. "Dan. Greg's over here. Come quick. I think his sedation is wearing off…"

Dan paced the distance of the ward, leaving the suspicious nurse in his wake and without a victim to berate. Dan took a close-up look at the large woman. Yes. Alison Saunders face was in there somewhere. She had the same bright blue eyes, the same cherubic lips, even the same tightly curled dark hair. But most of the original details were almost buried by the weight the dear woman had put on. Alison reached for him and hugged him to her. Dan hugged her back and only let go when she did. He felt her hungry need for comfort. In her situation, her husband inert in a hospital bed, providing a hug was the least he could do.

"Look at him, Dan. He's moving!" she said, with almost childish glee. "He's going to wake up."

Alison wiped her eyes and sniffed, keeping an arm around Dan as they looked at the figure in the bed. A nurse attended to Greg Saunders' stirring body, taking measurements and checking the tubes going into the big man's body.

"Come on, Greg," said the nurse, gently. "Your loved ones are here waiting for you."

Dan watched the big man's head turn left and right on the pillow. He lifted an arm and seemed to notice the wires attached to him. He waved them away, but the hinderance of the cables wouldn't leave him. The nurse steadied him.

"You're in hospital, Greg. You're going to be okay. But there are some important tubes attached to you to monitor your health. Please be careful or they'll come out."

Dan knew the message was for him and Alison as much as Greg, and the nurse gave them a look to say as much.

"I'll leave you for a minute."

"Thank you," said Alison, and the nurse left them alone.

Greg stirred again. This time he smacked his dry lips and his eyes flicked open.

He blinked at them with pin-prick eyes, lifted his arms, looked at the cables and tubes sticking out of him, then gazed left to the computer monitor above his head.

"What… happened…?" his voice was a croaky whisper.

"It's okay," said Alison. She left Dan and stretched a hand to touch her husband's face. "You're going to be okay."

"Alison," he said, and smiled. But his smile was short-lived. Dan watched his eyes begin to darken, the confusion replaced by something worse. "He hit me… the bastard hit me when I wasn't ready… he wouldn't go away, then he hit me."

"Greg," said Dan.

The man turned his head and saw Dan for the first time. Immediately, Greg tried to shift up in the bed, but failed.

"Steady, big man," said Dan. "Yeah, it's me."

"But… why? Why are you… here?"

"Because of what happened to you."

Greg struggled and frowned. This time he managed to sit up and look at Dan. He squeezed his wife's hand then waved away her attention.

"It's been a long time, Danny boy," said Greg. The big man looked down at the needles invading the backs of his hands. Dan sensed a flood of emotion behind his silence.

"Hey. Whatever happened here," said Dan. "It's not the end of the line. No matter what he said to you – or what he did – it's not the end. I promise."

"Due respect and everything, Dan… but what do you know? And what can you do about it?"

Dan's eyes narrowed, and he shook his head, not understanding.

"Greg, I'm here for you man. Don't turn on the people who want the best for you."

"I appreciate that, but you couldn't stop what happened to Carl, could you?"

"What?"

"Carl Proberty. I know you were there, Dan."

Dan blinked. His gut turned hard and cold. Greg knew he had been there, just like Geller knew he was there. But Greg's croaky voice ended his doubts.

"He told me, Dan. That's how I know. Before he smashed me on the head with the butt of that pistol, he told me about you. He told me you tried to stop him, but you couldn't. He said the only thing you managed to accomplish was to make everything worse."

Dan grimaced. "Greg. What are you even talking about? Some guy you've never see before comes around and what? Points a gun at you and so you start believing everything he says?"

Greg shook his head. His eyes were lazy and sleepy, but his voice was gaining strength with every word.

"Dan, I like you. I've always had time for you, you know that. But you're wrong on this. This wasn't the first time I saw this guy."

"Greg?!" said Alison. The man made a half-flail with his big arms and shook his head.

Dan stared at the man and waited for his response.

"He came to see me before. But last time I was at work."

"Work where?"

"Trailblazers Bar, Romford. I was working back then. But this guy got me fired. He threatened me. He threatened my family. Then he walked into the club and laughed at me. I totally lost it. I followed him inside and beat the living crap out of him. And after all those hellish insults he didn't even try to fight me. He just laughed at me while I hit him. After that, the bar kicked me out and the security agency suspended my licence…"

"You didn't tell me anything about that!" said Alison.

"Alison… we needed that job. What was I going to tell you? I beat up some arsehole for threatening you? You'd have told me to grow up."

Alison shrugged while the tears fell down her cheeks.

"When the guy showed up at my door I was surprised more than anything else. Yeah, he freaked me out. He took a beating without lifting a hand, and he took it easily. When he came to the house, I knew it was trouble, but I wasn't ready for what happened. He pulled the gun on me in five seconds flat. What could I do? I asked him to go. I begged him to go. But he wasn't interested in listening to me."

"What did he say, Greg?" said Dan, his face hard, eyes narrow.

"He told me all about Proberty. He told me how he had Carl snared like a rabbit. He told me how he turned Carl to dust. That's how he described it. Turned him to dust. And he said he was going to do the same to me."

"Greg," said Dan. "That's just words, man. This freak is all about intimidation. It's psychology, that's his trick. And when I see this man, I'm going to beat him. I'll bet this guy is no more than an old washed-up boxer with a grudge against Malachy. He's warped, that's all. But he's still human."

The numbers on the monitor beside Greg Saunders started to climb as the big man shook his head. The beep of his heartrate started to increase.

"You don't know, Dan. You don't know a thing…"

"Don't know what?"

"He's sick, yeah. But he means what he says. He broke Carl Proberty, didn't he? He broke him good. He made a champion into living dust."

"Those are his words. That's what he told you," said Dan.

"Dan – cut the crap now, okay? He showed me the photographs to prove it."

Dan shook his head as the coldness spread from his gut, blooming up into his chest, reaching for his throat too.

"Photographs?"

"He showed me Carl's body hung from the fricking ceiling. Dan, he showed me those things on the doorstep of my house. And he said that happened to Carl Proberty because you got in his way."

Dan's brow dropped low over his eyes. "You can't believe that, Greg. The guy's using you to mess with my head."

"Or maybe you are messing with mine. You mean well, Dan, but you don't know. And whatever you think you can do against this guy, I'm telling you, it won't work."

"What are you saying?"

"He showed me photographs of you entering that house. Proberty's house. He showed me photographs of you talking to Proberty in some seaside bar."

Dan's eyes flicked away. He turned cold inside at the thought of being watched the whole time he was with Carl Proberty. Why hadn't he noticed? Where the hell had he been hiding?

"He told me it was because of you that Carl had to die. I'm sorry, Dan. But that's what the guy said."

Dan bared his teeth and turned away.

"You can't believe that. I went down there to find Carl Proberty. I went there to see if I could find this monster, so I can stop him hurting people like Carl, like you, like me. And you believe what he tells you..."

"I know what I saw in those photographs, Dan. I'm sorry. And I know what I'm seeing in you right now."

"Keep it down!" called one of the nurses from the top of the ward. She moved towards them raising her hands for them to stop. But Greg Saunders ignored her. Her eyes flicked to the numbers on the black screen beside his bed.

"What do you think you see in me?" said Dan, quietly.

"This guy said he hurt you, Dan. You can't stop him. You think you can, but you're kidding yourself."

"He told you that. His words. Who do you trust, Greg? Him? Or me?"

Greg blinked at Dan. "He said he shot you in the guts because he knew you'd be trouble from the start. And he wanted to put the brakes on you, so he could do some things... before he came back to finish you off."

The cold hit him again, and Dan's mind froze. He remembered the eyes in the darkness. The flash of the gun.

"What the hell do you know, Greg?" snapped Dan.

"I saw those photographs, and I see the look on your face. You're hurting, Dan. I can tell."

"So, what is it? Now you want me to give up? And abandon you too? Abandon everyone else to fend for themselves against this evil piece of crap?"

"Dan. You're hardly better off than me. Admit it. He hurt you badly and he knows it. This son of a bitch is cruel, desperately cruel. He'll exploit your weakness. And then he'll hurt you as hard as he can."

Dan wanted to refuse Greg's words. He wanted to deny them access to his brain. But from a soft man like Greg, he couldn't help it – they went in all the way. Dan shook his head. They had been swallowed. But he hoped, not yet assimilated.

"That man has gotten to you, Greg. But don't worry, you're wrong. I'll deal with him. I know I can."

"Don't. If you do, he'll hurt me first," said Greg, his eyes dark and forlorn. "That's the point. That's what he said."

Dan growled with barely suppressed rage.

"I told you. I won't let that happen."

"But you can't stop him either. Don't try to be the hero on this one. Please. I don't want to end up like Carl Proberty just because you can't help yourself."

The words struck like a long sharp pin through his confidence. But the rage remained.

"I can't believe this," said Dan.

"Believe it…"

"Why is he doing this? Did he tell you that?" said Dan.

"Because he doesn't like us. Any of us."

"But why us? Why Malachy's boys?"

"The man pointed a gun at my head, Dan. He's a psycho. I wasn't in the mood to ask."

"Excuse me," said a female voice over Dan's shoulder. He turned and found the original hard-faced nurse close by.

"You're going to have to leave," said the nurse, in a forceful tone. She gave Dan a hard stare and looked for help from her colleagues at the distant end of the ward.

"Don't worry. I'm going. But before I do, Greg, one last thing. Tell me. And be honest with me. Did you know this man? Tell me."

Greg shook his head. The numbers on the monitor behind him stayed high.

"I never saw him before that night in Trailblazers. And after what he did to me at my house... I pray I never see him again."

Alison moved close to Greg's bed and seized his hand and squeezed his fingers. Dan's throat ached with a host of bitter emotions.

"He's killing our people, Greg. We can stop it."

"If you stop pushing this he might leave us alone."

"No. Come on! That's not how this ends," said Dan.

"It could be. If you let it."

"Is the man a fighter? Did you recognise him?"

"Dan," said Alison. "I thought this would be good for Greg, but it's not." Her eyes turned to the monitors behind the bed. "You'll have to go. Please."

Dan nodded and turned to leave. But he looked Greg in the eye one last time.

"Greg?"

"Okay. I heard you. I didn't recognise the man at all, but he's definitely a fighter. He's got a face that looks like it's taken shots in every gym, pub, and back alley from here to John O'Groats."

Dan nodded. It was a glimmer of light in a pit of darkness, nothing more. And the darkness was all around him. Bitter and cold.

"Thank you, Greg. I'm sorry."

"Don't be sorry. Just leave this alone."

Dan turned his back. "I can't do that," he muttered.

"Dan!" called Greg.

Dan turned back. "He killed Carl Proberty. He shot me in the stomach. He threatened your family, Greg. This thing is getting worse, not better. I can't leave it. I've got to find him and stop him before he hurts anyone else."

"And how much do you think you are helping so far, eh?" said Greg.

But Dan blinked his eyes shut as he walked away. Greg Saunders had a point. The monster had a point. The man was hurting people he knew. Killing them. And somehow, he had tied to it Dan, because the scum knew Dan was the only one who would come after him.

He thought about the threat – if he didn't stop, Greg Saunders would suffer the same fate as Proberty. Dan looked back once more as the nurses escorted him to the door. He hoped his eyes conveyed the apology he didn't want to repeat. It was an apology to the dead, for how he had failed them. And it was an apology to the living, for what he was about to do. There was no way he could give up. Not even if it cost him his life.

The scumbag had to be stopped.

Dan knew the man was a fighter.

He looked ugly and mean.

And he was as cruel as hell.

And that was the limit of all he had.

It was nothing.

But he had to make it count.

Right now, the last thing Dan needed in his life was Jonathan Parker. It turned out life had a wicked sense of humour. But these days Dan didn't find much of it funny.

Three

"This girl of yours lives around here?" said Dan, looking at Parker hunched in the back seat. Eva reversed her red Alfa Romeo into a tight space on the edge of the Leigh Broadway. A place where free parking spaces were as hard to come by as a pint of beer for less than a fiver. Coffee wasn't much cheaper either. But at least you had the theoretical comfort of having bought it in Leigh. Yes, a Leigh Broadway address was a luxury label.

"She lives here currently," said Parker.

"Currently?" said Eva, as she applied the handbrake and switched off the engine.

"Yes. She's a rolling stone type. And she seems very happy with that kind of life. I think it suits her."

"Well, I'm glad you're happy and doing so well. But I'm no clearer as to why you want to hire us," said Dan.

"Don't worry, all will soon be revealed."

"Good. Because I'm getting sick and tired of all the suspense…" said Dan.

Parker got out of the back seat with something of a bounce in his step. Dan sighed and slowly opened his door.

"You okay?" said Eva.

"Nope. But once I track down the psycho who's stalking Malachy's boys and snap him in half, I'll be right as rain again."

With Jonathan out of the car, Eva reached out and squeezed Dan's arm. "I want to help you."

"I know. And by being there you're helping. But I can't risk you on this one. I mean it. This guy, whoever he is, he's too dangerous. He might go for you first just to hurt me."

"But he might try that anyway. He wouldn't exactly be the first, would he? I can defend myself, Dan."

Dan nodded. "Yeah. You're probably right."

"I know I'm right."

"That's the trouble, Eva. This guy gets into your head first. And once he's in, he smashes you up inside. He got to Carl Proberty, and he got to Greg too."

"Then don't let him get to you."

"I'm trying, I promise you that."

"Hurry up, will you!" called Parker from outside the car.

"Do you want this case or not?"

"And Parker's already messing with my head. He does it every time," said Dan.

"You're only human," said Eva. They got out of the car onto the busy Broadway with its designer shops and flashy brands. Parker rubbed his hands with nervous excitement.

"Stop it," said Dan.

"Why?" said Parker.

"Your enthusiasm is disturbing. You're starting to freak me out," said Dan.

"Danny boy, it seems these days that you're the one who needs to lighten up."

Trouble was Dan couldn't argue with that at all.

***

The apartment was high above Broadway, directly above the garish menswear boutique called Strontium. Dan had blinked at the prices as he passed the window, with its stripe-shirted mannequins adorned with neon paisley ties. The prices were enough to bring a man to tears. He pitied the fool who wasted his money in a shop like that. The styles bordered on the ridiculous, with price tags to match. They passed along the side of the shop and climbed the outdoor flight of steps at the back. Dan blinked at Parker's tan coloured suit.

"JP, tell me you didn't buy that suit in that shop down there," said Dan.

"Why not?" said Parker.

"Because I think the place is an elaborate joke. Maybe they set it up in tribute to Jeremy Beadle."

"Jeremy Beadle? What are you talking about? I actually rather like this suit," said Parker, eyeing himself as he climbed.

"Eva," said Dan. "When we start discussing the fee for this case, make sure you double it."

"Now hang on," said Parker.

"Don't worry. Whatever figure we choose will still be cheaper than that suit."

At the top of the steps, Parker rang the doorbell of a white door. He ran his fingers through his oily mane as they waited. When the door finally opened, Eva's mouth dropped open. A very young lady with a long elegant cascade of brown hair and glossy baby-pink lipstick looked back at them blankly. If anything, she looked bored. As she eyed them, her fingers idly tweaked at a stone necklace she wore around her neck. Not a gemstone, but a plain grey rock clasped in precious metal. The girl looked at Parker and let loose a hint of a smile.

"Jonathan," she said, by way of hello. Then she retreated inside, leaving the door open. Dan and Eva studied her back. She wore a denim shirt, belted in the middle by a wide brown belt. Then there were the shining black leggings, finished off with a pair of black ankle boots and a lot of bangles on her wrists. The woman was so fresh-faced, it was hard to describe her as a woman. She looked more like a girl playing dress up than a real person.

"How old is she?" said Dan in a whisper. Eva's face said she was thinking the exact same thing.

"Why?" snapped Parker. "Age is but a number, is it not? And they say you're only as old as the woman you feel."

Eva frowned, and Parker's face tightened.

"We're all consenting adults here," said Parker.

"As long as we are," said Dan.

Eva frowned in a way which suggested her lunch was about to make a rapid reappearance.

"I take it you thoroughly checked her birth certificate before you made any, um, commitments?" said Dan.

Parker darkened. "Don't be such a prude. She just looks younger than she is, that's all. And there I was thinking you two were the leading edge of the new generation, not a pair of fuddy-duddies."

"Then I'm afraid you were mistaken," said Eva, as she walked into the apartment and looked around. The décor was appropriate for Leigh. Showy gilt framed mirrors in an otherwise understated room. A ceiling fan. A big splashy rug on a shining wooden floor, and a triptych of stylish flower prints on the wall. Eva stopped appraising the front room as the young woman turned away from the big windows and met her eye.

"Hi. I'm Eva Roberts. Pleased to meet you…"

Eva offered a hand. The young woman paused before she accepted it.

"Amelia," said the girl.

"Isn't she a dream?" said Jonathan, as he walked into the room. Parker gushed in the doorway, while Eva looked at the girl, trying to discern what she saw in an old man she herself thought of as an idle nuisance. Eva found a half-bemused smile appear on the girl's face. But when she noticed Eva's look, the smile wavered.

A firm hand appeared on Jonathan Parker's shoulder and yanked him back into the hallway. Dan gently twisted Parker back against the hallway wall.

"JP," said Dan, quietly. "That girl is young enough to be your granddaughter. Maybe your great granddaughter."

"How rude!" said Jonathan, testily.

"If you're insulted, that's your problem. I'm telling you the truth."

"Then you don't get it at all. That girl isn't some old man's idle fancy."

"No?" said Dan.

"No!" said Parker. "She represents a golden opportunity."

"Yeah. I bet her mother would be ecstatic to hear you talking about her like that."

"I don't mean that kind of opportunity! I'm not talking about man's baser instincts. Though, they may feature from time to time… I'm talking about a more traditional Parker type interest."

"What could be more traditional than a Parker getting involved with the wrong woman?"

"A Parker with his eyes on a once-in-a-lifetime investment opportunity, that's what?"

"The girl? She's an investment? Jonathan, are you out of your mind?"

In the front room, the girl and Eva shared an awkward moment. Glancing at each other, then avoiding each other's gaze. Eva could hear the tone but not the substance of the bickering. She decided it was her duty to cover it.

"Um. So how long have you been together with—"

"Excuse me," said the girl in a well-spoken voice. "Did you just ask how long we'd been together? Me and Jonathan? Are you serious?"

Eva frowned and gave a half-shake of her head. Confusion reigned supreme. "Well, to be honest, I did wonder if he was telling the truth."

"Together?" said the girl, smiling. "Well I suppose I may have let him get close once or twice."

Close…? Once or twice…? Eva's awkward frown returned. "Oh," she said and looked to the window. "Nice weather."

"Yeah. It looks nice," said Amelia. "But I haven't been out for a few days."

Eva arched an eyebrow. She hadn't been out for a few days. But the girl hardly looked unwell. In fact, she looked as fresh as a daisy. Now it was Eva's turn to wonder what was going on.

Out in the hall, Dan continued his interrogation.

"Come on then, what's the game here? Is she a prostitute?" said Dan. "You're not thinking of becoming some sugar daddy pimp or something are you?!

"What do you take me for?"

"You said it. You're a Parker. The Parkers I remember tend to let things slide in their old age."

"How dare you! That girl is too perfect to be a night-walking hussy. No, Dan. She's another kind of gold mine altogether. And she's my gold mine too. Just you wait and see."

Parker stepped away from Dan.

"JP. I'm lost here. Is there actually a case in all this, or are you finally going senile on me?"

"You should be grateful that I'm still willing to hire you at all. But I will. I'll do it out of respect for all that's passed between us. Come on in, and I'll tell you all you need to know…"

Jonathan led Dan into the room above the apartment, assuming a new demeanour as they walked into the room. Dan watched the old man walking taller and with far less of a stoop than he remembered from former times. The clothes looked ridiculous on him, but something about the girl had made the old man seem younger, sprightlier. The power of the male libido was an amazing thing indeed – at any age.

"So, you both want to know why I turned up last night, asking for your help," said Parker.

Dan looked around at the high ceiling, the imperial ceiling fan, and the old-style deep coving.

"Come to mention it, why you didn't stay here instead?"

Parker hesitated and looked at the girl.

"It's not always convenient," said Amelia, by way of explanation.

Dan narrowed his eyes and looked at Eva.

Eva shrugged.

"Carry on," said Dan.

"It's like this," said Jonathan. "I've been enjoying a lot of different kinds of experiences since we last saw one another."

"You don't say," said Dan.

Parker didn't bite. "Some good. Some bad," said Parker. "Some indifferent. But there comes a time when a man must think about not spending all his wealth, so he can reinvest it to harvest some more. And Amelia here holds all the answers I've been looking for."

"And this is you, thinking with your *head?*" asked Dan.

Amelia folded her arms.

"Are these people your friends or not, Jonathan?" she said.

"Yes, yes, indeed they are. One is a little rougher than the other, as you'll see. But they're just perfect for this, trust me."

"JP? Perfect for what?" said Dan.

"Look. I know we seem an unlikely match…" said Parker.

"Because we're not a match at all," said the young woman. "But I have the intellect to spot a good investment, and Amelia has the sharpest brain I've met in a long time. What she knows, combined with her contacts, I'm telling you, we'll be made for life. With the money I've got left we can convert it into something much greater. A measure of true wealth."

"Excuse me for saying, but I'm not sure if Amelia here is as committed to a long-term arrangement as you are," said Eva.

"Not true," said the young woman. "A business partnership is what I want. Maybe with some fun along the way. *Some very temporary fun.* But the business is what I'm interested in. Jonathan knows that. As for the rest… I think Jonathan is hoping and speculating."

Jonathan waved his hands. "Pah to all this negative talk. We haven't got the time for it, and we need to focus on the end aim."

"Which is?" said Dan.

"The accumulation of enough wealth to see us through a number of years, through using some very specific inside info…" said Jonathan with a grand, smug nod.

Eva replied first, saying what they were both thinking.
"Jonathan. That doesn't exactly sound legit…"
Before Eva had finished speaking, they heard the external
staircase rattling under feet at the back of the Broadway
apartments.
"Jonathan. That doesn't exactly sound legit…"
The sound of footsteps rattling the wrought iron stairway
grew so loud Dan looked back over his shoulder towards the
front door. When the noise was at its loudest, it suddenly
stopped altogether. Dan frowned. He looked at Jonathan,
who looked at Amelia.
"This is your place, right?" said Dan.
"For now," said Amelia.
There was a thud at the door. In the next second it was
smashed open, bursting at the frame, the door slamming
against the wall. A guy with a shaved head covered in short
stubble with a square jawline walked into the hallway. Dan
saw a knife glinting in his hand and sized the guy up in three
seconds flat. Dan guessed he was mid-thirties. He had mean
eyes, and a solid chin which looked like it could take a
punch. On a good day, Dan backed himself to win, even
with his stomach pains. But the knife in the guy's hand was a
big one. Dan was on the back foot. He had to tread carefully.
Dan raised his hands and blocked the doorway to the living
room with his body.
"I don't know who you are, or what you want," said Dan.
"But you'd better turn around, go back the way you came
and never come back."
"Excuse me?" said the stubble-head.
"You heard," said Dan. "Do yourself a big favour."
"I'm the one with a knife here," said the man in a gruff
London accent.

"You still need to back off," said Dan.

The man laughed.

"I don't think so," he pointed the blade at Dan, but his eyes flicked around the apartment. His gaze settled on the wooden console table by the door. As soon as he noticed it, the man ducked, seized one of its legs and hurled it across the floor towards Dan. A small vase and a print in a frame spun off the table and smashed on the floorboards. As Dan batted the table away from him, the newcomer charged in with a growl.

The man grabbed Dan's jacket collar and tried to pull him into the hall, but Dan pushed back against the doorframe and held his ground while closing off the living room behind him. His eyes flicked between the sharp edge of the oversized blade, and the man's keen eyes. Small, flinty, and angry, they kept searching beyond Dan's shoulder for the faces in the room behind him. Dan dropped his shoulder to let the man look. Then he took his moment. He batted the knife away and punched a hard fist into the man's knife-wielding wrist, knocking it against the wall. The invader groaned. But despite the pain etched over his face, the man somehow kept hold of the knife. Dan reached for it again, but the newcomer pulled back and jabbed the knife at Dan's chest. Dan stepped back.

"Ammie!" The guy with the shaven head called out. "I don't care how many of these idiots you drag into this. You know what I want, and you're going to let me have it."

Dan took a breath and looked for an opening, but the man's eyes were now fixed on his. There was no way to fight while the guy aimed a knife at his heart. Now was about damage limitation. Controlling the situation. And letting the guy know he wasn't ever going to be a pushover. Their eyes met and locked above the knife.

"Leave me alone!" screamed the girl from the room behind them. "You're a psychopath. I don't know what you're talking about…"

"Yes, you do know, Ammie. You know exactly what I'm talking about. And it's going to cost you if you don't give it to me. So, here's your chance. I'll give you an amnesty. I'll give you twenty-four hours, then I ramp this up in ways you just won't believe are possible. Do you hear me… and, Parker, I know you're in there too. You're going to get yours too, old man."

"You just leave the old man out of it. He's senile. Have you seen the suits he's wearing?" said Dan.

"Dan!" called Parker from behind him.

"Senile?" said the man with the knife. "I don't doubt it for a second. But the man's a scumbag too. And next time, you better keep the hell out of my way. I'm warning you…" The man pointed at Dan as he backed away towards the broken front door. When he was outside, the man turned and set off down the iron staircase.

"You know, I'm getting sick of getting warned off by every scumbag I meet," said Dan, taking a deep breath and walking into the living room. "And I'm getting tired of you, Jonathan, trying to hoodwink us into something yet again." The old man made a saintly face of innocence and Dan growled in frustration. He walked to the hallway and stuck his head out of the front door,

After checking the outside stairs were clear, Dan pushed the rest of the broken door against the jamb. It was the best he could do. Then he sighed, stepped over the smashed-up table and walked back into the living room. He saw Amelia standing with her arms folded, an irritated and arrogant look in her eye. Jonathan wore his familiar look of feigned victimhood and pained expression. Eva looked at him from the side.

"What was that all about?" she said. The old man didn't reply. "Jonathan?".

Parker shrugged and looked at Amelia.

"A long story?" he said, doubtfully.

"And let me guess," said Dan. "Is he part of your fantastic financial investment opportunity?"

Parker met Dan's eyes, and Dan watched him searching for an answer.

"No. Cadson is definitely not a part of what we're planning. Is he, Amelia?"

"No. He's definitely not."

Dan shook his head.

"Now listen here. If you want our help in any way – in any way at all – now's the time to come clean about what you're involved with here. That means both of you," said Dan.

"You said they'd help us, Jonathan," said Amelia.

"And they will," said Jonathan. "Sometimes they just need a little persuasion, is all."

"Jonathan?" said Eva. "That man knows you. He knew both of you. He wants something from you. So, what is it?"

"Information, of course. But he can't have it," said Parker.

"That information is trapped inside this beautiful mind right here. And we can't let him have Amelia now, can we?"

"You're saying he wants the girl here?" said Dan.

"The girl?!" said Amelia. "Please? What decade are we living in. I have a name you know."

Dan rolled his eyes to the ceiling.

"He's a scoundrel, Dan," said Parker. "And I mean an utter scoundrel. I implore you, both of you, we need your help. If not for me, then do it for the sake of Amelia here."

Dan looked at the girl and sighed. He put his hands on his hips and looked away.

"I've got a lot on right now, Parker."

"Yes, I know… that much is obvious… but this delicate flower needs me. And I need you. I can't do this on my own."

Eva and Dan shared another loaded glance before Dan gave the briefest nod.

"If you mess us around or try to pull the wool over our eyes like you did last time, I swear, I'll gift-wrap you in a ribbon and a bow and give you to that guy myself."

"No," said Parker. "You wouldn't do that. Not when you know what's at stake. Not when you know what I'd be willing to pay you…" said Jonathan.

"Until you tell us what's going on, it'll be a no," said Eva. "We won't take the job."

The girl tutted and sighed and shook her head as if Jonathan had let her down.

"Then let me tell you, Eva. And when I'm done you'll see that you'll be helping me to secure my final years, and the future of this lovely girl. It's the right thing to do. I swear it."

But Eva wasn't swayed by the bluster. She waited. Dan waited too.

"Okay," said Parker. "It's like this. Amelia here is a genius. A mastermind if you will."

The girl looked up and smiled

"I mean it you know," said Parker, warming to his theme. "She has the brain of a super computer and she's got a way with numbers that you and I won't ever grasp. That's what Cadson is after. He wants to take her from me, and use her, like some bloody slave. I managed to prise her from his hands and now I want to help her stay free, so we can build a bright future for her away from that awful man's hands."

"Wait a second," said Dan, turning to Amelia. "That guy was keeping you against your will? Like a prisoner?" said Dan, cutting through Parker's purple prose.

Dan tried to read the smile on the young girl's pretty face. It was cute, but smart too. Maybe Jonathan was telling the truth. Or maybe he was simply telling them whatever the hell he liked, making it up on the spot. Either way, the girl wasn't denying any of it. Dan held her in a steady gaze, waiting for an answer. Eventually, the girl relented under the weight of his stare.

"At the end, I was a prisoner, yeah," she said. "I had no choice but to do whatever he said. But I couldn't live like that. All the while seeing what he was doing. I couldn't live with myself."

"What was he doing?" said Eva.

"Cadson runs a card school. And much more besides," said Jonathan.

"A card school?" said Dan. "As in a gambling ring?"

"Yes. So I heard," said Jonathan.

"*So you heard?*" said Dan. "You're not back into gambling again, are you?"

Jonathan threw his hands up in the air. "What is this? No. I swear it! I'm a reformed man, and now I have the perfect reason to stay reformed. To help this fine girl keep her freedom."

Eva kept one eyebrow firmly arched in the air as she looked at Jonathan. "And you wouldn't be intending to exploit Amelia here in any way, would you, Jonathan?"

"Please," said Amelia, sharply. "He really couldn't if he tried."

"Yeah. But that's what everyone thinks," said Dan. "Until Parker shafts them too."

"Don't listen to them, girl. Their professional labours have soiled their minds and made them far too cynical for their years."

"You played your part in the soiling too, JP," said Parker.

"I still don't know what you want from us," said Eva. "Just what is the job here, Jonathan?" Eva's eyes flitted between the old man and the girl's blank-faced stare.

"That's simple enough. Help me protect this beautiful flower from that monster. Help me keep her free of him long enough so that she can work her magic on my resources. Then when the return on our investment comes in, Amelia will get a cut, I'll be able to pay you handsomely, and I'll get enough of a return to see out the rest of my days in the style to which I've become accustomed."

Dan stared at Parker to see what the man wasn't telling him, but if something was being hidden, Dan couldn't see where.

"What do you think?" said Dan, looking at Eva.

Eva's eyes fell upon the inscrutable Amelia. She met Eva's eyes without defence or apology.

"If this is *exactly* as you say…" said Eva. "If we're helping keep Amelia safe while she gets her life organised… then I suppose I don't see a problem with taking this on. Providing Jonathan pays us like he says he will."

"Of course, I'll pay you, my dear. And as for getting her life organised. Oh, this is so much more than that. This will be getting our lives organised for the foreseeable future, and in the very finest way possible."

"Save it, Jonathan," said Dan. "I've heard just about all I can stand. But seeing as you forgot to mention the guy with the knife until he kicked down the front door…"

"Cadson," said Parker.

"That part will cost you extra," said Dan. His eyes roved over the splintered wood, broken table and broken glass scattered across the floor. A breeze from the outside world plucked at the broken door and shook it in the frame. The movement caught Dan's eye. The same breeze plucked at a shred of paper on the hallway floor. Dan noticed the coloured piece of paper lying scrunched beside the skirting board. He frowned and slowly walked towards it to pick it up.

"What's that?" said Eva.

Dan picked up the scrap and flattened it out in his hands. It was a flyer, black with bright colours splashed across it. There was a picture of a racing dog running flat out with a number 6 on its side, with a scene of a firework-lit sky above. Dan turned the flyer over. On the other side in a rough black scrawl, was written *8pm*. Hmmmmm. Dan flipped the sheet and looked at the event information beneath the dog track illustrations. *Romford Dogs Relaunch Party! The best in local race sports entertainment is back in style!*

"What is it?" said Eva.

"Looks like a flyer for some event at Romford Dogs… there's a launch event and an after party." Dan looked back at the broken door and considered the scrappy flyer in his hand.

"I guess your man – *Cadson…?*"

Amelia nodded. Dan had the man's name right.

"It looks like he dropped it in the rush," said Dan.

The dog track event was billed for Thursday night. Today was Wednesday. Dan double-checked the date of the relaunch party.

"This event happens tomorrow night," said Dan. "Does this belong to one of you? Parker?"

"Hardly my scene," said the girl. From the look of her, she had a point.

Dan looked at Parker. The old man rapidly shook his head.

"I don't do gambling anymore. I told you," said Parker.

"Then this must belong to your friend with the knife," said Dan. "But does that make any sense to you?"

The girl nodded. "It could. He's involved with all kinds of gambling schemes. I wouldn't be surprised if he had something on with the dogs as well."

Gambling. Money making schemes. Investments. Shams, scams, and lies. It was enough to make Dan's head spin, if it wasn't spinning already.

"What will you do about the door?" said Eva. "You're not safe here anymore."

"Parker's got money. He can pay to get it fixed, right?" said Dan.

Parker muttered and let his words slip away unheard. Dan glared until Amelia intervened.

"No," said Amelia. "The guy who is lending me the apartment can fix it. He likes me. He won't mind."

"He likes you?" said Dan.

The girl nodded, with a coy smile.

"And he's lending you the apartment? The apartment that you just got trashed?" said Dan.

The girl smiled and tucked her hair behind her ears.

"Mitch, he's a doll. He owns Strontium, the suit shop downstairs. He's got money to burn. He won't mind at all. But you'll have to go first. In fact, you'd better go right now. Mitch will hardly be in the mood to help me if he sees all of you hanging around like a bad smell." She looked at Parker, but the old man seemed hesitant to leave.

"Go on. Go." she said. "I'll have to get this fixed myself."

"Trust me, Amelia," said Parker. "It'll be okay. I promise I'll come through for the both of us."

"Fine. But please go now. I need to get this fixed up. And I need time to think."

Dan could hardly blame the girl. If JP had promised to protect her, he had failed at the first hurdle. Dan had had enough of Jonathan's fantasy romance and his strange, desperate plans. He was keen to return to the normal world where people were often bad, but at least they made sense. For the most part, anyway. As Dan looked at the dog-racing flyer, and recalled Amelia's words, he couldn't shake the feeling that they were being played. Or were about to be played. The girl was a question mark with good looks – and not even Parker seemed to have all the answers. Amelia seemed like a victim. And at the same time, there was that smile, and that crafty confidence. And there was the fact that yet another man – the owner of the suit shop – seemed willing to drop everything to help her. *Help her in exchange for what? As if he couldn't guess.* The same thing the guy with the knife had been getting. The thing Parker was chasing like a horny teen trapped in a wrinkly OAP's body… Dan shook his head and stuffed the dog track-flyer in his jacket pocket.

"Are we leaving yet, Jonathan?" said Dan.

"If you insist," said Parker, wanly.

"*I* insist," said the girl.

Dan and Eva led the way out to the fresh air at the top of the wrought iron steps.

"I'm so glad that's over," said Eva.

"You agreed to take the case on, Eva. Which means it's only just begun."

"Yes, to help Amelia before anybody else takes advantage of her, that's the only reason."

"I'm not sure she's the one who needs help here, Eva," said Dan. "Anyway. It's too late. We've taken the case on. But if we're going to learn more about this Cadson guy – I think we could do worse than show our faces at this little dog race."

Eva glanced at the creased flyer tucked in Dan's pocket. He pulled it free and pointed out the handwritten note on the back. "I think Cadson is going to be there."

Parker emerged on the walkway behind them, his patent leather heels clanking on the metal. He did his best to close the remnants of the front door behind him.

"Dan," said Parker, setting his absurd trilby on the top of his head. "Why do you think the suit shop man downstairs is being so kind to Amelia like this?"

"I haven't got the faintest idea," said Dan. "Have you?"

"No," said Eva. "No idea at all." Before Parker could check her face, Eva coughed and stepped past Dan to descend the rickety steps. Their new case looked like the beginning of another Parker disaster. But at least it would put some money in the bank. Or so they hoped.

Four

Eva tapped one of her favourite chunky black markers on her teeth as she blinked at the flipchart board in their office. She quickly flipped past the sheet which made Dan feel bad every time he saw it, but the words still caught his eye. The names Malachy and Proberty stood out loud and proud on the grey-white paper. Just seeing Proberty's name made Dan's stomach burn. He still felt the weight of the ex-champion's body swinging past his shoulder. Dan had to work hard to block a tidal wave of ugly feelings. A moment later, his eyes blinked open to see Eva staring at a new blank sheet. Unless Parker opened up, Dan reckoned the page wasn't going to see much writing. Yet even if Parker continued to drip-feed them the truth, the old man still couldn't control events – and they'd already seen plenty of those. One way or another the truth would come out, and Parker's case would pay. Dan was sure about that part. Dead sure. Having taken on more of Parker's hassle, Dan was determined they'd get every penny. Eva stepped up to the flipchart and began to write – big, neat, dark letters with calm precision.

"Does she do this performance for every case?" said Parker. "Or is this just for my benefit?"

"Nothing here is done for your benefit, trust me," said Dan. "This is how we sift the wheat from the chaff."

Dan folded his arms as he perched on the back of Mark's desk. At his side, Mark was busy fielding the usual phone calls. There were plenty of unwanted sales calls, but little sign of new work, which made Parker's troublesome case a blessing in disguise.

"So, which am I, Eva? The wheat or the chaff?" said Parker.

"That's the problem, Jonathan," said Eva. "You're making it very hard to tell."

The rest of them scanned Eva's notes as she poured them onto the page in big black letters.

AMELIA – INVESTMENT OPPORTUNITY???

JOB TO PROTECT INVESTMENT? WHAT INVESTMENT?

THREAT FROM BREAK-IN MAN 'CADSON'. WHAT DOES HE WANT?

Underneath her words, Eva swept the marker across the sheet to make a giant question mark with a flourish of her hand.

"Do you see?" said Eva. "Questions, Jonathan. That's all you've given us here," said Eva, turning to face the others. Parker scratched an imaginary itch on his jaw.

"Look, I've told you what I can. The girl is a genius, I'm telling you – she has all the details of the plan and I don't bother to press her on them. I don't need to. That girl is in possession of a remarkable brain and she is going to help me turn my life savings into something to see out the rest of my days."

"Do you know how that sounds?!" said Dan. "It sounds like someone has just sold you a handful of magic beans. Come on. Try to think clearly, JP. Is there something in this, or have you been blinded by your libido?"

"What? Don't be so crude, man," said Parker, "Where money is concerned I'm never blinded by anything. The girl is sharp. That's why Cadson tried to keep her for himself. I know, she seems ordinary. Beautiful, but ordinary... well, ordinary if you ignore those stunning, youthful good looks of hers...."

Eva rolled her eyes.

"But she's a genius. I tell you she is."

"Yes, so you've told us a good number of times," said Eva. "But what you haven't told us is the nature of this investment or how the girl will broker it for you, if that's what she intends to do. Or whether it's a safe investment in the first place. Shouldn't you be trusting us to look into it for you?" said Eva. "Jonathan, you could end up flat broke!"

"Flat broke!" said Jonathan, pausing. "As if... I'm not a fool, Eva, even if I look it. My money is as safe as houses in this thing. All I need is to ensure this girl remains safe, and the rest is up to her. There's very little financial risk in it beyond that. I don't stand to lose money, but by helping Amelia I will be set for the deal of a lifetime. Which is good for all of us, isn't it?"

"It sounds like you're chasing a golden goose," said Dan. "And if you're not, then that means you're holding out on us. You're not telling us everything. Which suggests there's a problem. Like maybe the investment is a problem. Like it's *illegal...?*"

"No. It's not illegal," said Parker. "Not on my part at least." Dan sighed. It was his turn to roll his eyes.

"It's not a standard investment. Just think of the girl as the collateral," said Jonathan.

"Now that sounds worse than ever," said Eva.

"Not like that! No, no, no. The collateral is what she knows in that computer brain of hers. That's the thing. There's nothing sordid in this at all."

Eva's eyes remained set to sceptical. Parker recognised the look, cleared his throat and moved on.

"Nothing apart from you," said Dan, speaking Eva's mind.

"That's almost offensive, Dan," said Parker. "It's all kosher, I swear. And I don't want to be talked out of this by the likes of you two. And I don't want to start seeing more problems than benefits. This thing can work, but only if I believe in Amelia. She can do this, and so can I."

"You're worried we'll try to talk you out of it?" said Dan. "Do we need to do that?"

"No. You don't. But you'd still try, I know you would. Which is the precise reason why I've come to you as a client rather than a friend in need. By hiring your professional services, you can't tell me what to do, can you? But I can tell you how to assist me…"

"You're not going to tell us about this investment, are you?" said Eva. "And you're not going to tell us what this young woman knows either. Because it seems to me that's what you're fighting with this Cadson thug is all about."

"I don't want to. Not until we're done. Then you'll know everything."

Eva looked at Dan.

"How can we take on a case like that?" said Eva. "It's a blind alley with us taking all the risks."

"Don't see it like that," said Jonathan. "It's an opportunity for all of us."

"I don't like it, but he's put us through enough already. I vote we push on and get paid on this one. Parker owes us." Parker nodded with enthusiasm.

Eva sighed and turned back to the flipchart.

"I'm not convinced," said Eva. "But if we do take on your case, then hard as it is, it means we're going to have to trust you. Jonathan—we're going to have to take you at your word. Can we trust you?"

"Of course, you can," said Parker.

Eva's eyes lingered on the old man for a long moment before she relented with a smile. The old man looked very relieved to see it.

"Very wise, Eva. Very wise," said Jonathan.

"Then I sincerely hope you're not messing us around," said Eva, her eyes flicking to Dan. "It'd be a very bad time to do something like that. A very bad time indeed."

"Yes," said Parker, glancing at Dan. "I'm sure it would. Which is why you can rest assured this will end up being one of the easiest paydays you've ever had in your distinguished careers. Just trust me. You'll see."

"He's not going to crack yet, Eva. So, we'll have to work around him," said Dan.

"I am still here, you know," said Parker.

"Yeah. We know," said Dan.

Eva nodded. "Then let's look at what we *have* got." She turned back to the flipchart.

"This Cadson who broke into the apartment… the girl, Amelia. She acts like she knows something. Like she's in control, which is a little disconcerting," said Eva. "And you won't tell us what it is?" she said. Jonathan simply shrugged. "Which is one of the reasons I'm wondering whether Jonathan here is being had," said Dan.

"Stop it. I know Amelia is with me. We're together in this, I assure you."

"Your assurances are already wearing thin," said Dan.

"Amelia is confident because she's clever. Clever enough to get away from that man who was about to use her. And that's why she needs your help. To stay safe from him until she's able to release that money and get free of him for good."

Eva and Dan looked at Parker.

"That's still not enough to go on," said Eva. "If we're going to help you at all, we're going to need more information."

"But why? The job is simple. Protect us until we've set things up, protect us until we can draw down the cash. It's easy as pie. You really don't need to know anything more than that."

"No. But we need to be sure this isn't a con," said Dan.

"I wouldn't ever con you," said Parker.

"Funny. Last time we met you were pretty sure I was the one conning you..." said Dan.

"Those were very different circumstances, and I learned the error of my ways," said Parker, acting humble.

"Besides, JP," said Dan. "I don't think you're the one pulling the con. But there are a few people here who could be."

"You're wrong," said Parker.

"Maybe. But we need to know all the same. We don't know about the girl because you won't tell us, but we could learn something about this Cadson guy."

"Cadson? Him?" said Parker. "You don't need to know anything about him, either. He's a rogue. A criminal. That's all there is to it."

"It's not that simple," said Dan. "We have to be careful. The guy could be a one-man band, or he could be the thin end of a wedge going all the way to one of the big gangs. I need to know who we're taking on and why," said Dan. "I've got too many other issues going on right now. I don't need any new ones."

Parker shook his head. "Well then. If you can't take my word for it, what do you suggest?"

"Cadson," said Eva. "We've got a name. That's a start. We could always try the usual routes for information. PC Dawson might help us. Maybe DI Hogarth might even tell us something."

"I wouldn't bother with Hogarth," said Dan. "He'll start nosing around if you involve him. Anyway. I think we've already got a way we can learn a lot more about Cadson."

"How exactly?" said Parker. Dan noticed the pained look on the old man's face as he lifted the flyer for the dog racing event.

"Cadson's going out to the races. I think maybe we should go out too," said Dan.

"What? Follow a dangerous man to some stupid dog racing event?" said Parker. "What will that tell you?"

"Who knows? But it'll tell me a damn sight more than you have."

Jonathan blinked. "Dan. You can't talk to the man. He's dangerous."

"Funny how you don't want us to know a single thing about this case," said Dan.

"I'm serious, Dan." said Parker. "This guy is bad news."

"Then tell me about him. Does he work alone? Is he a front man? Is he connected? Is he a gangster? What?" said Dan.

Parker shook his head. "He's not in with the gangs. Cadson is too selfish to ever work for anyone but himself. But he's ruthless. I can't tell you more than that, because I've only ever known him as a vicious shark."

"Then how long have you known him?" said Eva.

"Only since I met Amelia," said Parker.

"Well that makes sense, I guess," said Dan. "She's at the root of all this trouble. So maybe you really can't tell us much about him. But whether you can or not, we still need to know who we're up against. We have to know more. Agreed?" Dan looked at Eva.

Eva nodded. "Agreed."

"Then that's it," said Dan. "The dogs it is."

"Well. It's your funeral. Don't say I didn't warn you."

"And it's your funeral too, JP, you're coming with us."

"What?"

"Don't wet your pants," said Dan. "We're not going to engage with the man. We're going to watch and listen and learn as much as we can. Then when we know enough we'll get out of there and get to work on the rest of this case of yours."

"With confidence, because we'll know who we're up against," said Eva.

Parker frowned and looked down at his shoes.

"Cheer up," said Dan.

"Why should I?" said Parker.

Dan tapped the front of the pictorial flyer. "Because this flyer says there's going to be free drinks to celebrate the launch."

But even the promise of free drinks didn't seem to cheer Parker, which wasn't right in itself. Dan frowned and chewed on his cheek while he brooded over Parker's mysterious attitude. Free booze had always brought a smile to the old man's face. If the promise of on-the-house drinks didn't cheer him up, Dan had to wonder how bad things were going to get. And there was another cause for concern too. Parker's investment plan. If the old man didn't have to put any money down, then why call it an investment? Where Parker was concerned, money was a fixation, as if cash was the elixir of eternal youth, the answer to all ills. Parker wasn't being honest with them about the investment. That much was clear. Now they had to hope the old man wasn't hiding any other skeletons in the closet.

Five

Romford dog track was a place Dan hadn't been to in years. And the new and improved Romford dogs turned out to be as glamorous as Dan had imagined. The interior hall was decked out in the very best of betting shop chic, complete with odd patterned carpets and garish Formica serving counters. Only the glittery decorations and the ambience of excitement matched the razzmatazz billing of the flyers. When they walked inside they found the venue crammed with people dressed in smart clothes that seemed a few levels above what the venue deserved, and which served to make Dan's standard jeans and leather jacket combo appear a little underdone. Eva's tweed suit was more than adequate, though she looked more management material than night-out punter. As for Jonathan, his bright suit marked him out more as warm-up entertainment than anything else. The three of them made a very odd set. But at least there were crowds in which to hide.

"Have you seen him yet?" said Dan, raising his voice to be heard above the chatter in the gallery. Parker seemed preoccupied. Dan watched the old man looking left and right and then back over his shoulder. Dan and Eva exchanged a silent glance.

"I said have you seen him yet?"

"Seen who?"

"Come on. You know who. Cadson. The man you say is out to kidnap your sweetheart."

"Kidnap? Did I actually say that?" said Parker. "I don't think I did."

"As a matter of fact, yes, you did. That's how you presented it to us, at any rate. Though to my mind, he seemed more interested in getting something out of you," said Dan.

"You're not about to change your story, are you, Jonathan?" said Eva. "Because if you are, that might force us to reconsider whether we can help you or not?"

"What?" said Jonathan, looking alert. "Changing my story? Why would I ever do that? I already told you. Cadson wants her brain. She's as smart as they come, and he knows he'll come unstuck without her."

"Sounds like you know this man better than you let on."

"Cadson... I know all I need to know," said Parker. "But I don't know why you even want to pursue this. We shouldn't be here. We should be with Amelia, protecting her, making sure he doesn't get anywhere near her."

Dan shrugged. "So long as we can see him, we know she's safe. Besides, I always like to know who I'm up against."

"He's a bad man. That's all I can tell you and that's all I want to know. He's best off being avoided altogether."

Dan nodded and looked around the shifting crowds as the punters went to place their bets at the bookies stalls or order a beer from the crowded bar. Not far ahead, the floor of the bar fell away to a cinema-style seating arrangement which looked out over the brightly-lit dog track through the gallery window beyond.

"Shall we get a table in the back?" said Parker, thumbing towards a huddle of plastic tables not far from the bar. "You'll be able to scope everyone from there. And they do table service for drinks. We won't have to queue at the bar."

Dan followed Parker's bony pointing hand to a small empty table at the back. The tables reminded Dan of the wipe-clean plastic bench affairs in the grim fast food joints of his teenage years. Relaunch or not, the dog track didn't seem to have many high expectations of its customers. And Dan had similarly low expectations of Parker. Dan eyed the position of the tables. The one Parker had selected was almost entirely out of sight from the whole venue.

"You really don't want Cadson to see you, do you?" said Dan.

"Don't be silly. I don't hide from anyone. Let's just grab that table before someone else does. I'm thirsty and I don't fancy waiting at the bar, that's all."

Dan relented and followed Parker. "You don't need to hide from this guy, Parker. That's why you hired us. And that's why we're here. To see what he's about so we can close a deal with him."

"Whatever you say. So long as you can keep him off Amelia's back until we're done, that's all that matters. In the meantime I think I'll have a drink."

"Done?" said Eva. "Until what's done?"

Parker paused and turned. "Until the investment is made and the return is received. The girl is a genius. Just you wait and see. I know she'll come through."

"It's all too vague, Jonathan. What are you investing in? How does it work?" said Eva.

"And is it legal?" said Dan.

"Questions, questions, questions! All you do is ask me questions. Is this how you treat all your clients?"

"No. Not all our clients. Only the ones who refuse to tell the truth," said Dan. But it looked like the old man wasn't going to be easy to crack.

"I've told you everything you need to know. I've already told you the truth."

"You've given us the bare bones."

"I've given you enough. I've introduced you to Amelia. And you know her predicament first hand."

Dan shook his head. "Fine. You sit down and hide here if you want to. I'll do a recce of the place and see what I can see."

"Cadson is a scoundrel, Dan. If he sees you... well, you'd better watch yourself."

Dan ignored the comment. Instead he looked at Eva. "Let him drink, but don't let him get drunk. That's the last thing we need."

"Eh?" said Parker.

"One drink," said Eva.

"One drink? How draconian," said Parker. "Meanwhile everyone else here can drink as much as they like."

"Everyone but us," said Dan. "We're here to work."

"Hang on. I'm the client. The work is yours, not mine," said Parker. But as he spoke, the old man's face changed. Dan watched Parker take on a sudden look of discomfort. He stopped speaking and shifted in his chair, moving left and right before finally hiding his face behind the plastic drinks menu.

"Jonathan? What is it?" said Eva.

Dan turned his head and looked back across the crowd until he spotted the cause of Parker's discomfort. Between the big gallery window and the busy bar a set of fresh faces were filtering in from the entrance. Four men in sharp suits with short haircuts. Dan put them in the thirties and forties bracket tops. But they didn't look the gangster type. They were too smooth. Too fresh faced, pale and soft. They looked more like professionals, people used to working in safe office environments. But following on behind them, in a suit which couldn't hide his rougher edges was Cadson. He was sharp-eyed and smiling, talking to the men with him. By his side, it was clear the men were cut from a different cloth. And to a man they were all taller than him. And the way the men looked back at him was almost deferential. It was as if he was in charge. *Or as if he was their host.* Three city suits were slumming it at Romford dogs with one urban hoodlum. What was Cadson doing now?

"Parker? Snap out of it. Do you know those others with Cadson over there?"

The old man peered above his drinks menu for all of five seconds before he ducked his face out of sight.

"No. I've never seen any of them in my life."

"And you're sure about that?" said Dan.

"Doesn't my word stand for anything these days?"

"The jury's out on that one. Wait here," said Dan. "I'll see what I can pick up on the grapevine then I'll be right back."

"Fine. But whatever you do, don't talk to him. He's dangerous. I mean it."

"You mean he can kill just by talking?" said Dan as he walked away.

"I mean it. Don't take the risk."

"Yeah, so you said" said Dan as he walked away. He snaked through the crowd. Beery breath and glassy eyes were already in evidence wherever he looked, and it was barely a quarter past eight. The screens above the bar said the big races were about to start

Cadson was holding court with the men in suits, pointing at the names of the racing dogs on the big screen above the bar. The men in suits laughed as if he had just told the best possible joke and it looked like Cadson thought his joke was pretty funny too. Dan could learn a lot about a man by the way he spoke, but he could tell a lot more by the words he said. Here was a golden chance to learn more than Parker would ever tell them. It was an opportunity not to be missed. Dan started a manoeuvre to take him looping towards them around the distant edge of the crowd by the bar. It worked for a moment, but then Cadson's eyes passed his way. Dan froze, cursing under his breath, believing he had been spotted. His chest tightened. He looked down to the floor. A long moment later he looked up and saw Cadson staring right past him towards one of the prettier barmaids pulling pints behind the bar. Dan scratched his forehead to quickly hide his face and made a sharp left past the bar. As soon as he got halfway there, he bumped into someone. He looked at them, ready to make the briefest apology before moving on, but then his eyes landed on a heavily exposed cleavage. The twin swells held his gaze for longer than he would have liked. Dan dragged his eyes away as fast as possible to correct the matter, before he found himself looking up into the eyes of the woman whose assets they were. The young woman was already looking at him, a knowing glint in her eye, her eyebrow raised, and a hint of arrogance about her smile. *Damn, damn, damn.* Dan recognised her, and immediately attempted to bury any sign of discomfort. It was Alice Perry, the young hack from The Record. The girl swished her well coiffured hair behind her ear and smiled brightly.

"Well, well, well. It seems fate does have a sense of humour," she said.

"You think?" said Dan, fronting it out. He glanced across his shoulder from the corner of his eye. Cadson and his guests were still in sight, but they were too far away for him to hear a word they said. And by now, his concentration was diverted in at least two other places, one of which Dan was determinedly struggling not to look at.

"Yes, remember? You said you'd call me and tell me why you needed Willard Burton's number in such a hurry. Surprise, surprise, Dan, you didn't make the call."

"Uh. Yeah. I've been a little busy the last few days, Alice."

"Maybe you have. Actually, you do look a little stressed."

The girl followed Dan's line of sight towards Cadson, but he altered his gaze and diverted her attention elsewhere. Perry shook her head and gave up. Dan frowned. Now he needed to be even more careful. The girl was young, but she wasn't at all naïve. It seemed she had tuned into his wavelength and was trying to read him. A dangerous and unwelcome development. If fate had a sense of humour, it seemed to be at his expense.

"I didn't think this would be your scene, Alice," said Dan, attempting to shift the conversation away from the places he didn't want to go.

The girl shook her head. "It's not. I could think of hundred thousand things I'd rather be doing right now. But an event like this tends to bring out the movers and shakers who might have a vested interest. And I don't mean the gamblers. Those kinds of people would be here whatever day it was. I mean the funders. The business people. The people who bankrolled the development."

"Why? You heard something?" said Dan.

Perry's eyes sparkled as she looked into Dan's. She shook her head. "Uh-Uh. Nothing like that. This is a speculative visit. When the business types of the town get loose with a few free drinks, you never know what you might overhear."

"Is that the reason for the...um... dress?" Dan made a hint of a gesture towards the girl's vest top without dipping his eyes.

"My choice of attire, you mean?" Alice was handed a glass of wine by another woman who was already drinking hers. The newcomer was a studious looking brunette, far less flash than Perry and he noted the camera bag clutched in her hand.

"Thanks, Yvonne," said Alice. The studious girl's eyes flicked to Dan from behind a pair of round spectacles.

"Oh – Yvonne, this is the man I was telling you about. The Southend PI. As in private investigator. He's the one who's promised to do the profile feature with us and is trying to wriggle out of it."

"Oh..." said the girl, with curiosity. "The topless shoot?" said the girl.

"Actually, Alice," said Dan. "I said I wasn't going to do that, remember?" said Dan.

"But that was when you promised to call me back and spill the beans. We agreed on an exclusive, and you're going to give it to me."

"Yes. And my word is my bond," said Dan.

"If and when you remember..." said Perry.

Dan looked back over his shoulder to check on Eva and Jonathan. He found them hidden from view by the movement of the crowd. Which meant they couldn't see him chatting with Alice Perry. Which was a relief.

"I said my word is my bond, didn't I?"

"I think I'll leave you two to it…" said the photographer woman.

"There's no need for that," said Dan, but the girl left them with a smile before sliding off into the crowd.

"See you at the photoshoot," she said, as she left them.

"Not happening," he called after her.

"Yes it is," said Alice. "But, moving on… seeing as you forgot to give me that Willard Burton exclusive, and as you didn't drop even a hint about that Croyde Crew business, you could at least tell me what you're doing at this high-class event." Perry eyed him over the top of her wine glass. She waited.

"Maybe I'm just here for kicks," said Dan. "Because I like a free drink."

"Not good enough," said Perry. "You're a private investigator and there isn't a drink in your hand. Sorry, but I don't believe you."

"PIs need downtime too you know," said Dan.

"Yes. And you can tell me about that when we do the profile piece. In fact, I'd like to hear *all* about what you do in your spare time."

Dan met the girl's eyes. He was unsure what she meant, so he let the comment pass.

"I bet you don't have much spare time, do you?" said Perry. "Which makes me doubly curious as to why you're here now."

Dan prickled but kept his smile in place.

"It's really not newsworthy, Alice. I'm not a story here. I'm here on a dumb errand to help a dumb friend who I probably shouldn't be helping."

"Now *that* has the ring of truth. And while it might not be newsworthy, it is still interesting, at least… see. That profile piece if going to be so much fun."

"Alice – I don't want to do it

"No," said Alice. "But you're still going to."

Dan frowned. "Why?" he said.

"Otherwise I might start to wonder why you used to be so very friendly with my predecessor, Gemma Cassidy – just before she got in all kinds of trouble and then died."

Dan shook his head, his face turning dark. "That's a very bad move, Alice. I'm telling you, you really don't want to go there."

"Don't I? Which probably means I do. I'm a reporter, remember."

"Alice."

"I know you had meetings with her," said Perry. "They were diarised on the office webmail. But I also know they weren't *always* diarised… as if they might have been clandestine. Tell me… does your partner know all about those meetings?"

"Alice… don't do this."

"Does she know that Gemma turned your head? Or that you got involved with her?"

"Involved?! Are you out of your mind? That's it. I'm out of here."

"Dan. Stop. I was only joking."

Dan stopped and looked at Alice Perry to check the look on her pretty face. Trouble was the girl was very hard to read.

"Hey," she said with a shrug. "The truth is I that don't care either way. It's really none of my business. And it's water under the bridge."

"You got that part right," said Dan.

"But I have to write something, don't I? You know that. So maybe, instead of blanking me and leaving me with all those empty columns to fill, you want to consider helping me out with that. Just saying."

Dan shook his head and turned away once more.

"Dan?" he glanced back. "Thanks for noticing my dress. I'll take that as a compliment."

Dan coughed. "Yeah. See you round, Alice."

"Call me," she said after him. "And don't leave it too long."

Dan gritted his teeth as he renewed his search around the crowd for Cadson. He looked left and right, but instead found Parker staring at him, nodding his head with an annoyingly smug glint in his eye. "Who was that?" said Parker.

"What?" said Dan.

"I mean the young blonde you were just talking to? The one with the... you know..."

"Parker? What are you doing over here? I thought you wanted to hide behind your pint glass."

"I did. But now I'd like to hide behind another another one."

"We said one drink, remember."

"Dan, I am not a child. I am your client. And for your information, I am no longer alcohol dependent."

"No?"

"No. These days I drink by choice, instead."

"AA would be so proud. Then get yourself another beer and sit down out of my way."

"Are there still some free drinks left at the bar? We have to pay for table service," said Parker.

"That explains the crowd at the bar. Go on then. You can hide in the crowd over there. I want to see what I can learn about your man Cadson and his little entourage."

"That's a total waste of time."

"And drinking yourself stupid isn't?" said Dan. "You go your way, I'll go mine."

"Now I know what you really wanted. Two minutes alone with that little blonde," said Parker. "But don't worry. I won't say what the butler saw."

"Parker – you're way out of line."

Parker chortled and scuttled into the pack gathered at the bar. A man of vast experience in the world of drinking, he slinked between the elbows of the men queuing to find himself a quicker point of service. Dan shook his head and his eyes found Cadson taking a seat by the gallery window. He lifted a 'reserved' card from a row of bright blue bench seats, and the suits with him gave a nod of satisfaction. Now they had a perch, Dan was happy. Eavesdropping would be a lot easier with the men seated. Dan moved through the crowds and found an empty bucket chair set two rows back from Cadson. Dan took the flyer from his pocket to use as a prop, and lowered his head to look at the flyer as if studying it hard. He turned his attention to the four men in front of him did his level best to tune in.

"…not exactly your usual night out, I bet, but seeing as the drinks were free, and it's so local for you, I thought you might enjoy a spot of sport among the common people."

One of the taller men raised his head and looked around. "It's certainly an eye opener. But as you can appreciate. We have a few other things on our minds."

"Yes. Yes, of course you do. But who said these meetings have to be boring, right?"

Dan watched Cadson's smile begin to strain. He had the man's profile in his sights, big jaw, and glinting eyes.

"It *is* safe, isn't it?"

Cadson hesitated and rubbed his stubbly chin. Dan could hear the sandpaper rasp of his skin.

"Of course," said Cadson. "Where could be safer than with me? If you lot had kept hold of it, it would have been next to useless. Think of me as your safety deposit box, with a few added bonus features," said Cadson.

"Bonus features?" said one of the other suits, with a nervous smile.

"Yes… such as the knowledge and contacts to turn that information into a cash machine which will keep paying out for years to come. Decades even." Cadson smiled. "Isn't that what you wanted to hear?"

There was a pause before the first of the suited men started to laugh like a chimp in a zoo. Dan glanced up at Cadson and saw relief show on his face. No doubt about it – Cadson was under pressure.

"Now… here's an idea to start the ball rolling. I've thought of a few names we could trial – just to test the viability of the whole plan."

"You really think we should start the draw-down this early?" said the nervous man, one with a squeaky, nervous voice.

"Why not?" said Cadson. "But you'll still have to wait a week. Just to give me time to make a few final preparations. That's all."

"So long as it's safe you can take as long as you need," said the calmest of the men. "But the chance of an early cash bonus does sound good…" said the tall one, laughing again.

"I thought it might," said Cadson. Dan noticed the sheets of paper in Cadson's hands as he handed them around to the other men. The sheets looked handwritten, yet the pattern of the writing suggested they were all the same. Which mean they were probably photocopies… maybe a list of names Cadson had planned to draw down from – whatever that meant. Dan had an inkling. But as yet he could only guess. To know for sure, he would need to get much closer. He needed to take a look at one of those sheets for himself. Dan looked back to the table where Eva was sitting at the back of the room. He struggled for a decent view, trying to catch her eye, but when he got it, he saw she was still drinking alone. Eva didn't look happy. Evidently, Parker hadn't bothered going back to the table as instructed. The old man was proving to be as awkward as ever. Dan tutted and moved on. He had other things to worry about. Next, Dan scoped the room for his latest concern. Alice Perry. Mentioning her suspicions about his supposed relationship with Gemma Cassidy amounted to blackmail, pure and simple. But there was nothing in it. Nothing at all. *So why then did he feel so guilty…?* Alice Perry was already getting under his skin. He caught a glimpse of Perry talking to her photographer friend nearer the bar. They were busy schmoozing with some other poor schmuck in a suit, sizing him up for a story no doubt. The guy was smiling and joking, while failing to notice that he was swimming with sharks.

More fool him. Dan guessed he was in the clear. He stood up and walked past the row of suits until he was ahead of them, his back towards them as he leaned against the gallery window to hide his face. He watched the dog trainers leading their sinewy hounds slowly towards the starting traps far below. It wouldn't be long now until everyone was focused on the race. Dan glanced back to his right and saw one of the printed sheets had been left on the floor nearby one of the men's feet. But Dan saw he would have to pass Cadson unseen to reach it. He waited and chose his moment. When Cadson turned his head to look back at the bar, Dan stepped past the front seats, and climbed up a few steps towards the last man in the group. He was one step away, the loose sheet of handwritten paper in his sights, but he had to make it look natural. Make it look like nothing. All Dan needed to do was duck, swipe it, and walk away and the guy wouldn't even know what was missing. Easy… he started to count time in his head. A private countdown for the moment when he made his move… 3… 2… 1…

He started to reach for it when suddenly, everybody froze. A shrill, ear-piercing electronic alarm filled the air high above the chatter and laughter. It was like a car alarm but far louder, far more intense. The crowds shifted and complained at the noise and looked around to see the cause. And as everyone looked around, Dan was caught out and exposed. The guy with the note at his feet looked up and found Dan too close. His eyes betrayed his suspicion. Dan looked across the line and found Cadson's eyes fixed on his. The game was up. Fortunately, Cadson looked the only one who posed any kind of threat. The alarm blared on and a few of the staff in blue polo necks appeared in the crowd.

"Ladies and Gents! Follow the signs! This is not a drill! Please make your way to the nearest available exit!" called the woman nearest them. "Don't run. Don't panic. Please walk calmly to the nearest available exit."

"What is this?" shouted a drunk as he passed the woman's shoulder.

"I don't know, sir. But it's certainly not a drill. Not on the opening night."

Dan maintained eye contact with Cadson as he ran up the last few steps back to the suddenly chaotic hustle of the main bar area. Cadson imitated him, bolting up the short flight of steps by his chair. As Dan got ready for the confrontation, he watched two burly security types in high-viz vests herding the crowd like sheep, away from the seating area. He saw Eva among them, the herd coming in a thick wave towards the crowded bar area. As Cadson tried to push his way up to the bar, the big high-viz men cut across his path.

"The bar's closed, sir. You need to take the nearest exit," said the biggest man. Cadson didn't like it.

"But I need to get my stuff," he said. "It's up there."

But the security man shook his head and put a palm on his chest. "Forget it. If this is a fire, your stuff stays. Out you go. The exit is down there."

Dan watched the security guy point Cadson and his friends to a door which had been opened in the gallery glass. A stream of punters from the gallery seating area were pouring out into the outdoor seating areas. Cadson watched but stood his ground, considering his options. The security man leaned into him and stared into his eyes. And while Cadson was stuck, Dan swept up past the security into the upper crowd.

He brushed past Alice Perry and her photographer lady-friend as they hustled towards the main exit doors. "Is this anything to do with you?" said Alice, with an arched eyebrow.

"Not this time," said Dan, cutting across their path.

"Of course not. It never is," said Perry. "Call me, remember."

Dan stayed quiet and pushed on.

As the bar crowd were pushed along by the tide, Dan caught sight of a garish rust coloured suit lingering underneath the signs for the toilets at the end of the bar. Noticing Parker's furtive movements, Dan narrowed his eyes. The old man was acting shifty. He was moving away from the toilets like he wanted to avoid being seen. But Dan didn't want to lose the old man in the chaos.

"Parker!" he called. He watched as the old man nearly jumped out of his skin and turned to face him, a look of guilt etched deep in every line of his face, a guilt which shone deep from the dark pits of his eyes. The look on Parker's face startled Dan for a second. Then suspicion got the better of him. Dan pushed through the crowds, reached Parker's shoulder and looked past him towards the toilet corridor at the end of the bar. He saw the single red fire alarm box mounted on the wall halfway down. The glass was shattered, and the light on top blinked red.

"You! You did this!" snapped Dan.

"Keep your voice down, or the punters will have me lynched," he whispered. "Anyway, it might not have been me."

"You virtually just admitted it. Why? I was right there. I was listening to Cadson and his people. I was just about to find out what he was doing here. He was giving out a sheet of paper to his people. A sheet with a bunch of names on it and he was promising he could draw money against them. Parker? Do you know anything about that?"

Parker shook his head and shrugged. "As if I know what that rogue gets up to. It'll be some scam or other no doubt."

"Please vacate the building!" called the security guard who was heading their way.

"Wait a minute…" said Dan. He looked into Parker's eyes. "You knew! You knew I was getting close to him, and you intervened just before I got my hands on those notes. You never wanted me to get close to him, did you? Is that why you hit the fire alarm? Just to stop me?"

"You're far too suspicious for your own good, you know. It must be your line of work. Most unhealthy."

"You two! Move along!" The security man thrust out his arms in a wide gesture, to usher them on.

"Yes, yes, we're going," said Parker. "And we'd better go this way too. Cadson's gone down through the stadium. If we go this way, we'll be out in the clear."

"Scams, Jonathan… your words, not mine. Why do I feel like I'm smack bang in the middle of another one?" said Dan, as he started walking at the old man's side.

Dan caught Eva's eye halfway across the hustle and bustle and waved her towards him. She started to weave through the people on their way out.

Parker opened his mouth as if to speak but seemed to think better of it. But his words eventually came as they skipped down the main steps for the exit and the car park.

"Dan, I would never embroil you and your dear Eva in anything underhand or iffy… you've helped me far too much to ever do that to you. The way I see it, I've hired you for this job as a way of saying thanks for everything you've done for me."

"Yeah? Then why did you hit that fire alarm?" said Dan, as Eva drew up at their side. The car park was full of people.

"What? He hit the fire alarm?" said Eva, looking at Parker. "You started all this fuss?"

"Why not broadcast it a little louder, eh?" said Parker. "Come on… there's a quick way out on that side. The side street over there should take us back towards your car without that psycho Cadson seeing us.

Parker moved like a man possessed, skipping away from them at a rate of knots, head tilted down, like a track sprinter. Dan stepped up his pace to follow as Parker cut across the car park towards a low side wall. Eva followed suit.

"So why did you do it?" called Dan.

"You know why. Because I don't want us having any dealings with that man. He's the enemy. There's nothing good to be learned from him. He's just best avoided at all costs. All I want from you is to keep him away from me and keep him away from Amelia until our work is done."

Dan gave Eva a sideward glance, signalling his displeasure with a shake of the head.

"There's always something to be learned by watching your opponent… that's what every boxer does. It's what people do in every sport and in every walk of life. It's a skill to work out what your opponent is trying to hide. What don't you want us to know, Parker?"

"Sport isn't always a useful metaphor for real life, Dan," said Parker. "I want you to trust me. That girl needs your help, and so do I. You'll have my eternal gratitude if you only do as I ask."

"Gratitude?" said Dan. "I think we'll take a cash payment instead, thanks."

"And you'll get that as well. When the boat comes in, so to speak."

"Now hang on… *when the boat comes in?*" said Dan, as Parker swung his leg over the car park wall.

"It's another metaphor. When I get paid, you do too."

"We never agreed on a conditional payment or anything like that," said Dan.

Eva sighed. "Wait here, will you? I don't need you two bickering in my ear while I fetch the car."

She hurried off down the side street leaving Dan and Parker standing by the wall of the dog track stadium. Dan looked at Parker and shook his head. But Parker was already acting up again. He stood up on tiptoe like a meerkat to peer about the dispersing crowd. When he finished, he ducked back down and hunched out of sight like a kid playing at being a spy.

"What is it now? What are you so afraid of?" said Dan, looking back into the melee. But he couldn't see any sign of Cadson.

"Sorry. I seem to be experiencing a little anxiety lately. I think it's just old age or something. I'll have to go back to the quack and ask him for some of those beta blockers."

Dan watched as a shiny black Jeep pulled away from the chaos in the centre of the car park. The Jeep seemed to be heading for the exit, then it stopped and doubled back in a wide loop which took it close to the side wall. A moment later, Dan realised the Jeep was heading right for them. Dan strained his eyes to stare though the dark windscreen. His heart thudding harder in his chest, he fully expected to see the shaven-headed Cadson behind the steering wheel. But when his eyes made sense of what he saw, Dan was almost relieved. There were two Asian men in the front of the Jeep. Thin looking guys in tracksuit tops. Then Dan noticed the two men looked extremely unhappy. Parker blinked at the black car as it cruised towards them. A look of concern started to crystallise among the lines and wrinkles.

"Parker…?" said Dan, staring at the Jeep. As it got nearer it began to slow down. The driver turned the Jeep, so its side doors were facing towards them, just on the other side of the car park. The low wall was the only barrier between them.

"Parker…? What else haven't you told us… who are these guys?"

Side on, Dan could see there was another man in the back of the car who looked like a smaller, dumpier version of the others. They wore their hair cut in an old-fashioned schoolboy style – short back and sides with a side parting. And they all wore the same dour-faced frown.

"Don't tell me, Jonathan," said Dan. "Last time you came to Romford, you walked out of a Chinese restaurant without paying the bill."

Parker looked up at the black Jeep as the doors started to open, and the men inside stepped out.

"Oh no. Bad luck. It's those three…" said Parker, glumly.

"Those three. Who are they?"

"It's got nothing to do with any unpaid restaurant bills, I can assure you. But it just so happens that they're from Thailand. Funny that."

"Funny?!" said Dan, as he watched the young Thai men slam the doors on their Jeep.

"I didn't expect to see those boys ever again. I doubted they'd ever set foot outside Chang Mai."

"Chang Mai?"

Parker smiled at him, weakly. "Yes. I happened to spend a little leisure time in Thailand soon after we got that money out of Hither Green. I had a great time. Really rather wonderful, actually. At least it was at first."

"At first?" said Dan, his face scrunching into cynical readiness for what was coming.

"Yes," said Parker. "It was just a shame I couldn't leave on such good terms."

"JP – what the hell am I supposed to do with you?" said Dan.

"Don't worry about me. I think you should worry about them," said Parker.

"Parker," said the small dumpy man in a clipped Asian accent. He took the lead at the front of the two other, younger men. Now that they were near, Dan saw they had the look of close family. The same eyes. The same mouth. The men had to be brothers.

"Anuman!" said Parker, with a jolly air. "How the devil are you? So good you could make it to Blighty to sample the fine culture of English dog racing."

"Don't you dare talk like we are friends, Parker. You know what you did. You owe my family. You owe all of us."

Dan looked between Parker and the approaching trio.

The little lead man swung a stiff fat leg over the wall to step closer to them. The other two men stepped over the wall and folded their arms. While the little man devoted his full attention to Parker, the other two seemed far more interested in Dan. Dan met their eye and nodded. The two taller brothers didn't respond.

"What did you do, Parker?" said Dan, not taking his eyes from the brothers.

"Not much, really. I did what any visiting Englishman does when they go to Chiang Mai."

"What?" said Dan. "You saw the sights. You went on a jungle safari. Sampled a few curries. Enjoyed the sunshine."

"Oh yes. And the rest."

"Talk to me when I'm talking to you!" snapped the little man. "Don't you dare disrespect us!" said the little man.

"And the rest?" said Dan. "JP literally everyone we meet seems to hate your guts. Have you ever stopped to consider why?"

The small man shook his head, then moved fast. He stepped forwards and smashed a deep body blow into Dan's stomach. Ordinarily, the blow would have simply hurt. But against his badly healing scar, the strike sent a shockwave of pain flooding through Dan's body, filling every synapse with a molten agony. The world had stopped and was filled with pain. While Dan doubled over and groaned, the little man stepped back to his original position.

"You, be quiet!" said the Asian addressing Dan with a pointing hand. "This is between him and us. You open your mouth again, we hit you harder, understand?"

Dan was too busy enduring the pain to hear. Out of nothing more than self-respect, Dan managed to pull himself upright. Grimacing, Dan wiped a tear of pain from his eyes.

"You dishonoured us, Parker. All of us. You gave us no alternative but to come to this country to take back what you owe us."

"Son of a bitch… that hurt," said Dan, as his breath returned.

One of the brothers stepped forward and lashed a punitive strike against Dan's cheek. This time there was no pain. Dan took the hit, stepped back, and straightened his shoulders.

"Hey, that's enough," growled Dan. He stood back and jabbed a finger of warning at all three of them. "You hit me again, and I'll give you a few reasons to book the next flight home."

The little man nodded an instruction to his brother. Another punch was coming his way. This time, Dan swiped the thin man's bony fist away and gave him a flat-handed slap on the cheek in reply. An eye for an eye. It was enough for now.

"Let's not do this," said Dan. "If you've got a problem with Parker here, we can sort it out another way."

"But we are already fixing it. We don't need your involvement," said the smaller man. "This is what Parker must do. Listen. You owe my family ten thousand pounds. And now you owe us another five thousand to cover the cost of our flights to London, and another five thousand for the cost of our flights home."

"Ten thousand for three return flights to Chiang Mai!" said Parker almost choking. "Did you charter a private bloody jet?!

"Think of it as compensation," said the dumpy man. "That's twenty thousand pounds, Parker. You will give us twenty thousand with no excuses. We came here to get that money, and if we don't get it, we'll take our compensation by other means."

One of the brothers spoke in thick Thai accent. "A photograph of your dead body would be a suitable alternative to take home. Our mother is very, very angry."

"*Your* mother always is," said Parker.

The little man frowned, and the brothers tensed. Dan threw up his hands and stepped between them.

"Hey. Enough is enough. We'll work something out."

"Shut your face," said the little man. "He pays or we kill him. Twenty thousand pounds. Forty-eight hours. We'll be watching you, Parker… come on."

The little man stepped over the low wall with some difficulty before his brothers helped him and they walked back to the car.

"What the hell did you do in Thailand?" said Dan.

"I did what every red-blooded male does at some point in their lives. I took a risk."

"Then stop taking risks, please! Your risks hurt other people. And stop being so damn vague and start telling the truth. What is wrong with you?"

"What is wrong with you, more like," said Parker. "I hired you as my professional protection, but you can't even take a rabbit punch from an angry Thai dwarf. What kind of help are you going to be exactly?!"

Anger flashed in Dan's eyes. The pain was echoing around his gut.

"You watch your mouth – and I'm not your protection, either. You hired us to help you with the girl on your mysterious investment mission. The way I see it, you've lied to hire us for a dodgy job and financial caper, all wrapped up with your lust for a girl who is a quarter of your age."

"That's not it at all! You've got me wrong."

"Whatever, JP. I'm tired of dressing this up. I'm saying what I see. And if I'm wrong, then it's time you started telling me otherwise. And as for those Thai guys, do they have a point? They sound seriously aggrieved."

"I did just what any other Englishman abroad would have done. I don't intend to be blackmailed or bullied for it."

"Jonathan, why don't you just offer them the ten thousand to get them off your back? Clear the basic debt and I'm sure they'll go. Come on. You've got plenty of dough these days, and you really don't need those guys on your back while you're setting up this other deal. Who knows what could happen with them around? They could make things go very sour for you."

"Then it's a good job I've hired you to help me, isn't it?" said Parker. "I tell you, I'm not paying those greedy brothers a single penny."

Dan stared into Parker's small moody eyes. The old man sighed.

"Some things are about more than the money, Dan. Some things are a matter of principle."

"Principles? You?" said Dan. "You're kidding me, right? Since when have you ever been concerned with principles…?"

Eva's red Alfa Romeo drew up at the kerb beside them. Dan couldn't remember the last time he'd been so glad to see her. The driver's window slid down.

"What's happened? Are you okay?" she said, looking at the exasperation on Dan's face.

"Ask him," said Dan. "See if you can get a straight answer out of him, because I've had enough of trying."

Dan scowled at Parker as he walked round to the front passenger door. Parker sighed and got into the back seat.

"I'm sure you don't treat all your clients like this."

"No," said Eva. "And with very good reason."

Eva gave Jonathan a hard look in the rear-view mirror, then turned the car out into the street and drove off with Parker quietly humphing in the back seat.

Six

The next day.

At half past eleven on Saturday morning, Dan parked the Egomobile on Distra Lane, Basildon, and walked to the gate of the terraced house he had last visited almost fifteen years before. He blinked at the white painted wagon wheel left on the front lawn and the concrete gnome, its nose grown with bright green moss. The white wagon wheel had been neat and crisp when he last saw it. Clean and ornamental. But today the wheel's whiteness had succumbed to a browny grey, and a few of the spokes had rotted and fallen through to the lawn below. Death and decay had been captured in that wheel. Fifteen years back, Malachy would have kept that wheel in good order just like he always had. Order, discipline, focus. They were the watchwords of Ed Malachy's whole life but it looked like things had changed. Dan pressed the doorbell and noticed how small the house seemed. A whole minute seemed to pass before a small pale figure shuffled to the door and pressed his face to the distorted glass. There was no mistaking that lined face and hawkish eyes. Ed Malachy opened the door and looked at out at him with a wry smile.

"You're like a freaking homing pigeon. I knew you'd get here soon enough. Well, come on in then. You'd better come in now that you're here."

As welcomes went, it was pure Ed Malachy, and Dan was already beaming. Fifteen years dropped away like a discarded robe. He stepped up into the hallway and was immersed into a fug of greasy cooked food, old man's aftershave, and menthol oil. He walked straight down the narrow hall feeling almost nineteen again, following Ed until he got to the kitchen at the end, fully expecting to give big old Mary a cosy embrace, and ready to accept one of her homemade buns.

But there was no embrace. Mary wasn't there. Dan turned to look at Ed and his smile dropped away. Malachy nodded slowly.

"Go through, son. Go through," said Malachy, his words were quiet, and loaded with emotion.

Malachy gestured to the open door which led them out to a little lean-to conservatory that smelt of damp.

"Mary passed six years ago. She had a stroke, and then not long after she had another massive one. It was the second one that got her. Mary, my sweetheart. Yep… life can be very hard, Danny boy. But I guess you know all about that, by now."

"I'm sorry, Malachy. I wish I'd known."

"I wish I didn't," said Malachy. "And I'd love to offer you one of those sugary buns, but I can't, son. She always knew I didn't want you fighting boys eating that crap anyway, but Mary just couldn't help herself."

"Too much of a mother figure," said Dan.

"Too bloody stubborn, more like – and she didn't care what I thought either way."

Dan grinned.

"So… what brings you home, kid?" said Malachy.

Kid. Hah. Dan hadn't been called that in a while.

"Come on, Ed. You know why I'm here. And you know all there is to know… I've told you most of it. I went to see Greg Saunders. He was in hospital. Did you know about that?"

Malachy blinked and nodded. "Yeah… poor Greg. Why the hell would they ever pick on him?"

"It's not a *they,* Malachy. It's a him."

Malachy swallowed, his Adam's apple bobbing up and down on his saggy neck. Malachy's eyes stayed on Dan's. They were sharp now. Keen.

"I've seen him twice now. I caught a glimpse when he shot me. Then I got a second look at him after I found Carl Proberty down in Devon."

"Yeah… Carl. That was bad. Very bad. It's been all over the news, too. The body of an ex-world champion found hung in his little bedroom. The police are suggesting that he took his own life."

"Bullshit, Ed. You know that, and I know that."

"Yeah… but he was in debt. Big debt. That's what they are saying caused him to do it."

"That's a very convenient lie," said Dan.

"Ain't it?" said Malachy. "I know he was murdered, Dan."

"He was. And I saw one of your old training gloves on the floor beneath his body."

The old man's eyes blinked wide open.

"What?"

"I think the killer tied him up and used him for a punchbag."

"No. That's sick."

Dan shrugged. "That's what it looked like to me."

Malachy turned pale and shook his head.

"I saw the man's eyes, Ed. He's a cold-blooded killer. The man is a psychopath, pure and simple. Carl described this man as a monster and I thought he'd lost it. I thought Carl had grown weak and fearful, because we were never scared of anyone. Not back in the old days. But Carl was right. I saw that man's eyes. His is a monster, Ed. He's seriously dark. But that still doesn't mean there's no motive behind this. There has to be a reason why he's targeting your people."

"My people? Our people, Dan. But if you came here for answers on that, then sorry to disappoint you, you've come to the wrong place. I don't know anything. I'm just an old man with my best days behind me. Look at my home, Bradley. You can see the life I've led. I put it all back into the boys' club. Every penny."

"Then maybe this isn't about money. If it was money, he could have gone straight for the big time. Chris Geller has got be worth a few million by now."

"Easily," said Malachy. "But The Slick left my stable a long, long time ago. He wasn't one of my fighters any more, Bradley. He's not one of us."

"You can say that again. Geller's gone all showbiz and arrogant as they come. With an ego like that it won't be long before he falls."

Malachy shrugged. "Maybe. But I still wouldn't wish this guy on anyone."

Dan bit his lip and shook his head.

"What is it?" said Malachy.

"Oh… it's nothing, Ed."

"Bullshit, son. Out with it," said the old man. "You drive all the way out here for the first time in fifteen years… you've taken on this psycho and your face looks like you're seeing ghosts… Dan – don't you leave here without saying what you came here to say."

Dan nodded and forced a smile. Ed Malachy was still the same tough old man he always had been.

"Yeah. I guess you're right."

"Of course, I'm bloody right. Well what is it?"

"It's just that if this man wants to hurt us so much – if that's all this is about – then there really isn't a way to stop him, is there? Do you see?"

"What do you mean?" said Malachy, sitting back in his chair. The old man looked upset.

"I mean, money, Malachy. That's easy to understand. That's a motive you can deal with, one way or another. Pay up or don't pay. Settle the dispute another way until it's done. End of story. But if this guy is just out to punish us for God knows what – or if he's on some kind of vendetta, then he won't ever stop until he wants to. There's no way you can negotiate with that. He won't stop until he's done what he set out to accomplish. And if that means hurting us, well who knows how long that could take? He could keep coming back for more… it might never end."

Malachy nodded gravely. "You're beginning to sound like Carl Proberty. You're worried about your girl, is that it?"

Dan's eyes locked onto the old man's. He nodded. "That's part of it. But not all. I'm worried about me too. I'm don't want to end up like Carl."

Malachy nodded. "And you won't. You're a different prospect."

"You think so?" said Dan. From the dark space he occupied, his mind was hungry for encouragement. He needed a chink of light. Malachy was the best he could hope for.

"Yes. You're Dan Bradley, remember? You're the one who never gives up."

"I don't give up…" said Dan, his voice loaded with doubt. Malachy shook his head. "No," he said firmly. "You don't." Dan nodded and let the words sink in before he spoke again.

"Malachy… Greg said this bastard showed him a photograph of me talking to Proberty just before he died. He showed Greg a photograph of me going to Proberty's house after he had him hung…"

"Then let's hope the police never see those or they might link you to the murder."

Malachy's words were like an electric jolt through his body. He'd never considered those risks before. Dan saw he was under pressure from every angle. The killer had all the cards and was controlling the game. He was the only one who knew what the rules were.

"Greg said the guy told him that he only killed Proberty because I was onto him. And he told Greg that if I didn't give up pursuing him, that he would kill Greg too."

Dan met the old man's eyes.

Malachy sighed.

"He's trying to put the brakes on you, Dan. And from the look of you, it sounds like he's succeeding. He's doing a job on you, just like he did with Carl," Malachy looked Dan in the eye and reached for his hand. He seized Dan's wrist to make sure he had his full attention. Dan couldn't look anywhere else but into Malachy's watery eyes. The old man raised his voice and breathed mentholated vapours all over his face.

"The bastard did a job on Carl, didn't he? He chased the man three hundred miles out of town and crippled his bloody mind before he finally took the man's body. That's torture in my book. That's inhuman. And that's what this man did. And he's been hitting a lot of people and their families too. There's no respect in that. No honour. He's a cruel man hitting all my old boys. A lot of your friends, Dan. From what you just said, he's done a job on Greg Saunders too. So Greg is telling you this is your fault? Well it's not. It's all on the man who's doing this. All of it. Every single bit. You're not to blame in the least. Why? Because you're one of the victims. Now this scumbag may have gotten into Carl's head and he may have gotten into Greg's head… hell, let's be honest… he might even have gotten into this lonely old man's head. I live alone, Dan, I have too much time on my hands. It was bound to happen. But you? You? No way. You're Dan Bradley. You're a fighter, Dan. Don't let him see that you have a weakness. Not even for one single minute. You know how this fight game works."

"A weakness…?"

Malachy nodded. "You care for people, Dan, and sometimes you care too much. Don't let this bastard see it, or it could be your downfall."

"I have other weaknesses, Ed."

"You're afraid. So what? Fear always made you fight like a tiger. So use it. Fight. Don't be controlled by this man. Don't be controlled by your fear. Go out there. Avoid Greg if you need to. Avoid anyone who trips you up in this."

"Ed… I thought you didn't want me to take this on."

"But now I see that you're the only one who can. Whatever this bastard wants from us… he has to be stopped. This can't go on."

"You think I should find him?"

"You have to. If you don't, who else is there? Besides, if you stop, this thing could eat you up like it did with Carl. You could end up like him. And that's not who you are. It never was."

"But Malachy, what if he kills Greg because of me? I'll have that on my conscience too."

The old man shook his head slowly. "It won't be on your conscience. It'll be on his. You mustn't stop, Bradley. If you do, others will suffer worse. You know it's true. You're the only one who still has any fight left in them."

Dan looked deep into the old man's eyes. His pupils were no more than pin-pricks in the centre of his pale blue irises from all the worry and strain. Dan imagined he didn't look much better himself.

"I know people have been suffering, Malachy. That's why I've been trying to draw everyone together. I wanted to create a united front between us. Without that, I don't know if I can do it."

"Don't know…? Or scared that you'll be alone."

"I'm hurt Malachy. I don't like to admit it, but that bastard hurt me bad."

Dan looked into Malachy's unrelenting eyes, and the years fell away again. He felt like he had when he was back in the ring in those ABA days, when Malachy would be building him up, telling him the other guy was ripe for the taking, if only he could believe and stay the distance.

"I don't like being scared, Ed. You know… I've faced death before…"

Malachy's eyes trailed down to the stump of Dan's little finger, then returned to his eyes.

"Looks like you have. It looks to me like you've been hurt bad before. But you came through it, and here you are."

"But this man almost killed me – he almost killed me just to send me a message. I've never dealt with anything like that before."

Malachy reached out and slapped Dan's bicep.

"Don't talk yourself out of it. That's what Carl Proberty spent his time doing. You can do this. You're the only one who can. Forget Chris Geller. Forget Carl too, if you can. And as for Greg… Greg let his guard down. He's let this scumbag get into his head. But you? You can't afford to do that. We're all relying on you."

"And? What if Greg ends up dead because of it? Because of me? You think I'll be able to live with that?"

"Dan… come on! What choice have you got? You remember what I always said to you out there – in your corner of the ring. Get up. Get back up and box on. Box on, son! Box on! Trust yourself. Come on, Dan. Deep down, somewhere, you know you can stop this man… right now you're the only one who can."

Malachy looked into his eyes searching for the fire of Dan's self-belief. But it seemed he couldn't find it, because the old man added. "I know you can do it. I believe in you."

Dan smiled, and stood up.

"That's good, Ed… thank you. Because right now, you're the only one who does. I'll be seeing you."

"I think you will," said Malachy. "But don't wait fifteen years next time, okay."

Dan grinned. "Okay."

"See yourself out, will you. It's a long way for these old legs."

Dan nodded and paced down the narrow hall corridor, as Malachy watched him leave. The old man sighed when the door was shut and ambled into his kitchen. He opened a cupboard and pulled out a half-empty bottle of Scotch and pulled a mug off the little wooden mug tree. He poured a generous three-finger measure and took a big gulp. Scotch was a lonely man's last comfort… and after hearing Bradley's lack of confidence he needed a stiff drink more than ever. With Bradley shot to pieces, there was no telling how this might end.

***

Dan jumped into the Egomobile and sank deep into his seat. His eyes tracked past the broken, rotting wagon-wheel in Malachy's front garden. It seemed the sun was setting on another great life, but Dan didn't want the man to suffer in his final years. *Box on, son, box on.* The words echoed around his head, taunting him for his fear. Fear used to be his friend. It had spurred him on to fight. But the fear of death felt so heavy, Dan thought it might crush him. For the first time in a very long time – the prospect of failure seemed tangible. And if he failed… the consequences were obvious enough. The man had already pulled a trigger on him once. He wouldn't hesitate to do it again. Dan faced his own eyes in the rear-view mirror. He was back in the territory of kill or be killed. And this time, he had to do it alone.

His mobile phone rang in his pocket. Dan pulled it free and saw Eva's name on screen.

"Eva. You okay?" said Dan, as he answered.

"I'm okay, yes. But we need to watch him like a hawk."

"Who?" said Dan stiffening in his seat.

"Jonathan, of course," said Eva.

"Oh. Yeah. You didn't need to remind me."

"He's gone off sulking, Dan. He went off in a huff because apparently we're not taking him seriously enough."

"So what? Let him sulk."

"But he's not just any other client. He's Devon's brother, Dan. We owe it to old Devon to look after his brother. We've still got to treat him with kid gloves."

"I don't like kid gloves."

"Then it's best you remember the job. The money," said Eva.

Dan tutted. "Okay. I get it. So where's he gone?"

"The Railway Inn."

"That dive? It suits him."

"Dan…" said Eva.

"Okay. Okay, I'll go and fetch him and try and talk some sense into him."

"Thanks, Dan. So how did it go with Malachy?"

"About as well as I could have hoped."

But Dan's tone of voice said it didn't go very far.

"Okay…" said Eva. "Let's get Parker out of our hair, then I'll help, I promise."

"I don't think you can, Eva. I need to keep you away from this one."

He could feel Eva preparing to contradict him, but Dan was in no mood for an argument.

"I'll get the old man and I'll see you soon, okay?"

Dan ended the call before Eva could say anything else. Such bluntness wasn't going to help matters between them, but Dan decided he would deal with the fall-out when the time came. He started the engine and set off along the fast, drag-strip roads of Basildon back towards Southend, just another stressed out boy-racer in a hurry. The Railway Inn? At least it wasn't The Sutland Arms, the dark and sweaty fleapit where scallywags and snitches idled away their time. Small mercies and all that. But Dan had forgotten one important aspect about drinking at The Railway. Its proximity to The Record newspaper offices…

Seven

The Railway was busy with a good mix of barflies and flouncers. There were the kind who wore leather waistcoats, a garment Dan couldn't remember being seen in any clothes store for at least twenty years. Then there were the over grown rock 'n' rollers and the mature students who had never graduated past the beery excitement of their first halcyon drinking days. Then there were the students pure and simple, the ones dodging lectures to drink the day away. Finally there were the pin-eyed alcoholics propping up one end of the pale brown wooden bar. The Railway was a big pub, wide but not deep, with a narrow customer seating area stretching all around it. And with the spring days getting warmer, the pub didn't smell too pleasant. The stink of slops stale sweat and smokers' breath hit Dan as soon as he walked through the old wooden doors, but he was committed to the cause. He wouldn't walk back out until he'd found the man he was looking for. Dan glanced around, blocked his ears to the drunken chatter and hunted for the face he wanted. There. He saw JP standing in a corner beside a grey plastic payphone which must have been teleported in from a previous decade. But then the whole pub looked lost in the time/space continuum, much like its drinkers.

And JP was the worst of all. A rogue Doctor Who, wearing the worst of all imaginable costumes. His snazzy orange and brown suit. And by now he looked drunk to boot.

Dan cut his way through the drinkers until he was beside Parker, who was busy talking to the barman. The barman wore nothing on his torso apart from a well-worn leather waistcoat. He leaned on the bar with both wiry tattooed arms, exposing his hairy armpits. The barman stopped smiling when he saw the mood music written on Dan's face. Parker turned to see who the barman was looking at, and as Dan looked over Parker's shoulder, he was forced to squint in the light reflected from the grey windows of The Record newspaper offices. Alice Perry appeared in his mind, and his gut burned. Dan tried to put the thought aside.

"What are you doing, Jonathan?"

"Me? Taking solace with a few new friends. At least these people don't berate me all the time."

Parker picked up his pint and took an enthusiastic gulp. His eyes were glassy. Dan wondered how long he'd been drinking.

"Berating you? We're trying to help you, Jonathan."

"Yes. For a price, mind…" said the man, making his point in front of the barman.

Dan ignored the comment. "And you're not making it easy. You won't give us the tools we need. We've got no information, which leaves us guessing as to what's going on. You've got people after your blood, Parker. You want us to protect you and Amelia – whoever she is – and then you run away like a spoilt child."

"I didn't run anywhere. I told Eva and that intern kid of yours exactly where I was going. I knew very well that you'd come to fetch me. It was all perfectly planned. And now, as you're here, you may as well join me for a drink."

"No thanks," said Dan. "One of us needs to keep our head straight. Besides which, I'm driving."

"You keeping your head? I don't think so. These days you look more strung out than a string quartet. Well? Doesn't he?" said Parker, thumbing towards Dan's face so the barman would look and agree. The barman glanced at Dan, but something in what he saw warned him not to comment. "Enjoy your drink, Jonathan," said the barman, slinging his bar towel over his bare shoulder. "I need to serve the other end of the bar."

The guy nodded at Dan and slunk away.

"See the effect you have on people with that stressed out face of yours?" said Parker. "You're still a young man, Dan. You should relax more. Enjoy the best that life has to offer. What do you think dear old Devon would say?"

"Devon would tell you to put down that pint glass and get a grip of yourself."

"But Devon loved a drink or two."

"Devon worked his whole life and he worked hard. The drinking came when the job was done. And then his problems came with it."

Parker frowned and put his glass to his lips.

"You're becoming a grumpy old man ahead of schedule, Mr Bradley."

"And I'm sad to say you haven't changed a bit since the last time we met," said Dan. "Now, are you coming with me, or do I have to make an example of you."

"I am not your child."

"Then stop acting like one."

Dan's eyes tracked to The Record building across the street. For a moment, he imagined he could see a shadow watching him from the window. He looked again, straining his eyes but saw no one behind the dull glass. He'd imagined it, that's all. Parker was right. He *was* strung out. He needed to get back to the office, to focus on the job for a while…

"Okay, okay, I'm coming. Just give me a few minutes to enjoy the rest of the pint, then I'll be done. Deal?"

"Five minutes, and not a minute more. And, JP. You could have chosen a better pub than this."

"Snob. That's one thing about me. My brush with wealth never changed me, Dan. I know that I'm no better than these people in here irrespective of all the money I had."

The words pricked Dan's ears.

"Had?" said Dan, his eyebrows arching high at the use of the past tense. "Did you say all the money you 'had'?"

"Oh. I meant have, of course. It was just a slip of the tongue brought about by the old drink. Don't start fretting now."

Dan shook his head. His phone vibrated in his pocket. Dan slipped out the phone and stared at the text message, keeping the screen angled away from Parker's prying eyes.

"You've become enslaved to that silly thing," said Parker. "Maybe that's what your problem is. All this modern life is killing you…"

"Modern life is killing me, is it?" said Dan as he scan-read the text. "Jonathan, you read me so well…"

The text was from Alison Saunders – pretty much the last person he was expecting to make contact. Especially after Greg and the hospital nurse had insisted on his departure from Basildon ICU. Dan dumped his jacket on the barstool by Parker and stepped away to get a better view of the screen. As soon as Parker was out of his eyesight, the old man raised a hand across the bar to get the barman's attention for another beer. The words of the text bothered Dan, so much he had to read them again.

I know it didn't go well before, Dan. But what you said has me worried. I've seen a man walking past the ward. He's been past twice, and he stared at me both times. He doesn't look like a doctor. I never saw who hurt Greg, and I'm scared, Dan. If you can come by the hospital, it would really help me feel better. Sorry for before. Alison x

Dan read the message through twice and felt his gut tighten as if someone was tying it into a knot. *The bastard was there.* So Malachy was wrong… the threat to harm Greg was no idle one. The killer would certainly target Greg if he kept pushing. But maybe there was a chance Alison was wrong – after all, she had every reason to be as stressed and paranoid as Dan. Her husband's life was on the line. The woman needed to be reassured. But so did Dan. If he left Greg to chance, no matter what the man said to him in that ward, it would be like abandonment. He couldn't do it. Malachy was right on that score. He had to box on. His instincts wouldn't let him do anything else.

"Looks like that message contains bad news," said a silken voice close beside Dan's ear. Heart thudding hard, Dan wheeled round to see Alice Perry standing beside him, gazing up at him with sparkle and appeal. The girl was probably just over half Dan's age, and he had to admit she scrubbed up well. From the look of the make-up and the styled hair, Alice was certainly trying to impress somebody.

"Alice…" said Dan, forcing a smile to hide his discomfort.

"That's more like it. The profile piece will come out so much better if we're on friendly, first name terms."

Dan shook his head. "What?" Dan glanced at his phone screen but saw Alice Perry's eyes track towards it. He dropped the phone out of sight. Behind Alice, Dan glimpsed Parker being handed another pint by the barman. Alice Perry smiled as she saw anger flash across Dan's face.

"You do seem a bit testy at the moment. A bit under pressure, maybe. You know what they say. A problem shared is a problem halved," said Perry with a chuckle.

"Except in your case, it's a problem multiplied."

"Now, now. No need to be rude, remember?" said Perry.

"I wasn't being rude. I was being honest. You're a reporter, Alice and you're not interested in reporting news. If I share anything with you, I might as well go to the top of the high street and use a loud speaker instead."

The girl shrugged and tilted her head to one side.

"Not true. I do have some loyalty to my best, most useful sources. If they show a willingness to cooperate on a regular basis."

"What are you doing here?" said Dan. "Today's Saturday. Don't you have a home to go to?"

"Yes, I do. But my work is my passion. Like you. I'm always at work."

"Yes, you are," said Dan. "Look…" he said, trying to turn away.

"I saw you from the office, Dan. I've got no idea why you might be in a pub like this, but seeing as you are, you may as well buy me a drink and talk to me. It looks like your friend back there is going to be a little while yet…"

Parker watched Dan with a hint of suspicion and amusement glinting in his eye. When the girl referred to him, Parker raised his pint glass and nodded at them both.

"Oh, don't mind me," called Parker. "Don't mind me at all. I won't listen in. Promise."

"See?" said Alice.

"That stupid old man doesn't know what's good for him," muttered Dan.

"But you do, don't you?" said Alice. "So I'll have a vodka tonic, thanks."

"I'm not buying any drinks, Alice.

"Fine then. Not in here," said Perry. "Somewhere else then. So where are you going to take me? There's a nice quiet place just around the corner from here…"

***

Parker smiled. Dan looked like he was struggling. The sassy young journo wanted more than a story, that was for sure. As far as Parker could make out, she wanted to get Dan into the sack. So far, the boy seemed to be playing hard to get. He was loyal to Eva. Good for him. With a woman at home with smarts and beauty like that, who could blame the boy? But as Parker eyed the girl's assets he wasn't so sure if he would have put up as much of a fight. Parker sipped his fresh pint wondering whether Dan might eventually cave in. And as he continued to cast his eye over the buxom young blonde before him, a man at the bar bumped hard into his shoulder. Parker was shunted against the bar top, and a slosh of cheaper lager landed on his shoe. Parker turned to complain then immediately thought better of it. It was Cadson. His stubbly head and mean eyes were so close he saw all the gritty detail, down to the first few silvery dots at the man's temples, Cadson leaned closer on the bar beside him as if he was just another barfly shooting the breeze. The old man licked his lips nervously and looked back at Dan. But Dan was still busy with the journalist girl. Parker was relieved and petrified at the same time.

"Don't think you can play me anymore, old man…" said Cadson, quietly.

"How did you find me in here?" said Parker, his whispering voice shaking.

"Because I'm smarter than you. And because I'm watching you, of course. Why else would I ever appear in a hole like this. I came to see you."

Parker sipped his beer.

"Look at you. You're a total waste of space. You're the kind of man I wouldn't even use to wipe bird shit off my shoe."

"You do say the nicest things," said Parker.

"I don't have to be nice, not to you. And after what you've done to me, I'm going to be a lot less nice than I am being now. Unless you give me back what you've taken from me."

"I have literally no idea what you're talking about," said Parker, defiantly.

"Oh, you lie so very badly," said Cadson with a grin. "Yes, you do."

"Amelia's free of you. Accept it. She's an adult. She can do whatever she likes, and you can't force her to do anything."

Cadson sidled closer until his shoulder pressed hard against Parker's frail bony chest.

"We both know I can do anything I please. I've got a knife right here. And, if I wanted I could open you up like a suitcase and walk away with a smile on my face, knowing I'd done the world a great act of service. But if I did that today, I know I wouldn't get what I want."

"I already told you," said Jonathan, whispering as he shook.

"Stop blagging, old man. You know I don't need that girl back, so quit stalling. I want what you took from me. Both of you. I know you've got it, and you're going to give it back, or you won't live to see Monday morning."

"But I haven't got it. I haven't!"

"It's not on you. I know that, because you're not that dumb. But I want it by tomorrow night. And if you don't give it to me... I'll show you that knife."

"I don't even know what you're talking about."

"Enough with the lying. Don't use up the rest of your life with lying. You'd be far better doing what I've asked. And I'm warning you – what you did at the dog track hasn't exactly helped your standing with me, either."

"I didn't do anything..."

Parker felt a sharp point press against his scrawny stomach.

"It's high time to stop all the lies. And as for that second-rate bodyguard of yours, well, he's not working out very well, is he?"

"I suppose not," muttered Parker.

"So – the penny finally drops. You'll give it back to me. And you'll give it to me by tomorrow night, along with the cash… or you and your bargain basement bodyguard over here are going to end up very dead. Understand?"

Parker nodded.

"Good man," said Cadson, as he withdrew from Parker's personal space and patted the old man hard on the back, causing a large slop of lager to land on his shoes. "Enjoy the rest of your drink." Cadson adjusted his collar and sauntered away. Parker grimaced and poured the remains of his pint down his gullet until it was gone. He put the empty glass on the bar and looked back. Dan was still busy fending off the blonde… or egging her on. It was hard to tell. Good. Dan's distraction gave him an opportunity – an opportunity he couldn't afford to miss.

"Sorry, old bean," whispered Parker. He stuffed his hand into the folds of Dan's leather jacket on the barstool beside him, and pulled out Dan's brown wallet. The wallet looked full enough, but when Parker opened it he found as many receipts inside as bank notes. He took out all the bank notes, slid out the best-looking bank cards, and closed the wallet. But then he froze and considered his grim reflection in the dirty bar mirror. He tutted at himself. "No. I just can't do it," he whispered. With a quick shake of his head, Parker opened the wallet and put exactly half of the money back in place. And he replaced the cards too - all bar one, then he quickly slipped the wallet back into Dan's pocket and skulked away across the bar. Moments later, the saloon door swung shut and Parker was gone.

Dan gulped on a dry throat. "Alice, I've got a lot on right now. I'm sorry. I don't have time for this."

"As far as I can see you're always busy. You're an action man, Dan. A risk taker. The kind of person my readers would love to read about. Especially my female readers… all I'm asking is for a few minutes of your time. At least let me have the basis for the profile piece. Where's the harm in that? It's a fluff piece. No controversy to be had there."

"Yeah. So you tell me now."

"I promise," said the girl, sparkling at him. "Cross my heart." She drew an imaginary cross over the top of her chest to draw Dan's eye. He saw the gesture but looked away just as quickly.

"I'm sorry Alice. That's a no," said Dan. He pushed past the girl to reach Parker, but he found Parker's position at the bar empty. Dan growled and looked around.

"See. Now we've got plenty of time."

"No, Alice," said Dan.

"So, is this who you are? A man who gives his word, and then who constantly breaks it? Is that the reputation you want? Because you must know by now, your reputation can be shaped or broken by a journalist's pen."

Dan frowned. "What?" said Dan wheeling round.

"I told you before. You asked me for help, and you got it, didn't you?"

"I asked you for a telephone number. A telephone number, Alice," said Dan.

"Yes. And I got you Willard Burton's number exactly when you needed it. But it was always quid pro quo. You were supposed to give me information on that case and then help out with the profile feature. But instead you gave me nothing. There are now rumours of another investigation into the Leroy Burton killing, which means whatever you could have given me is already yesterday's news. That's no good at all. That would have been a huge scoop. You let me down. So, the least you owe me is that profile piece."

"Leave it, Alice. I don't owe you anything like that."

"No. I won't leave it. That's what I'm saying. It's time you cooperated and it's only in your best interests to do so."

"We're back to threats? Is that what we're doing here?" said Dan.

The girl looked into his eyes.

"Buy me that drink, Dan. You owe me. I know you bought Gemma Cassidy a drink when she was doing this job. So buy me that drink."

"It was a drink, nothing more, Alice. You're reading too much into things. And besides, you and Gemma are very different people. And you certainly weren't ever friends. Please. Don't push this."

The girl frowned for an instant before she brushed it off with a smile.

"I'm sorry, but I'm going to have to push. What you do – who you are, Dan – that can sell papers. And in my job, that matters. Now, I happen to know some of the cases you were involved with were… how shall I say, intriguing. They were murky. And I think there's a lot of potential public interest there. And guess what I heard? I even heard that some of the people you dealt with… some of them, and this isn't well known, some of them even ended up dead. But you never had anything to do with that, did you?"

Dan blinked, his eyes taking on a haunted look.

"I find it very interesting how no one ever really looked into that... or put it into print. Don't you think?"

"Alice, I've got nothing to hide. Nothing at all," said Dan, but the truth hurt. He struggled to keep his composure.

"Are you sure about that. Yes. You look pretty sure. But maybe I should look into it," said Perry. "Just in case."

"No one ever cries when bad people die, Alice."

"Can I quote you on that, Dan?" said Alice.

Dan fell silent.

"Did you cry when Gemma Cassidy died?" said the girl. Dan swallowed and watched the girl's eyes follow his Adam's apple up and down in his throat.

"It's old news, Alice. And it's over."

"So you say," said Alice. "So there's really no chance of a drink today, then?"

"No chance in this world," said Dan. The girl swished her hair and shrugged, before reaching out to touch the neckline of Dan's plain white T-shirt. She tugged the seam, revealing his collar bone and a few chest hairs. Dan pulled his T-shirt back into place.

"That article will happen, Dan. The only thing you get to decide is which article I write. The friendly one. The puff piece for the local ladies. Or the exposé. So, if I were you, I'd decide to play nice. Next time, I think you'll buy me that drink." She turned away from Dan, ready to head for the door.

"You're playing a dangerous game, Alice," said Dan, watching the girl's back as she walked out of the bar.

"Now who's making threats?" said Alice, opening the bar door. Dan didn't say a word.

"If this is a game, Dan, I'm going to win," she said, then she walked out, leaving the door to swing shut.

Dan stretched up on his tiptoes to look around the bar, but Parker was nowhere in sight. Dan guessed that with so much booze inside him, the old man must have gone to take a leak. But then remembered that Parker had slipped away from him before. He decided to look in the toilets, and as he grabbed his jacket from the barstool his wallet thudded onto the wooden floor, spilling his bank cards. Dan stared at it and frowned. His frown deepened. He picked up the wallet and opened the cash compartment and counted off the tens and twenties. Eighty pounds was missing.

"Parker...?!" Dan snarled when he saw his credit cards jumbled. He went through the pack
and picked up the rest from the floor. His Mastercard was missing.

"Parker!" shouted Dan. Half the bar turned to watch Dan stalk past their backs. Dan yanked opened the bar door and slammed it against the poster strewn wall before he walked out into the street.

Parker's case wasn't a case.

It was a sting.

And as far as Dan could see, the only ones getting stung were them.

Eight

When Dan walked into the office, the glass shook in the window frame as the door rattled the timber. A fraction later, the office's old-fashioned door chime caught up with the news of Dan's arrival and made a short sharp "brrrrrring". Eva stood up from her desk, stuck her hands on her hips and waited for the news. At the front of the shop, Mark nearly jumped out of his seat.

"Problems?" said Eva. Her eyes roved around behind Dan's back, checking the street. He knew who she was looking for. Dan shook his head to say the old man wasn't with him.

"Parker's back up to his usual tricks."

"He wasn't there?" said Eva.

"Oh, he was there alright..." Dan considered mentioning Alice Perry, but the girl was one problem too many. Eva didn't need to add another to the growing list.

"I got distracted by a text from Alison Saunders. She said there's some character hanging around Greg's hospital ward and she's worried."

"She thinks it's him?" said Eva.

Dan nodded. "Then while I was reading the text, JP bailed on me."

"What does he think he's playing at?" said Eva.

"And that's not all. Did you notice how cagey he's been when it comes to talking about his money?"

Eva considered Dan's words. "He's made plenty of promises to pay us when the time comes."

"Exactly," said Dan, "*When the time comes... when the boat comes in...* all of that. And I caught him talking about his money in the past tense. Like it was all gone."

"All gone? Surely not – you saw how much he had."

"Yeah. I remember it well," said Dan. But his doubts showed in his eyes.

"You think he's been hiding the fact he's brassic?" said Eva. "That's why he's been so vague about everything."

"Partly, yes. And the other part is because this thing of his is probably as dodgy as hell. My head's telling me we should get out while we still can. But I'm not going to let him get away with it. Not this time."

"Sorry. Get away with what? Deceiving us again?"

"If only it was just the lies. He stole half the cash in my wallet and one of my credit cards while my back was turned. He took them right out of my jacket."

"That's cold," said Mark. "Considering everything you've done for him…"

"That's Jonathan Parker down to a tee," said Dan.

"But," said Eva, hesitating. "Even after all he's done, he's still in danger…"

"I know. And by rights we should leave him to face it all by himself. But if Cadson or the Thai boys stick his head on a spike, I'd have to live with myself."

"The Thai boys?" said Mark.

Dan squinted and pinched the bridge of his nose. "Long story, kid. Suffice it to say that Parker has got more secrets than you get hot breakfasts."

"Don't you mean hot dinners?" said Mark.

"No," said Dan, adding a lopsided grin.

The cogs of Mark's mind slowly ground away until he remembered Joanne's morning visits. Mark blushed so deeply he had to look away.

"Then are we still going to help him?" said Eva, ignoring the innuendoes.

"Yes. Because we have to," said Dan. "And because he made us a promise, and this time he's going to keep it. *We're getting paid, Eva.* Even if I have to sell his worn-out kidneys on the black market to get it, that's what I'll do."

"But if he's gone off with your credit card, he could have gone anywhere," said Eva.

"Not likely."

"Amelia," said Eva.

"Yeah. He won't go too far with the dream girl still in his mind. She with the amazing computer brain – as if! The girl looks like she has to think hard before she chews a stick of gum. I don't know what she's got that he needs, apart from the obvious – but it's clear he can't do without her. And they've got something which Cadson won't give up on."

"I don't buy the super-computer line either, Dan, but Amelia certainly isn't dumb."

Dan shrugged. "Either way, Parker needs her. He won't give up on that deal. It sounds like it's worth much more than my ripped-off credit card." He turned to the kid, whose blushes were finally beginning to subside.

"Mark?"

"Yes?".

"Is there any way you can help us locate the old man?"

"From here you mean?" said Mark.

Dan nodded. "Any way at all?"

"You said he's nicked your credit card?" said Mark.

Dan nodded.

"Well, if he's been using it, there might be a way to see where he's been…"

Dan nodded grimly. "Fine. Try it. You can have my credit card log-in details. See what you can find. Latest transactions, the shops, any cash withdrawals. Hopefully he won't use it, but if he does, I want to see where."

"Okay," said Mark. "There's no guarantees that your account will update fast enough for us to use, but I'll do what I can."

Dan scribbled down his card details and handed the note over along with the website password and credentials.

"He'll show up sooner or later," said Eva.

"I know he will. But I'd rather stop him cleaning me out before he does."

"Want a coffee?" said Eva.

Dan read the concern in her eyes. It went deeper than concern for his caffeine needs. She stood up and he followed her through to the small kitchen at the back of the shop, and they slid the door shut.

"You okay?" she said.

"I've been better."

Eva leaned forward towards him and laid a hand on Dan's chest. "You really didn't need Parker on top of all of this, did you?"

"It's okay. He's going to pay us, Eva. I promise you he's going to make this right."

"He bloody well better do or he'll have me to answer to. I've been far too nice already."

She leaned close against Dan, pressed her cheek to his chin, then drew back and looked into his dark eyes.

"You said Alison texted you about this stranger at the hospital…"

"Yeah. And it didn't go well last time I was there. Greg was angry, and the nurses wanted me kicked out. She must be terrified to be asking me to come back. I need to go and check it out."

"If you need to go, go," said Eva.

"You think I should?"

"Yes. But, Dan. No matter what you say, I'm coming with you. I can't risk losing you to this psychopath. If he's there, I'm going to help you handle it."

Dan looked into Eva's eyes and saw there was no talking her down. And there was no point arguing. If he left her behind, he knew Eva would soon find her own way there. He relented.

"Okay…" he sighed. "But I'm not happy about it."

"I know," said Eva. "And I know why too. But you're not handling this on your own. I won't let you." She kissed him on the lips before sliding away to pull the door to the office back open. Dan watched Eva check herself for signs of the kiss – adjusting her red hair, wiping her lips. Dan smiled then called after her.

"Okay, Eva. Then you better grab your stuff because it's high time I went. Alison sounded in a state. Parker's wasted too much of my time already."

Eva nodded as she finished wiping her lips.

"Let's go."

***

Greg Saunders had been awake for a while now, but when Dan saw him the big man looked in worse shape than ever. His skin was pale, and his face tired, but the worst of it was in the eyes. He looked afraid. Greg Saunders was beginning to remind him of Carl Proberty, which wasn't good. Alison looked in better shape, although Dan and Eva saw through her fake smile and nervous excitability. The woman was bordering on hyperactive – almost as jarring as the look in Greg's eye.

"Thanks for coming back, Dan... and wow... Eva! Look at you! You've barely changed at all in all these years."

"Oh, I wouldn't say that. Put it this way. I'm very familiar with the seven signs of ageing. Every single one of them," said Eva.

Alison smiled. "Not as familiar as me, I'd bet. Anyway, it's good to see you again. And I think Greg has something to say to you, Dan."

Dan stuck his hands into his jeans pockets and fortified himself for another volley of abuse or an equally uncomfortable forced apology. Greg met his eyes for a fleeting second and rubbed his nose.

"Sorry," said the big man. But Dan knew his nose scratching was a classic tell. Greg really wasn't sorry at all, and Dan really didn't mind in the least.

"It doesn't matter, Greg. I'm just glad you're well."

Greg made a half-hearted sneer. "Well? I wouldn't go that far. Well, Alison. You've dragged the man back into this, so you may as well tell him what you saw."

"I did that already. By text," said Alison.

Dan nodded. "Yeah. But I need details. That's what I need more than anything. If this guy is who we think it is, I could do with a description."

Alison put her hand to her chubby cheeks as she struggled to think. "It's difficult. I saw him through the glass over there," said Alison. "It's a way off – you can see that. And those ward lights reflect off the glass."

She was right. The bright ward lights in the ceiling bounced off the corridor windows, making a decent view of the passing medical staff all but impossible.

"But you saw him – otherwise you wouldn't have texted me."

"Yes, I swear I saw something. I saw a man in dark clothes stop by the glass. Twice. He looked through the window and he stared right at us. Right at me. It was like in the movies, when you see something and the feeling changes – I just zoomed right in on his face. I could feel him staring right at me. It was awful. It sent me cold, Dan."

Dan grimaced. He knew the feeling well. "Okay. So, what did he look like?"

"I can't give you details. But I can tell you his hair was short, really short, and dark. His head was tanned, and he had this big ugly jaw. He had a big chin and a big forehead. Honestly, he looked frightening…"

Greg rolled his hand at his wife as if he wanted her to get to the point.

"You saw him twice," said Greg.

"Yes," said the woman, emphatically. "Yes. The second time the door opened, and it looked like he was going to walk right into the ward. He kind of hung around behind one of the porters with the food trolley, but when he saw me looking, he stayed back. I know he saw me. Our eyes met. Then he turned away. Do you think he was waiting for me to go? Do you think he's trying to get to Greg?"

Greg shook his head in a show of slow derision.

"It's not him. It's just some weirdo, Alison. Just a coincidence," said Greg. His eyes flicked to Dan, letting Dan see the lie.

"Greg?! Why are you saying that? Surely you don't believe that…" said his wife. But Greg gave her a long solid stare.

"Yes. I do. This is a public place. They let anyone into hospitals. Who knows how many fruit loops and junkies are walking around these wards at any one time."

Alison gave a weak nod, then turned to Dan.

"I know what I saw, Dan. That man was staring right at me."

"It's okay, Alison. I believe you," said Dan.

"Then why doesn't he?!" she said, looking at her husband.

"Honey. Leave me to talk to Dan, will you? Just give me a minute, please."

"Only if you don't get angry with him again," she said.

"Whatever. You go and get yourself a coffee. Just stay away from the weirdos, okay?" said Greg, forcing a smile.

The big woman passed Eva and gave her a sad, appealing eye, hoping Eva understood the long-suffering experience of a hard-man's wife. Eva gave the woman a sympathetic nod. In many respects, she did. But Eva was a fighter too, and she knew it.

As Alison left the ward, Greg pushed himself up in the bed and took a good long look at them. All humour had drained away from his face. He looked sweaty and pained.

"He was here, wasn't he? It was him," said Dan.

"Yeah. And it was worse than Alison knows. He came in when she went for a break."

"Then you've seen his face," said Dan, with excitement.

"You do know what he looks like."

Saunders nodded, and his eyes glazed.

"He looks so full of hatred, like you wouldn't believe. I don't even know this man, and he hates my guts like he wants me dead."

Dan nodded once. "Who is he, Greg. What does this man look like?"

"He's just like Alison said, only worse. The guy is a boxer through and through. He's got a head like someone chiselled it straight out of a quarry, and there's so many scars on him it looks like he's been in a war zone... but the broken nose, and those eyes. Yes, he's a boxer. An old boxer. A warhorse who's seen a lot of action."

Dan nodded. It matched his suspicions – and the fleeting parts of what he could remember from his fateful morning run.

"How old is he?"

Greg shrugged. "He's balding and what he's got left is slicked back. His nose has been broken in a couple of places, and there's a scar all the way down his forehead. If I had to guess, I'd say he's in the fifties bracket."

"And do you have a name for this guy?" said Dan.

"A real name? No. This man doesn't introduce himself. He just gets nasty from the word go."

Dan frowned.

"What happened, Greg?"

Greg paused and dragged his fingers down his hefty, stubbled chin, as if he was having trouble framing the words. As if he didn't want to say it.

"Greg...?" said Dan. "The first time, when you told me to go away. You wouldn't tell me anything at all. You just wanted me to leave you alone. So, what changed?"

Greg looked away. "He came back. He walked in here when the nurses were away, when Alison was calling the childminder. He walked straight up to me and pretended he was happy to see me like one of the regular visitors. Like an old friend. He picked up that chair over there and slid it right to my bedside, like an old friend. He even sounded like one too. He asked how I was doing, how I liked the hospital, all of that crap, and I couldn't do anything but play along, because of everything he was saying in his eyes. The man is a walking time bomb. If I'd blown the whistle and called the nurse, who knows what he would have done to Alison."

"His eyes," said Dan. His mind flashed to the glaring eyes he'd seen above the window of the black BMW outside Proberty's house in Cornwall. He blinked and found Greg Saunders watching him. It felt as if Greg had seen the darkness inside him.

"Dan… I hate this guy. I mean, I hate him with every fibre of my being. He's hurt me, that's obvious, but what he's put my family through – my babies – my wife – it's sick. I got at angry at him. I asked him why he was doing it. You made me wonder why. You want to know what he said when I asked him? He told me that it was none of my business, but then he said this – 'I know why. And so does one other man and all of this is his fault.' Then he said. 'This only stops when the past has been atoned for.' That's it. That's what the man said. Like any of that makes any sense at all. The guy is sick in the head."

Dan listened.

"I tried to reason with him, Dan. I told him I hadn't wronged him. I told him I'd never even seen him before he hit my house. But it didn't matter what I said. I could see he didn't care. When I saw he wouldn't stop, I decided I wanted to hurt him before he hurt me again. What could I do from here, a broken man trapped in a hospital bed, tied to these machines. What could I do?"

Dan could feel Saunders building up to something, but his eyes were averted, cast down to the blue hospital floor. He just couldn't say the words.

"What did you do, Greg?" said Dan, pushing him on.

Saunders met his eyes.

"I wanted him to be scared."

"Greg?" said Dan.

"I exaggerated a bit. That's all."

Dan waited for more. But Greg Saunders started to fidget with the cables going into the backs of his hand.

"He doesn't like you, Dan," said Greg.

Dan's stomach started to burn. He looked at Eva and saw his anxiety reflected in her face.

"And?" said Dan.

"He showed me that photograph of Carl Proberty – the one with him dead and hanging from a rope – and he threatened that to do it to me if you kept on coming. I guessed it was because he was worried that you were still coming after him. The second time he said it, I wondered, what if it was more than a threat? What if he was worried you were on to him. It was the only thing I could think of. I wanted him scared. It was a dumb thing to say, I know it was, but the guy was trying to get into my head and I needed to get out and leave me alone… so I said it without even thinking."

"What did you say, Greg?" said Dan.

"I told him you'd promised me you wouldn't back down."
The cold feeling poured over Dan's skin, and down his
spine. He felt the sweat prickling from the skin on his face.
"Well? It's true isn't it? That is what you said…"
"What else did you tell him, Greg?"
"I said you wouldn't stop no matter what he did. I knew that
was true. Deep down I knew you weren't going to listen to
what I said. And I enjoyed telling him. I enjoyed watching
him getting angry because he couldn't have it all his own
way. And it's true… isn't it, Dan? I know you're in a bad
way, Dan. I can see it on you. The pain shows on your face.
But I remember what you were like in the old days. You
always kept coming, even if you were getting hurt. It was the
one thing we all knew back in the old days. That was the one
true reason you could have been a champion. But you gave it
up for her," said Greg. He nodded at Eva.
"You told him what?!" said Dan.
"I told him that you were coming for him, just you like told
me. And I told him you wouldn't stop until he was finished."
Dan swallowed and took it all in. Slowly. His eyes were wide.
He drew air into his lungs, cold and slow.
"And what did he say back?"
"The usual. He threatened to kill me. Alison. My kids. My
whole family. But for one moment, it all felt worth it. That
one instant when I wanted to kill him. But all I could do was
say that you would do it instead."
"And then?" said Eva.
"And then he got up and left."
"And that's it?" said Dan.
"Yeah," said Saunders, nodding. "That's it."
"But then Alison saw him hanging around outside?" said
Dan.

"No. She saw him before he came in. I guess he was waiting to see me alone."

Eva stepped towards Greg's bed. "And you haven't seen him since?" her voice was serious, and worried. "When did this happen?"

"Two hours ago," said Greg.

Eva and Dan looked at one another.

"Dan, I'm sorry, but I just had to say something. I wanted to hurt him like he'd hurt me. I wanted him scared."

"It's okay," said Dan, quietly. But it was anything but okay. Eva saw the worry swirling around Dan's head.

"Greg, I've got to go. There's every chance this guy is going to react. I need to get prepared."

"Look," said Greg. "I didn't think about that then. I'm sorry…"

"Forget it," said Dan. "But if he comes back, you call me right away. Call the police, do anything, but whatever you do, don't leave it. What you've said will provoke a reaction against someone. I've got to go." Dan turned away for the door, Eva joined his side.

"Hey, Dan…" called Greg.

"Don't worry. I'll be back," said Dan. "Stay safe, okay?"

They walked out into the corridor passing a half dozen faces: nurses, doctors, and one tense Alison Saunders. The woman was walking along holding two take-away coffee cups. She blinked at Eva and Dan as they drew near.

"He didn't upset you, did he?" said Alison. Dan's eyes flicked past her to the exit doors. They needed to go.

"No. It's not like that," said Dan, in a half-lie. "Just look after him and I promise I'll see you soon." Dan walked on before the woman could question him again. Eva gave her the best parting smile she could muster, but it came across far less than sincere. She felt the same kind of worries Dan was feeling, crushing in on all sides. The danger had ratcheted up another level. Greg had just lit the blue touch paper and stood well back. Instead of dealing with his own share of the problem, he had thrown Dan well and truly into the frame.

"Greg shouldn't have done that," said Eva, in an angry voice. "He's thrown you under a bus."

"I know exactly what he's done, Eva. But the man was coming for me anyway. All Greg's done is make it happen sooner. Either way, we'd better get ready."

"You really think this psycho is going to react to this…?" said Eva.

Dan nodded. "I've no possible reason to think otherwise. Trouble is we don't know how he'll react, and we don't know when…"

Dan's words had them rushing through the hospital grounds faster than ever. They walked along in silence, side by side, minds whirring the whole way.

***

So far, Mark confirmed there had been no new transactions on Dan's Mastercard, and the kid had refreshed the screen often enough to be sure. With current cases so slow, the phone only ringing with call-centre sales calls, the office empty, and no sign of the runaway, Parker, Mark was at a loose end. It wasn't long before temptations came calling, in several different guises. First, Mark clicked into Dan's most recent credit card statement, and started to nose around the list of purchases, noting the random shops, online clothes purchases and frequent petrol buys. So far, so boring. The card in question looked to be reserved for meeting daily needs. There were no firearms purchases from dodgy international suppliers, and there was no further insight into Dan and Eva's private life – the stuff which Joanne was really interested in. There were no restaurant bills. No purchases from online suppliers for anything remotely private or sexual. He wasn't checking for himself, of course. His investigation was on Joanne's behalf pure and simple, to track down any insider gossip on the private lives of the two PIs. In truth he felt a little seedy for prying like that… and yet, he didn't stop. He felt a sordid desire to look back further. It was an almost compulsive need. What else did they get up to? Surely if the evidence was to be found anywhere, it would be found on one of Dan's credit cards. Mark looked back through another month's transactions and found a restaurant bill for one of the Arches restaurants on the seafront. The forty-pound price tag suggested lunch rather than dinner. Mark reckoned Joanne would have had much better success with the prying. The girl had a real nose for it. Besides, if she came to the office, with a little spare time on their hands, who knew what else they could get up to? Maybe a stolen moment in the kitchen? Joanne certainly knew how to make life more exciting. In fact, the girl was pretty addictive in herself. It was wrong, he knew that. But where Joanne was concerned he really couldn't help himself. Mark picked up the handset and dialled Joanne's mobile. She answered in three rings.

"Hello you," she said. "Are you finished up yet?"

"No, and I think I'll be here a while longer too."

"What's the matter? Don't your bosses believe in weekends anymore?"

"Who? Eva and Dan. They never stop working, you know that."

"No. But you should. We need to live a little. I miss you," she said.

"That's exactly what I'm calling about. I miss you too. And I've got something for you. I've been tasked with keeping an eye on Dan's credit card bill. With access to his online credit card account details to be precise…"

"Really?" said Joanne, intrigued.

"See. I know how nosey you are when it comes to these two. I thought you might want to come and help me. You never know what you might find. Besides. I'm feeling lonely."

"Lonely, eh? Sad little pup. Is that what you call it?" said Joanne. "Okay. Fret no more. I'll be along soon. Put the kettle on and we'll see what we can find… *before we see what we can find*…" she said with a chuckle.

Mark smiled as he hung up the phone. Spending time with Joanne would certainly make the work far less dull, and she was bound to find some spice on Dan's credit card account to keep her happy. And if Joanne was happy, well, he was bound to have a good time. Mark put the phone down and slapped the desk with both hands in excitement. His weekend had been rescued – which called for a little celebration. A cup of tea and a walk into the backyard for some much-needed spring sunshine. No one was calling the office today. He'd be okay for a few minutes.

Mark put the kettle on and walked out into the main office in order to put the bolt on the front door for his tea break. He reached the front door, and yawned, hand resting on the bolt, while he took an idle look out onto the busy Southchurch Street. The cars flew by, as did the kids on their bikes. The first hint of summer was in the air, and Mark couldn't wait. The way things were going, he fancied this would be his best summer yet. He smiled at the prospect, and started to slide the bolt, as a shining black saloon glided into view. It slowed to a halt immediately outside the shop, and Mark's mood dropped a notch. A client maybe. An inquiry at a time he really didn't want one. Mark considered hurrying to lock the door. If he was quick he could slip away into the kitchen before the driver had seen him. But what if it *was* a new case? The cases paid his wages, and he knew all too well that paying work was a rare thing at present. And if old man Parker welched on them – as now seemed likely, Mark guessed there would be a cashflow issue sooner or later. So he sighed and waited by the door. He hoped it was a letter drop-off, something quick so as not to ruin his plans for Joanne. But when he saw the meathead in the tight suit get out of the car, all bets were off. He blinked at the figure as he straightened out his suit and tugged at his shirt collar. The man was stocky, with slicked-back hair and a hard, businesslike face. A mean looking face. The kind of face you could use to hammer nails. When the man's head turned, and the guy caught Mark's eye across the roof of the BMW his breath hitched. The man had a rough looking face – rugged didn't do it justice. It was almost too hard, too raw to look at without staring and being repulsed. And yet the beastlike face wore a smile which seemed to be friendly and polite. A smile which said *I'm here to see you*. The man nodded and raised a finger to ask Mark to wait one minute while he ducked to get something out of his car.

"Don't s'pose I have a choice…" muttered Mark as the sound of the boiling kettle grew louder in the kitchen behind him.

He waited for the man to stand up and shut his car door, then watched as he rounded the back of the long saloon. Strange. The guy had dipped back inside his car like he was going to pick up a parcel or a letter for handing in, but Mark saw the man's big hands were empty. The guy had long arms which swung low by his hips, and as he walked to the door, he kept his thin-lipped smile in place, showing a glimpse of sharp white teeth. The closer he got to the door, the worse he looked. Mark tried to keep his stare neutral – a challenge in itself.

When the man stood blocking the daylight in the shop door entrance, he waited a moment before tapping on the glass, then smiled and pointed to the door bolt in Mark's hand.

"Oh, yeah…" said Mark. "Sorry." He slid the bolt back and opened the door. A waft of street sound and exhaust fumes rode the warm breeze into the office. Mark pulled the door open.

"Yes? Can I help you?"

The man took one step forward, forcing Mark to take a step back.

"You're looking for Eva Roberts or Dan Bradley…?" said Mark.

"Yes. I was. But instead I've found you."

The man's voice was rough-edged, and gravelly. It was unpleasant to hear.

A cold prickling of nerves began high in Mark's chest.

"Actually, I really shouldn't be here. This is my day off. I was going to close up and…"

"Bummer," said the man.

"What?"

"I mean, it's a bummer for you, that you're here instead of Dan Bradley."

The cold feeling prickled deeper. Mark gripped the door tighter in his hand. "You could always come back on Monday," he said, his heart thudding hard as he felt the man's gaze begin to cut deep into his. As if the man was trying to invade his thoughts. He thought of closing the door, but his way was blocked. The man was effectively inside the shop already. The guy was in.

"But I don't want to come back on Monday," said the man.

"But Dan Bradley isn't here," said Mark, confused and feeling the panic rising inside.

"And that's why it's such a bummer. Because you've drawn the shortest of straws."

"What? What do you mean?" said Mark, his voice shrinking as he spoke.

"Don't worry. I'll show you."

He bustled Mark forward, stepping through him as if he wasn't there. When he was fully inside, the guy turned and shut the shop door behind him. He slid the bolt and locked it.

"Hey. You can't do that!"

"I just did," said the man. The sound of the kettle reached a crescendo, its loud bubbling peak. The man straightened up and peered towards the back kitchen and the light pouring in from the backyard. "Anyone else here?" he said.

Mark blinked at the beast, wondering what the best answer was. But the man read his mind and smiled.

"Did I hear a kettle boil?" he said.

Mark looked him in the eye.

"I was about to have a cup of tea."

The man shook his head slowly. "Not anymore, you're not. We're going to need that water. For what comes next, I think we'd better shut that back door too."

The kettle clicked off and Mark gulped. He thought about running and remembered the incident on the seafront. The synapses clicked into place. He remembered Dan's unseen man hiding behind the beach huts. The man who pulled a gun on Dan and almost shot him dead. *What had the man retrieved from the front of his car?* For the first time, Mark had an awful inkling. But beyond all other hopes, Mark hoped he was wrong. He was young. He had a wonderful girlfriend. Summer was coming. He wanted to live. He wanted anything but this. But he knew there was nothing he could do to stop it. Pain was coming. The promise of pain was in the maniac's terrifying eyes.

***

Joanne checked her reflection in the cycle shop window as she passed it by. She saw she was smiling, laughing inside at what she imagined Mark really had in mind when he'd called her. She had a feeling the credit card was just a ruse. Really no more than verbal foreplay. Yes, it would be fun to sneak a look at Dan's credit card account, but the truth was Dan was pretty predictable and boring. He was a guy. The most he would have ordered was a pair of jeans or a new pair of leather boots (though probably not, looking at how worn-in his current pair were) or maybe a subscription to a sports magazine. Dullsville. Joanne didn't hold out much hope for excitement there. But Eva… if they had Eva's credit card statement, that would have been something. No woman could be as serious, controlled, and so utterly work focused as Eva without having a few personal little vices to fall back on. Joanne kidded herself about it. What would it be? Leopard-print underwear to release her inner-Amazonian? Or maybe Eva was the dominatrix type? The thought brought images to mind which had her chuckling under her breath. Eva with a whip in hand? Please! But who could tell? But she still doubted it. Shame. Of the two, Eva was the one who needed to loosen up a bit. She was a great woman, one of Joanne's idols, but no one could be that heroic and wholesome without having a little streak of bad somewhere in them. And having a liking for a large glass of cold white wine wasn't vice enough. There had to be something more beyond the Pinot Grigio. Joanne decided she would work it out one day. But not today. Today was about her and Mark, stealing some private time in paid hours to make it even more fun. Joanne made one final check of her appearance before she crossed the last side street before Eva and Dan's office. But when she saw the parked BMW outside the office doors, and heard the ticking of its cooling engine, she knew their plans had suffered a setback. *A visitor had arrived. A very unwelcome visitor.* Still, Joanne was good at playing the business game – and her time in the council offices had given her a lot of practice in getting rid of unwanted people. Mark was far too polite, but he'd soon learn. Joanne was in a hurry. She walked a diagonal across the pavement straight towards the recess of the old shop's front door. But just as she was about to cross into the shade of the shop, she heard Mark's voice, and the tone of it shocked her. It was unmistakably Mark, but his voice was high, wild, and desperate. Joanne froze and peered into the dim interior, seeing the shadowy shapes moving towards the back of the shop.

"Please… please don't do this!" said Mark.

Joanne froze. She watched as the large figure bustled him back, herding him deeper into the back-room kitchen, as Mark's limbs spilled out from the edges. He was like a frightened lamb, trying every effort to escape.

"Mark…?" she whispered. Joanne's eyes widened, and her mouth formed a terrified 'O'. The shapes made more sense the more she looked. A strong looking guy in a suit was pushing Mark into the kitchen, and Mark couldn't fight back. The man was too strong. She caught a glimpse of Mark's pale, terror-stricken face as he was shoved into the bright kitchen and saw the daylight from the backyard over the beast's shoulder. She walked deeper into the entrance recess and pulled at the door. It shuddered in the doorframe. She peered around the doorframe and saw the bolt had been locked. Mark wailed. It wasn't a sound of pain. Not yet. But a sound of struggle. Something very bad was going to happen, and Joanne couldn't let it. She turned and looked back at the street, but all she saw was the traffic rushing past in the Saturday sunshine. No one out there would stop, and even if they did, she knew they wouldn't stop in time to help her. *So what could she do?* Her eyes traced over the gleaming black BMW and suddenly she had an idea. A desperately bad idea, but it was the only one she could think of. She looked around the street and saw nothing she could use… just rubbish… beer cans flattened in the gutter… crisp packets… nothing substantial enough for her purpose.

"Please, no!" she heard Mark cry again. Her time was almost up. There was a chance the back door was open. Maybe she could get in there... but what could she do then? Surely, she'd become a victim as well, and make things even worse. She had to do something. She had no choice. Joanne ran around the side of the shop onto the side street. And there she saw it. A single piece of timber sticking out from behind Dan and Eva's backyard wall. She burst into a sprint, running along the yard wall and grabbed the piece of wood. In her hurry, she passed two bewildered young men. One was forced to duck out of her way, as she ran back up the street with the wood in hand. "You got trouble sweetheart?" called one.

Joanne ignored the question... then stopped and thought better of it.

"Trouble...? Yes. Yes, I've got trouble! There's a man in there – attacking my... my brother! Can you help us?" Joanne knew men well enough – if they knew she had a boyfriend, their motivation would be halved, or removed altogether. But a brother was no threat at all to their interests.

"Of course. How can we help?" said the most forthright of the two. Joanne's smart eyes sparkled his way.

"All you need to do is get into the yard. Just do anything you can to get in there. If he sees you in there, this nutcase might stop."

"We'll stop him alright…" said the tall one, with a nod of conviction. His mate didn't look so sure, but Joanne wasn't investing much hope in them anyway. If they did anything at all they would be useful as a distraction. Joanne raced back around the corner to the front of the office, her eyes focused on nothing but the vast sleek black BMW. Her heart lurched. She felt sick. She snatched a deep breath and raised the lump of wood high in the air above the car bonnet. She hesitated for a second as the wood hung in the air. A scream from the shop pushed her over the edge and she gritted her teeth hard and smashed the wood onto the bonnet. As the screaming started again, she thudded the wood down hard again. She watched the bonnet dent and distort. *It wasn't enough.* She needed to do more. She needed to make him stop. She had to be louder. Joanne stepped around to the side of the car, and swung the wood in a wide sideways arc watching with frightened glee as the wood met the windscreen, bit into its surface and cracked it apart. The glass misted and imploded. Shards fell around her feet, and the sound of Mark's scream was drowned out by the sudden ear-piercing noise of the car alarm. The discordant noise filled her ears, but Joanne didn't stop. She walked around the car and clattered it again and again with the wood. Paint creased and flaked. The doors dented. The bonnet crumpled and complained.

"Oi!" the shop door was wrenched open behind her, and a big man in a dark suit stepped out into the bright sunshine. He stared at her with eyes like two tiny stars. His head was shaped like an ogre, but those eyes were the most menacing things she'd ever seen. Lizard-like blue eyes – tiny and full of menace. On instinct Joanne backed away and pointed the lump of wood towards the man in self-defence. The big man looked at his car.

"You stupid rotten bitch," he said, and moved towards her.

"You better not have hurt him," said Joanne.

"Him?" said the man, frowning for a second before he stepped towards her grinning.

"Of course I've hurt him. He's in the kitchen, crying his heart out. But after what you've just done, honey, I'm going to hurt you even worse."

"Just you bloody well try it," said Joanne. She jabbed the wood at him as he came towards her. As Joanne backed away, she turned her eyes back to the street. When she looked at the man, she saw he had paused, a grimace on his face, his lips twitching in thought.

Close by, the thick stream of traffic was slowing down with the weight of the cars heading towards the seafront, and as the cars slowed, the heads in the passing cars turned towards the pretty young woman with the piece of two by four in her hand standing beside a smashed-up BMW. Then their eyes turned to *him*. The beast in the suit. The man blinked at the faces passing in the traffic, then he stared at Joanne. She met his eyes and felt a shiver. Joanne was sure she had been disliked by almost no one in her entire life. But for the very first time, she felt the full weight of someone else's hatred.

There came a sudden noise from the back of the shop, a clatter, a few words, and then the hammering of running feet as one of the young men from the side street burst through the shop doorway only to stop abruptly on the pavement behind the monster. He looked at Joanne with a heroic look set on his face, but his act was blown apart the moment his eyes fell on the face of the man in the suit. His eyes blinked wide with shock. His voice wavered.

"Your brother's been hurt, but I think he'll be okay. The bastard hurt his hand badly."

The thug turned to look back at the young man standing in the doorway, and as the youth's confidence seeped away altogether he became speechless.

The ogre looked at them both and shook his head.

"You made a mistake here," said the man in a deep, rasping voice. He jabbed a finger at Joanne. "This was intended to be a warning. But you've used up the last of my goodwill. This is the final one. Tell them to back off, or next time I see Bradley he won't be so lucky. Next time I'll aim for his face."

Joanne gasped, and the wood fell from her hand. It was him. The man who had shot Dan. She watched as he walked over the shattered glass from his car, opened the driver's door, and got inside. He started the car. As it shunted forwards and bobbed down from the kerb onto the street, the young man in the doorway found his voice again.

"Yeah! Get out of here!" he called, drawing up by Joanne's shoulder. "Don't come back!" The young man shot off a few swear words for added effect and looked at Joanne for her reaction. She dropped the wood from her hand as the battered BMW roared away up the street, heading away from the seafront to the faster roads at the back of town.

"You okay, hun?" said the youth, reaching for Joanne's arm. She shrugged him off. Trembling inside, she raced into the dim office. She stared into the bright kitchen and saw Mark's feet sticking past the edge of the door, but she couldn't see his face. He was sitting on the floor. The other young man was crouched in the kitchen beside him, talking in a quiet tone. Joanne felt the tears pushing their way out, but she didn't want Mark to see her crying for him. She gulped on her aching throat and walked into the kitchen doorway. There he was. Mark sat on the floor, his back pressed against the oven. He cradled one hand wrapped in a red-chequered tea towel, his face pale, sweaty, and pained. The second lad stood up to make away for Joanne and she took his place beside Mark.

"He was like this when we found him… only his hand wasn't covered… it was awful…"

Joanne ignored the words. She saw the sharp thin line of blood on Mark's face – across the width of Mark's forehead. Blood had seeped from either end, but the wound itself looked clean. But his eyes – Mark's eyes looked haunted, and he clutched his wrapped hand to his chest as if it was broken. Joanne eyed the tea towel and reached for it, seeking permission with her eyes. But Mark shook his head.

"Please. Just call an ambulance. Please call one now."

"What has he done to you?" said Joanne, her voice full of pity and fear.

"The kettle… he used boiling water, Joanne… he cut my face with a knife, and then he used boiling water on me. The man is an evil monster, Joanne… there's no other word for it…"

Joanne leaned in close to bury her sobs in a kiss. She kissed his cheek, and then she reached for his lips with hers as Mark groaned in pain. Behind her, the taller, vocal young man appeared in the kitchen doorway.

"Hang about… I thought you said he was your brother?!" Joanne glanced at up him once with a disdainful eye before she turned her attention back to Mark.

"Yes. We're very close in our family. Just call an ambulance will you, you can see he's in pain."

The taller youth grunted, shook his head and walked away. A moment later they heard a sullen male voice on the office phone requesting an ambulance.

"That's the end of it, Joanne…" whispered Mark "I mean it. I've had enough. I can't do this anymore."

"What?" said Joanne.

"That's the end of my time here. It's too dangerous."

His pained eyes blinked at hers, waiting for a response.

A moment later Joanne nodded. Mark had the seal of approval. The decision had been made.

Nine

The first thing Eva and Dan noticed were the shards of glass scattered across the pavement outside their office. Dan kicked at the two by four lying on the concrete and frowned. "We're too late. Something's already happened," said Dan. "Thanks, Greg," said Eva, peering into their dark office. "He panicked, Eva…"
"And now we'll have to pick up the pieces. Whatever they are."
Eva walked into the office, the door chimed, and she blinked as her eyes adjusted to the light. Dan walked in behind her. The bright golden light outside failed to make it far into the interior. The anxiety inside had Eva searching rapidly for Mark's face. It was too quiet. The front desk was empty, but the door was open. Mark had to be somewhere.
Dan appeared at Eva's shoulder, looking around. "Mark? Hey, Mark? Kid, are you here?" said Dan. A movement from the back kitchen made them jump. Dan stiffened and took a step forward to deal with the situation. But before he could go any further, Joanne appeared and leant against the doorframe. She looked worn out, but her eyes were wide and accusing. Her lips wee pinched. She tipped a mug to her lips and sipped as she stared at Dan. He blinked at her, trying to discern where the attitude was coming from
"Where is he?" said Dan. "And what happened?"
"Where were you, more like?" she replied.
"Investigating…" The girl's question irritated him, but something about the way she asked made Dan play along. "We were called to see an old friend. A boxing pal of mine, from way back. He got attacked. His wife said she saw the attacker lurking around. We had to go."

"An old boxing pal?" said Joanne. She searched both their faces, looking ready for an argument. Eva nodded.

"We think it could be connected to the man who shot Dan in Shoebury."

The girl's eyes flared, but she held her tongue. "Connected?! I'll tell you about connected!"

"Joanne," said Eva. "What happened?"

"The man who shot you came here! The man you've been hunting out there. The man who shot you! While you were busy out there dicking around playing PI, he came here, and he attacked Mark!"

"No!" said Dan.

"Yes, he did. He attacked Mark. And wasn't it lucky that Mark called me before it happened? If he hadn't asked me to come who knows what might have happened? He could have been killed, that's what! I saw him through the glass. The guy had him trapped in the kitchen, but I couldn't see what was happening." Joanne's eyes misted, and she put a hand to her lips. "I could only hear him scream. I didn't know what to do. I panicked. *You should have been here! You should have helped him!* He's your apprentice. You were responsible for his safety!"

"Joanne…" said Dan. "The guy we saw. I think he said some dumb things which provoked this attack. If I'd had the slightest inkling of what he'd done, I would never have left anyone alone here…"

Eva stepped forward to catch Joanne's eye. She wanted to get back to the point.

"What happened, Joanne. What did the man do to Mark?" Eva's face was serious. Joanne saw the trepidation in her voice.

"He cut Mark's head with a knife. He's got a cut from here to here," she said, swiping a pointing finger across her brow. "But that's not the worst of it. The guy poured boiling water all over his hand. Eva, he's in so much pain right now…"

"Oh no," said Eva. "Where is he?"

"He's been to A&E. They discharged him already. But you know what they're like these days. They're too busy to help anyone. They told him there was a four hour wait and A&E then told him to go and sit and wait at the drop-in centre for help. That's where I left him. Hopefully he's finished by now."

"We'll go and see him" said Dan. "We'll make sure he's okay."

"No!" snapped Joanne.

Eva frowned but spoke softly. "Joanne… I know how you must feel right now. But we've got a responsibility to Mark. We need to see him."

"Responsibility to him? You remembered now, have you? You bet you did. He was your apprentice, Eva. Your *apprentice! He wasn't* your receptionist and he wasn't your *bloody human shield!*"

"Joanne. Stop it. That's out of order," said Dan, jabbing a finger at her.

"Is it?" said Joanne.

Eva shook her head. "No. I think we probably deserve that."

"Yes, you do," said Joanne, her voice quiet and filled with anger. "Besides… Mark doesn't want to see you," she added softly.

Eva sighed and nodded. "When do you think he'll change his mind?"

"I doubt he ever will, Eva. He's quitting the job," said Joanne.

"What?" said Dan.

"You heard. He's quitting. His decision, not mine. He thinks the job has become too dangerous for the pittance he gets paid. So he's finished."

"That's it?" said Dan. "No discussion. No right of reply? He won't even speak to us?"

"Can you blame him?" said Joanne. "I only stayed around here to tell you because he asked me to. It's dangerous here now."

"I'm sorry, Joanne," said Eva.

"Did you see him?" said Dan. "Did you see the attacker?"

"See him? I damn near fought with him out on the street. The only way I could stop the guy form hurting Mark any more was by smashing up his car to distract him."

"His car?"

Joanne nodded. "He parked a black BMW out on the pavement outside. I saw the car there and realised someone was in the office with Mark. Then I heard him crying out… well, I smashed it up pretty good after that… and then the guy came outside. This man looks like something from a horror film. I mean it. His head looks like it has been beaten out of shape… but for the most part what gets you is in his eyes. If looks could kill, this guy would kill everyone every time. The man's sick. I swear it. As sick as they come…"

Dan took in every word. "You smashed his car up. So he came at you… then what?"

"It was too public for him out there. He took off in what was left of his car."

Dan nodded and took a long deep breath. He nodded in appreciation. "You did good, Joanne…" he said, and he meant every word. The girl had done more than most of Malachy's boys who had encountered him.

"I don't care about doing good! I only did what I had to, that's all. And you know what? I think Mark is right to quit this place. I don't want him working here again. Don't forget, I know what happened to him the first time."

"Mark put himself in danger that time. But… if that's his decision," said Dan. "Maybe he's right. Maybe he's too vulnerable for this line of work."

"Is that all you can say?" said Joanne. "Mark risked his neck for you – more than once."

"Mark is family here. His job is still open," said Eva.

Joanne ignored Eva and stared at Dan.

"He idolised you. Is that all you can say. He's gone. So good riddance?"

"That's not what I said at all," said Dan. "Give me a chance here, will you? I'm still thinking what to do about all of this. That bastard is off the leash. Who knows what he might do next…?"

"I can tell you what you're going to do about this."

"You're angry," said Dan. "I get it. But don't overstep the mark, Joanne."

"I don't care what you say," said Joanne. "Mark is hurt, and you're going to help him. Because you're the target, Dan. Not him. Mark was the substitute."

"This guy said that?"

"Near enough – that's what he told Mark. So the best way you can help is by making sure that psychopath is taken off the street as fast as possible. He threatened you, Dan. He threatened to come back and kill you if you keep trying to get him…"

"So now what? You want me to hold off until Mark feels better?" The frustration and anger in Dan's voice came through loud and clear.

"No. You've got to stop this man. He's an animal. If you don't stop him I think I might have nightmares the rest of my life – about what he might do to me or Mark…"

Dan nodded once. His anger subsided into relief. "Don't worry. I'm going to find him."

"Yes, I know you will. And I'm going to help you."

"No, Joanne," said Eva. "You've said it yourself. This man is too dangerous."

"Yes, he's dangerous. But with Mark quitting, I know you need some help. Don't get excited. I'm not offering you much. Just a pair of hands, part-time, between my other shifts until you bring this man down. Whether you like it or not, I'll be going to help you find him."

"We can't put you at risk, Joanne," said Dan.

"Don't worry about that. I'm not going to be a sitting duck for this psycho. I'll help you remotely. I'll help you from my desk at the Civic Centre, whatever is needed. I'll even work here if you put those shutters down."

Dan shook his head. "Thanks for the offer, all the same."

With an air of defiance, Joanne walked out to the front desk and dumped her cup by Mark's laptop. She pressed a few buttons and twenty seconds later the printer at the side of the room clicked into life.

"But I've already started," she said. "The police came by asking about the incident. I told them it happened outside. Some local yobs having a fight smashing up someone's car but they're all gone now. You won't have any trouble from the police."

Dan nodded in thanks.

"But what about Mark?" said Eva.

"A&E weren't exactly interested in details and there's no police incident number. No record of a crime there. Everything that happened here happened off the radar, which is exactly how I knew you'd want to keep it."

Dan offered a grim smile as Joanne met his eye. She handed him the sheet of paper from the printer.

"But when you find this guy, I want you to deal with him. Properly."

"And what's this?" he said, his eyes dropping to the sheet in his hand.

"I said you'd need help. This is your other case. The old man who's ripping you off. Mark told me all about it. He asked me to carry on looking for you because no matter what happened to him, Mark still doesn't want you to fail. I don't think Mark will be very happy to hear that I'll be helping you for a while, but there it is. It's my choice. I'm hoping you can deal with your Parker problem, because the way I see it, he's nothing more than a distraction. Then you can get back to fixing your main priority."

Dan scanned the print-out from his credit card activity. At the top he saw two brand new transactions, each with a very recent time-stamp from the afternoon.

Strontium Menswear £495.

"What?" said Dan in disbelief. "No way... Parker's gone and spent five hundred quid with that joke in Leigh. And he's done it on my credit card! The son of a—"

Joanne cut across him and pointed at the transaction beneath.

"Look," said Joanne. "That transaction is brand new. Do you see?"

Dan scanned the next entry down and Eva crowded in by his shoulder to read it.

Estuary Brewery Ltd £18.68

"He's dining at my expense too?" said Dan.

"Look at the time of the transaction, Dan. That one came in twenty minutes ago. There's a chance he might still be there."

"So where is this place?" said Dan, pointing to the entry for the food spend.

"That'll be the Estuary Arms," said Joanne. "The pub on the corner by the old Grand Hotel."

Dan glimpsed the pub in his mind's eye as he looked at Joanne. It wasn't the first time she had impressed him.

"Thanks, Joanne," said Dan.

"Don't thank me. Just deal with it so you can get back to what really matters."

Dan nodded.

"This psycho… you've got to stop him, Dan…" said Joanne. "You can stop him, can't you…?"

Dan nodded. "I can barely think about anything else. Okay. Let's go and get this over with…" Dan walked towards the door before he paused and turned back. "And Joanne…?"

"What?" she said.

"Tell Mark, I'm sorry."

Joanne nodded. Satisfied, Dan walked out of the door into the street, his boots crunching on the glass as he walked.

"What are you going to do, Joanne?" said Eva, lingering by the door.

The girl shrugged. "Call me. I'll be waiting."

Ten

Leigh Broadway on a late Saturday afternoon.

The sun was shining, and the streets were buzzing with the enthusiasm of the crowds willing summer to arrive. The young women wore short skirts and short-shorts, and some of the older women had followed suit. Young men strutted around in chino shorts, posing around the pubs, bars, and bistros. It was a good day to be seen on the Broadway – a place where money moved quickly and where nothing was cheap. The trouble was Dan's money shouldn't have been moving anywhere. Which explained the stormy look on his face as they roved the busy Broadway. There were other reasons for his mood, but Dan was determined to lay them aside until Parker had been dealt with. As Joanne had said, the man was a distraction.

Dan had left his leather jacket in the car. It was too recognisable, and Dan needed any advantage he could get. If the old man was still stalking the street with Dan's credit card in hand, Dan intended to catch the blighter red-handed. The Strontium boutique had been quiet but for young office types. And Parker had already done enough damage there. So, with the smell of hot meat and fresh fries from a kebab shop wafting past them, Eva and Dan peered across the street towards The Estuary Arms – the polished dark wood and brass pub on the opposite street corner. The chrome bistro-style tables outside were packed with jolly drinkers in skimpy clothes. Other drinkers stood in clutches stepping out of the way of passers-by. None of them were Jonathan Parker.

"If he's got any sense, he won't be here," said Eva. "He's got a half dozen people after him, including us."

"If he had any sense he wouldn't have tried to rob us in the first place," said Dan. "He's not out here with the posers. Let's try inside. But walk behind me in case he recognises you first. He's got a sharper eye for the ladies than anything else."

They crossed the street and walked in through the pub's big corner doors. Unlike the Railway, the Estuary Arms was bright and clean inside, and packed wall to wall with men in polo shirts and women in strappy tops. The bar was full of raucous chatter and laughter. Eva and Dan stared around the edges of the bar, meeting the eyes of the drinkers who looked their way. The big screen TV was on, showing an international athletics event, with football scores scrolling across the bottom. Dan caught a sudden movement at the far end of the bar, heading towards the toilets at the back. He turned and cut through crowds as fast he could. Noticing a thin crack between the toilet door and the door frame, Dan slowed to a halt still some way off.

"He's in those toilets. See? I think that's him hiding in there," said Dan.

"Could be," said Eva.

"Don't look at the doors. Look at something else until we get close…" said Dan. Eva nodded and made a point of looking at the exit door on the right, pretending not to be aware of the toilet doors as they came close up on their left.

"What are you going to do?" said Eva.

"When dealing with Jonathan? Whatever comes naturally…" said Dan.

As far as Eva was concerned, that didn't sound good.

They walked past the busy pub tables into a space before the toilets – a walkway of brown carpet. As they walked between the exit door and the entrance to the toilets, Dan saw the door was now firmly shut.

"Now," said Dan. He turned abruptly to the toilet door, shoving it hard without pausing to consider anyone behind it. The door swung back and thudded hard into a body standing right behind it. Dan pushed harder until the door pressed the unseen figure tight against the wall.

"Sorry…" said Dan without any tone of apology. He stepped into the small anteroom of the toilets and peeled the door back to reveal Jonathan Parker in a silvery suit. Dan looked at the material more closely. As Parker peeled himself off the wall, the surface of the material seemed to shimmer, and show a hint of black which moved across the suit in a subtle wave.

"Oh, Dan… thank goodness it's you."

"Who else would it be? Four hundred and ninety-five pounds. Really? You look like a silverfish. Did you really spend four hundred and ninety-five pounds of *my money* on *that?* I wouldn't be seen dead in that."

Parker grinned obsequiously. "It's what they call a difference of tastes. I'm going for the distinguished, suave, look these days. Whereas you still plumb for the classic, well… Dan look."

Dan grabbed Parker by his shirt collar. He pulled the old man out into the bar and tugged him towards the exit.

"Hang on. I haven't even finished my beer!" said Parker.

"Oh, yes you have. I paid for that beer, I'm telling you it's done. Outside. Now."

Dan yanked the exit door open and swung Parker out onto the side street opposite the old boarded-up hotel. Dan followed, leaning into the old man's personal space, getting a face full of beer breath and fermenting barbecue sauce.

"So come on. Tell me what else you had at my expense. A few good beers. And what did you eat?" said Dan.

"Hunters Chicken, actually. With chunky chips. To be honest, I've eaten better, but it was fairly nice."

"Do you really think I care about what you ate?" said Dan. "You stole from me. You took money *and* a credit card from my wallet while my back was turned. If you were any other guy, if you were any kind of man at all, I'd knock you from here to next week. The only reason I'm not going to do that is because you're an old man and we used to be friends. Jonathan, we used to be like family! Even if you won't respect that, I still will."

"That's very big of you, Dan, that really is…"

"Don't push it, Jonathan. I want my money back. Every penny. The cash and the card."

"Well, it's a bit late for that."

"The cash!" said Dan, snapping his fingers.

"I happened to make a small wager at the bookies as I passed down the street, but here, you can have the rest."

Parker dug a hand into his pocket and pulled out a fistful of notes and loose change.

Dan scowled as he took every penny.

"How much?"

"That's the best part of thirty pounds right there."

Dan growled. "Fifty pounds is missing – on a bet at the bookies! I'm adding all of this onto your tab. You're going to pay us. You may not think you are. Maybe you think you're going to welch on me like you've welched on those Thai boys and your man Cadson too, but I warn you Jonathan, trying that on me will be worse than both of those put together. Now come on."

Jonathan opened his mouth to speak but Dan wasn't interested. He pushed Jonathan towards Broadway and started walking. Eva stayed close by Parker's side in case he tried to wander off.

"But where are we going?" said Parker. "I'm due back to see my good lady any time now. She's waiting to see me. I mustn't disappoint her."

"Are you sure she'd be disappointed?" said Eva.

"A low blow, Eva. But I understand you're not happy. She'd be very happy to see me. Happier than you two at any rate." Dan leaned back and seized Jonathan's wrist like a child, dragging him alongside as they walked.

"I can't walk that fast. Where are we headed, for crying out loud?!" said Parker, loud enough to get heads turning.

Dan stopped. "First, we're going back to the joke shop to return that suit. I want a refund."

"Now, please don't do that. That's not a good idea."

"Why not?" said Dan.

"Because the shop owner is a friend of Amelia. And happens to think I'm in a strong financial position, as does Amelia, and for the sake of this whole project, that perception needs to continue…" said Parker.

"Here it comes!" said Dan, stopping in the street. "You're skint, aren't you? You've got no money left at all, have you? And you're letting that girl think you're so rich that you can do what? Be her sugar daddy and take all the added benefits to boot!"

The old man blushed. "It's not quite like that."

"You know, the way you just said that makes me think it definitely is," said Dan.

"Jonathan, is this true?" said Eva.

"Which part? The sugar daddy or the financial side," said Parker.

"The sugar daddy side is bad enough…" she said.

"Eva, I had you down as a bit uptight, but I didn't have you down as a prude," said Parker.

"The money, Jonathan!" said Eva, exasperated. "You hired us. You made firm promises. How could you do that when you knew you were broke?! Why did we ever agree to any of this?"

"Now see," said Jonathan, looking around the busy street, and lowering his voice. "It's like this. I'm not *entirely* broke. But the money I have left is all spoken for. It's tied up with our forthcoming investment. And I only have twenty thousand left…"

"Then you can pay us back with that," said Dan.

"Not possible, I'm afraid. That money is tied up in the investment. I can't take it out. But when this investment pays out – well, in a few days' time, both myself and Amelia will make many times what we've paid in. I'll be back to a standard of living which suits my temperament, and you'll get your fee, as agreed."

"So, let me get this straight. You're using our money – the money you stole from me – to give a false impression of the health of your finances?!" said Dan. "Have you ever been honest with anyone at all? Tell me how we can trust a single word that comes out of your mouth…"

"Look," said Parker, raising both hands in surrender. "I know I've let you down before, but I promise I won't this time. This investment is real. It's golden. And as sure as eggs are eggs, I'm going to get paid and so will you. But until then I mustn't look impoverished or everything could go wrong. Looking the part is feeling the part, and Amelia has fallen in love with the new me, not the old me. These days I have certain standards I need to keep."

"I rather doubt she's fallen in love with you at all," said Eva.

"That's not a very nice thing to say," said Parker.

"After what you've done I think I'm entitled to be frank," said Eva. "What is this investment, Jonathan? If you're asking us to go on supporting your charade, we need to know. I mean it."

"Fine, fine, fine… if I must. But please, not here. Away from the public ear. Let's step over here. And she does care for me, you know."

Dan shook his head and sighed as they followed Parker. He led them to a quiet spot beside a charity shop and leaned close to the window.

"You saw those people at the dog track," said Parker.

"The Thai boys," said Dan.

Parker shook his head. "The men in suits who Cadson was entertaining that night."

"Of course I saw them," said Dan. "Then you hit the fire alarm. You didn't want me to see or hear what they were up to."

"Only because I didn't want you jinxing my investment! I need this. Amelia has some resources, And I have the twenty k. Between us we can reach the threshold required for a very specific stock exchange transaction."

"A specific stock exchange transaction?" said Dan. "And how did you come by this knowledge?"

"How do you think?" said Parker. "Amelia of course. She heard all about it when she was living with Cadson. The man's an awful boaster. He told her time and again how he was going to live the life of Riley after a series of investments he was planning to make. I don't think he was aware how much he'd told Amelia over time. He'd boasted so much, and Amelia, with that super smart brain of hers, was able to assemble the detail herself. Honestly, the last month with him she spent entirely devoted to gleaning every last bit of information she could about his investments. And what a memory she has! The right portfolio names, the right codes to use for the purchase... the necessary down payment. She's a genius."

"And how is she going to buy these stocks and shares?" said Dan.

"She's smart, Dan. And it's not exactly hard these days. She has a trader account all ready to go."

Eva frowned. "Living with Cadson? That's what you said. That she was living with Cadson. I thought you said she was trapped by him, that she was practically being tortured."

"For all intents and purposes, she was. Make no mistake, Cadson is a very cruel man. Deadly too, as you'll no doubt have seen. One of the reasons I left you in that pub, schmoozing with that pretty little journalist—"

Eva turned a quick and questioning look upon Dan.

"Alice Perry," said Dan with a shrug. "She surprised me, Eva. She wasn't supposed to be there."

"Perry? And what does she want?"

"Another time," said Dan. "Don't let Parker off the hook here."

Parker's eyes glimmered with mischief. Dan's frown took another downward twist.

"Cadson showed up in the pub right when you were so distracted... he threatened me. And he threatened to harm you too unless I paid up," said Parker. "I suppose I panicked, which is half the reason I swiped a little cash to calm my nerves. I need this to work, Dan. Can you see that? I need Amelia to believe in me. I need this investment to work so I can clear the decks and start over again. So I can pay you back too."

"This investment," said Eva., "Amelia stole the information on this investment from Cadson?"

"You can't steal knowledge, Eva. This is an investment. Like a bet at the bookies. And you can't steal a hot tip. You simply hear it and then you'd be a fool not to lay a wager."

"Then why does Cadson want you dead?" said Dan.

"Because he's the jealous type, and Amelia is with me now," said Parker, with a shrug of his shoulders. "How am I supposed to know?"

"You owe him money too," said Dan. "I know you do."

"Maybe a little. But I can pay him off with this too, you see?"

"You stole info from him..." said Dan, struggling, "so you could pay him back?"

"I didn't... but Amelia did. So she could get free and start again. Where's the harm in that?"

"There are so many problems with what you've said, what you've done, that I can't even begin to list them," said Eva. "But you pretending to be rich just so Amelia sleeps with you must be pretty close to the top of the list."

"Stop that! You're misjudging me, "said Parker. "I haven't lied. It's just about presentation, that's all."

Eva shook her head.

"Now will you help me? Please?" said Parker. "Help me keep this girl safe from Cadson until the investment is made and we can sell those shares? So we can make a new start away from this man?"

Dan narrowed his eyes. "This *is* legal?"

"Buying stocks and shares? The whole London Stock Exchange gets away with that caper every single day and no one minds. I should think so."

Dan looked at Eva. "Then we'll help. For a short time," said Eva.

"And this better be the truth this time," said Dan.

"A few days. That's all we need. Just a few days to enable the girl to make this work."

"Funny," said Eva. "I haven't heard of many short-term investments which guarantee a multiple return. You are sure this is a stocks purchase?" said Eva.

"Cross my heart," said Parker. "Where's your faith, Eva?"

"We'll do it," said Dan. "But there's a new condition."

Parker rolled his eyes. "What now?" he groaned.

"Your fee just got doubled. And you'll also reimburse every penny you stole off me on top of that fee. Understand?"

"Double? How's that even fair?"

"Think of it as a liar's tax. You can read it in the small print when we add it to your bill."

"How very irritating," said Parker. Dan shrugged it off.

"And I've got one more question for you, JP," said Dan.

"If you must."

"Amelia. The girl rinsed Cadson for information, got what she needed, then cut and ran. Think about it. Cadson is half your age and wears better suits. What's to say this Amelia isn't going to do the exact same thing to you when this is done?"

Parker grinned. "When it comes to the opposite sex, you've become a real cynic, Danny boy. Eva, whatever did you do to him?"

Eva gave Parker the full force of her hardened green eyes, but the old man seemed oblivious.

"Amelia won't run out on me," said Parker. "I know it. For one thing, there's my charm and my classic good looks…"

Dan raised his eyebrows and coughed into his fist.

"Two. I bring money to the party."

"My money," said Dan.

"No. I've brought my twenty k, remember. Thirdly, I promised I would protect Amelia from Cadson until the money has been made."

"Protecting her from Cadson? That's back to us," said Dan.

"Yes, for which you will be handsomely rewarded. But I think it's mostly down to my class and good looks. The girl simply can't get enough of me."

"Except for when she's telling you to go away?" said Eva.

"She has her mood swings, just like most women I've ever met.

Eva shook her head. "I'm prepared to give you one more try," said Eva. "But if you're using us for any type of illegal trade, I'll drag you to the police station myself and tell them every single thing you've done."

"You're a hard woman, Eva, hard but fair. Now can I go and see my Amelia now? True love. Surely, you younger ones must know how it is…?"

The look on Eva's face said she didn't want to consider it at all.

"We'll play chaperone… if we must," said Dan.

Eleven

They headed along Broadway past the dandyish men and the trendy girls. Dan wasn't in the mood for trying to look good, so he did his best to ignore the posing crowds as he passed them by and instead he looked at the cars. It had always been an idle interest. He'd had so many different cars through the years, he was almost a connoisseur. A Lamborghini passed by with a showboating roar. A template BMW cruised past. Not gleaming, not black. Shortly afterwards, Dan caught sight of another black car. Parked up beside the bank on the opposite side of the street was a black shining Jeep… there was no one in the car. It was probably just a coincidence… after all, a Jeep was a poser's car these days, and there was bound to be more than one Jeep in Essex this weekend. But Dan's brow still crumpled. He thought of mentioning the sighting, but he wasn't sure it was necessary. Probably just a coincidence…

Finally, they reached the parade of shops which housed Strontium, and they took a right turn down the side street for access to the stairs behind the flats.

"I think I could get accustomed to life around here, you know," said Parker. "I think it suits Amelia. And it suits me. It's like one of the nice places in London – but far smaller, of course, and with seaside views."

"You're not moving in. No way," said Dan. "Besides, the locals wouldn't let you. With those suits and the hassle you'd bring there would be a crash in the housing market."

They passed the last few shops picking up the dregs of the main road's trade before they turned left into the lane behind the flats. And then they stopped dead. Their way was blocked. Standing right before them were the three Thai brothers. The men from the Jeep, leaning around like a trio of standard issue British villains with a twist. As Dan weighed up their threat, he guessed they couldn't have been waiting long. The shopkeepers with CCTV would have reported them to the police as soon as they saw them. Dan checked their hands, the bulk of their clothing. He didn't notice any sign of weapons. Not yet.

"Dan?"" said Parker. The old man stepped aside until Dan was at the front of their number. Dan's stomach twinged with remembered pain as he glared at each of the brothers in turn. The trio shuffled and stood upright to block their way.

"What's now?" said Eva, as her eyes roved across the men's mean faces.

"It's about Parker," said Dan. "And as ever, it's about money."

"You have the money?" said the shorter brother in his heavy Thai accent. The little man stepped forward to the front of the trio.

"No... not quite," said Parker. "But my representative here can explain all."

Dan raised his eyebrows and made a silent tut at Parker's audacity.

"Yeah, I'll explain things alright," said Dan.

"We told you before. Be quiet," said the smaller guy, shooting Dan a look of warning. From the look the clothes they were wearing, the Thai boys had been sightseeing. The shorter guy was wearing a *'I heart Leigh-on-Sea'* tourist T-shirt. One of the taller brothers was decked out in a T-shirt with a striped deckchair on it. If not for the memory of the ache in his gut, Dan might even have laughed.

"Sorry to break it to you, but I'm not the quiet type," said Dan.

The shorter man fixed his eyes on Dan, then turned his head back towards his brothers. The other men took a step forward. *Here we go again*, thought Dan. He tensed his gut and took a breath. They brothers came at him slowly, stalking like predators.

Eva and Parker were too close for comfort, so Dan decided to take the initiative. He leapt forward to meet the men as they closed in. The man on the left leaned across his older brother's body to swing a punch at Dan's head, but he blocked it with a swipe of his arm and saw the shorter man aiming a punch at his gut. *Not this time*. Dan stepped back, swept a blocking arm through the downward punch, then rocked the short guy with a crashing blow against the side of his jaw. It made Dan's knuckles sting with pain. The third brother stepped past him and took a few hasty, panicking steps towards Dan. Dan had to hold back a smile. He saw the gap in the man's uncertain defences and sent one probing punch through the man's soft guard, then smashed a hooking punch right around the back of it, driving through hard into his face, sending him crashing down to the floor. Dan took a breath. With fists still raised, Dan stepped back to take stock. The dumpy man's eyes flared at him. The other two hung back to lick their wounds.

"Parker must pay! This is about my family's honour. He has insulted my whole family and disgraced my sister… this is not our way!"

"Poppycock!" said Parker. "Your whole family used your sister as bait for a husband-bagging honeytrap. It was pure entrapment designed to separate me from my wealth."

"Liar!" snapped the short man. The little man's face was dark and shaking. He jabbed a fat finger at Parker's face as if it was a gun.

Dan stepped between them, with raised flat palms. "Hey… let's hold fire here," he said. "Jonathan, what's your version of the truth in this?"

But the short Thai spoke first.

"That man proposed to my sister. They were living together, Parker and my sister, in Chang Mai. She accepted his proposal for marriage. The date was set – the marriage was to go ahead for last month. But then he tried to get out of paying the dowry! The money he promised for taking my sister's hand. He took advantage of us all and insulted my family's honour."

Dan looked at Parker. The old man wore a new sheepish look on his face. He scratched his scrawny neck and pulled at his shirt collar.

"Jonathan?"

The old man said nothing, so Eva turned upon him.

"Jonathan, is this true?"

"They must have had it planned the whole time, Eva. It was entrapment, pure and simple. They only cared about my money. All of them Phee-lau too. I was lucky to get out of there before they drained me dry and sold my organs to boot."

"But you *were* engaged to this woman? Their sister?"

"After a fashion, yes. Phee-lau was a nice girl. A lovely girl. What can I say? There are plenty of married ex-pats out there. But none of them act as if they are married, I can tell you. I thought it was a common-law thing, a folk marriage. Not a contract so the brothers here could rinse me for all I was worth."

"But you did ask the girl to marry you?" said Dan.

"Surely, you of all people will understand, Dan? You're a red-blooded male, Dan, and I know it. I've seen you in action."

Dan dragged both his hands back over his head and blew out a long weary breath. The Thai brothers looked at Dan as if he might have finally understood.

"What are we going to do here?" said Dan, looking at Eva.

"I'll tell you what we're going to do. Parker's going to pay them..." said Eva.

"What?" said Parker, looking aghast. The Thai brothers smiled and looked at one another in relief. "But I can't pay them," said Parker.

"When this deal of yours comes off, you can. Jonathan, you can't just go around the world proposing to women so you can have your way, then dump them when you're done. You made a promise to marry that girl. If you can't honour it, you'll still pay this family what you owe them."

"But... but..."

"The dowry? It was ten thousand?" said Dan.

The men nodded.

"Then that's what he'll pay. Ten thousand pounds. No more, no less."

"But we had to fly here to collect it!" snapped the dumpy man. "We had expenses!"

"And as an investment it was well worth it. You'll get your ten grand. Job done. And then you're quits. Parker pays, you go home, and you don't come back. Agreed?"

The short man glowered at Parker. "That old man lied to us every step of the way. How can we trust him at all?"

"Because we'll make him pay. You think I want you three running around hassling me forever? Parker will pay you because I say he will," said Dan.

"And you'll guarantee it?"

"Guarantee it? I can't guarantee anything where this man is concerned. But he's due some money. When it comes, I'll make sure he pays."

The short man nodded in acceptance. "Then you guarantee it. How long?"

"If Parker here doesn't pay you back within one week, you can do what you like with him."

"Hey!" said Parker.

"But you'll pay, won't you, Jonathan?" said Dan.

The men nodded with glee. The shorter man extended his hand to Dan and they shook hands.

"At least some people in this land have honour," he said. "One week, old man. That's all you've got. Make sure you pay."

Dan turned to watch them walk away, taking care to guard his stomach in case the Thai brothers changed their minds.

Eva, Dan, and Parker kept watch until the Thais reached the Broadway kerbside to cross the street.

"You're not really going to make me pay those awful people, are you? It's blackmail."

"If you don't pay them, they'll never go away. It's that simple," said Dan. "And those guys could scupper your whole investment without even trying. Think of the interference they could cause. Or what Amelia would think."

Parker nodded. "Hmmmm, yes. I suppose I hadn't considered that. Still. Once the money is in, I could take flight before they knew thing about it."

"Jonathan," said Eva, in a voice of warning. "You dumped their sister. You made a false marriage promise and took advantage of her. And I bet you knew about that dowry the whole time. Didn't you...?"

Eva looked into Parker's eyes and saw him squirming. "Then you'll pay them what you owe. End of story."

Eva turned away, to walk down the back lane towards the iron steps of Amelia's apartment. Dan gave Parker a wry smile.

"She's fiery, isn't she?" said Parker.

"And then some," said Dan. "That's a side of Eva most people don't see. You're a privileged man."

"Really?" said Parker. "Then why at this particular moment, do I feel like the most disgusting man alive?"

"Look in the mirror, Jonathan. That's a question you need to ask yourself."

Twelve

The girl opened the door and smiled. It was the same smile as before. Pretty and bright, though not entirely warm. And Eva detected more than a hint of condescension hidden inside it.

"My protection is back," she said, with a hint of sarcasm. "Oh joy. I do hope you make a better fist of it from now on. I'll only need your help for a few days. Then I can put this awful business behind me."

"We can *both* put it behind us," said Parker.

The girl gave Parker an enigmatic smile. When she saw he wasn't entirely satisfied, the girl opened her arms to him. Parker gratefully walked into the girl's embrace. Eva watched with a vague look of disgust. Dan scratched his temple and looked away, but in the end, their investigator instincts had them both watching for the details. The old man sought a sloppy kiss with his wet, puckered lips, but the girl moved past it, and leaning her head on his shoulder, she kissed his cheek. Parker's lips found nothing but the girl's long flat brown hair.

"Yes, the both of us," she said. She stepped away from Parker towards the new console table which had been set up as a desk beneath the big window which looked out over the top of Broadway. The window presented a sun-drenched view of the estuary all the way across to the misty Kent side in the far-off distance. Eva's eyes glanced at the expensive white laptop which was open on the console desk, its screen bright. Beside the laptop was a plastic punnet of strawberries and a jar of Nutella. It seemed the girl had been luxuriating in the finest things as she worked. A few eaten strawberry tops – tainted with chocolate spread – had been dumped into a wastepaper basket beneath her desk. Eva noticed the girl's attire. She was still wearing the same oversized denim shirt, belted at the middle. It looked like a man's shirt, but Eva supposed that could have been the style. Her sleeves were elegantly rolled up, and the shirt hem stopped at her lower thigh. On a closer inspection, Eva decided the look was a good one. It suited her. Even with just a denim shirt, the young lady managed to make her clothes look far more than they were. She noticed the diamante studs on the shirt collar and the epaulettes on the shoulder. It wasn't any old denim shirt, after all. Then Eva noticed the cellophane wrapping discarded by the bin, and the white sticker on its surface. An empty string-handled boutique bag sat beside the bin. Both the sticker and the bag wore the classy branding of the shop below. *Strontium*. The girl noticed Eva's eyes moving over the elements from her shirt to the boutique bag, from the strawberries and chocolate, to the untouched prosecco bottle and clean flute glass by her desk. The thin smile on the young woman's lips said she thought Eva was jealous of her. Eva sincerely hoped she wasn't, though she couldn't guarantee jealousy wasn't a part of it. The young woman was certainly conducting a secret symphony of some kind, but none of them could hear the music. Not even Jonathan. Not quite. Not yet. When the girl flicked her hair, Eva noticed the curious stone pendant the girl had been wearing before had been taken off and left on the desk beside the computer. At first Eva thought it had been dumped and abandoned. Maybe the necklace had been just another unwanted item from her suitor in the shop downstairs. But another look suggested instead the necklace had been left close at hand for safekeeping. Her laptop and the necklace. Two precious items left close together. The girl stopped smiling when she saw Eva's green eyes peering at the desk. She moved her laptop to one side, tilting the screen away from Eva. The laptop nudged the necklace with it and Eva looked up and met her eyes.

"So, Jonathan… why did you bring the protection in here?" said the girl. "Surely, we're better off with them outside, you know, *protecting.*"

"Yes, Amelia. But they're not merely hired help. They are my friends too."

The girl gave Eva another appraisal before folding her arms. "I'd prefer not to have to discuss our plans in front of them. No offence," she said.

"None taken," said Eva.

"What have you told them?" she said.

"About the investment. About the multiple return. That you have a stake and I have a stake, and that it runs through the stocks on your online trader account. That was okay wasn't it?"

The girl swished her long brown hair back and thought about it.

"It would have been better if you hadn't told them anything, like we said before. This is a sensitive operation. They must see that, with Cadson hanging around. He's doing all he can to sabotage things."

"Does Cadson know that your investment is based on his knowledge? That you're going to invest in the same stocks?" said Eva, searching for the right phrases.

The girl's eyes glazed. Her thoughts turned inward and thoughtful for a moment before she returned to the present. "Does he know? Of course. It's one of the reasons he keeps coming after me here."

"The way I heard it, Cadson came here to get something that you took from him," said Dan. "He said that when he came here. So, it can't just be about what you know," said Dan.

The girl frowned at him then turned her frown on Parker and shook her head.

"It's about information, too," said Dan. "Don't worry. I believe you there. When I heard Cadson talking to his contacts at the Romford dogs, they asked him if it was safe. He replied that the information was safe with him. Which was an out-and-out lie. He told them he was like a safety deposit box or some other spiel. I think they bought it, but I remember the look on his face. Cadson didn't look convinced. He knows you've got this information – whatever it is."

"The information on *the investment*," said Parker, dismissive and irritable.

"Yeah. You've got the information, haven't you?" said Dan. "But Cadson can hardly ask for that back if it's in your head. So what else have you got?"

The girl's pretty eyes turned dark.

"I told you. These friends of yours ask too many questions. If we're not careful they'll ruin everything, and this won't work. You hired them, Jonathan, so you should be able to control them. Stop them asking so many bloody questions."

"Dan… Amelia has a point…"

"We're private investigators, Jonathan," said Dan. "We ask questions. We investigate. That's what we do."

"Then try not to. Not until this thing is done."

Dan was barely able to contain his rage, but the look in Eva's eyes called to him. He looked across at her and she shook her head. It was a barely noticeable gesture, but Dan swallowed his anger and folded his arms.

"I guessed that Jonathan owes him some money," said Dan. "I'm pretty sure the man wants that back."

"I do owe him a little, I suppose," said Parker, reluctantly.

"But I'm still sure there's something else," said Dan, staring at Parker, who offered nothing in return but a blank poker face.

"Leave it, Dan," said Eva. "We know enough for now, I suppose." She turned towards Amelia who was still seated at her desk by the window. Dan's brow dropped over his eyes. Eva couldn't mean what she had said. They didn't know enough by any measure. But Dan held his tongue. Eva must have known what she was doing.

"As Dan said, we're investigators," said Eva, her words aimed at Amelia. "It's in our nature to ask questions, to solve problems. You hired us to protect you, so it's natural for us to look at the threats ranged against you. But to deal with all the threats we need to know why they're there… That's all we've been trying to do."

"Yes," said the girl. "But as you said, you know enough to do the job."

"Hmmmm…" said Eva. Her eyes trailed to the white laptop and the necklace, the screen just out of reach. Before the girl could see where her eyes were directed, Eva looked away. "I suppose you're right," she said.

"Yes. I am," said the girl more brightly. "Strawberry and chocolate anyone?" she said, offering Eva the punnet of strawberries and the jar of chocolate goo.

Eva shook her head. "Thanks anyway. Where did they come from?" said Eva. The girl paused to evaluate her answer before she spoke. Eva detected a shrug.

"From the man who owns the shop. My friend Sebastian."

"He gave you chocolates and strawberries— *and the prosecco?*"

The girl nodded. "He knows me so well." She ate a strawberry and put the punnet down.

"I see the console table has been replaced too," said Dan.

"Sebastian," said Amelia, by way of explanation.

Parker frowned at mention of the name. There was a loud knock at the door, the metal knocker striking the plate outside. Dan turned towards the hallway, but the girl strode past them towards it.

"Should you be answering the door, Amelia. It mightn't be safe?" said Jonathan.

"But I know who it is…" she said as she walked down the hall.

"Let me guess," muttered Jonathan. "It's Sebastian…"

Jonathan turned towards the hallway. Eva bit her lip as she stared at his back, willing him on, wanting him to take a few more steps to leave the living room free of watchful eyes. In the hallway the front door latch clicked and the door creaked open.

"Oh, Sebastian… thank you!" said the young woman, cooing on the doorstep.

"Sebastian," said Dan, with a smirk. But Eva wasn't paying attention. She watched until Jonathan finally crossed the threshold into the hallway. As soon as he was out of the room Eva didn't waste any time. Fast as she could, she moved to the laptop and angled the screen back towards her. The necklace tumbled to one side, making the smooth grey stone pendant catch her eyes. It was a curious piece of costume jewellery, she thought. But Eva's eyes honed in on the laptop screen. She moved her finger across the mouse pad, opening the desktop, finding two computer applications ready and waiting. One of them was a web page – all empty space and clean lines, white and blue. A very fancy and up-market minimalist design. Basilica Holdings? Eva rolled the words around in her head, then clicked through to another page beyond to read the company profile.

The London Based Arts Buyer - Procuring Art for Clients of The Finest Tastes

Clicking around the site, Eva saw images of pictures and paintings presented in vast and ornate gilt frames. She was no expert, but Eva recognised the stylised brushstroke of a Van Gogh when she saw it, and the mottled sunlit colours of a Monet. If the images she saw weren't Van Goghs or Monets, then they were almost certainly by artists from the same schools. And if Basilica Holdings shifted art like that, it meant money was changing hands. Big money.

"Thank you, Sebastian. You must have read my mind…"

"I thought you'd be hungry by now," said a deep male voice from the hallway.

 But… where's the mayonnaise? Mussels and chips need mayonnaise with them. Surely you know that. Good rich mayonnaise, freshly made…"

"Oh," came a deep male voice. "Sorry, I forgot that part. But no problem. I can get you some mayonnaise."

"Fresh mayonnaise," said the girl with emphasis.

Then Jonathan's voice cut across him. "No, no, Sebastian. Leave it. I can get the mayonnaise. You've got a shop to run, after all…"

Inside the front room Dan leaned over Eva's shoulder as she scanned the Basilica Holdings website.

"This is an art dealer?" whispered Dan, the light reflecting a pale glow on his skin. "An art scam with a man like Cadson? And these two? I never saw that one coming…"

"Who said art was anything to do with it?" said Eva, as she clicked back to return the browser to the original page she'd found it on. Then she saw the message at the top right-hand side of the web page. A simple four-word message. *You Are Logged In.*

"Look," said Eva. "She's logged into the Basilica Holdings website," said Eva. "She's got internal access… that means passwords. Insider knowledge…"

The fuss out at the front door began to die down.

"No, it's okay. I'll get the mayonnaise," insisted the man with the deep voice. "I know where to get the best stuff. Be back in a tick."

"You know I like the best," said Amelia, as the door clicked shut.

"That man!" snapped Parker.

"What?" said Amelia, with a hint of smugness. "Don't you like Sebastian? But he's one of my friends."

They heard the girl's bare feet gently slap on the wooden floor as she paced back down the corridor towards them. They were out of time, but Eva couldn't help herself. She left the website and moved the mouse pointer to the bottom of the screen, where the tab for another program was open and waiting. She clicked it and up popped a spreadsheet. At first it seemed like nothing but a grid of meaningless numbers, but then Eva scrolled sideways, and a column of names appeared. But she barely had time to register any of them.

Anjay Asagi
Benjamin Astley
Jonathan Atterton

The footsteps came ever closer. Eva's eyes worked fast. She scanned across the columns to find a continuing series of numbers against each name. But time was up. If she risked another half second, the game was up – Amelia would see everything. Eva clicked out of the spreadsheet, returned to the web browser on screen and angled the laptop back towards the window. She stepped away from the machine into the centre of the room and snatched a breath to right herself, as she tugged her hair and composed herself as the girl returned holding a small steel bucket and a large white plate of French fries. Steam curled up from both dishes. "Moules et frites," said the girl. "One of my absolute favourites. I used to eat this whenever I went to Bruges…"

As she spoke her eyes happened upon Eva's awkwardness, and she stopped smiling. Eva felt exposed and guilty. It must have shown in her face. The girl glanced to her laptop and placed the food down on a chair near the door.

"The Belgians eat their fries with lashings of mayonnaise," said Eva.

"And so do I," said Amelia, her voice growing distant.

Amelia walked past Eva and leaned over her laptop. The glow of the screen filled her face and lit her eyes. She looked at the screen, tapped the keys and then stood up once more. She seemed satisfied. Eva coughed delicately into her hand to hide her relief. It was as Eva turned away, that she noticed the small white USB stick – a micro USB – sticking out of the side. It was barely larger than the chip housing the data it contained, and it was the same colour as the laptop, which explained why she hadn't seen it before. It looked a half-inch long at best. Damn it. If only she could have seen what was on that micro. Eva had seen too little to determine what was on those spreadsheets, though her mind was already toying with a guess or two. Names and numbers. Things which made the modern world go round… but Eva needed more, and that micro USB promised the lot…

Sebastian was due back with his fresh mayonnaise. Maybe there would be one more chance to learn more.

"This Sebastian is really looking after you," said Eva.

"Yes," he is," said the girl. She picked up a chunky chip and bit off a piece. She pointed the other half at Eva.

"I know what you're implying, by the way. But it's not like you think it is. You think the same as Jonathan does. But you're wrong. You're all wrong," she said with a smile. "Not that Sebastian wouldn't mind that happening, of course."

The girl was a user, just like Parker. Maybe they were made for each other. Two con-merchants of the lowest order dressing themselves up as high class. One glamorous and devious, one old and lecherous. A match made in heaven. *Or in the other place…*

"Chip anyone?" said the girl. "I can't eat all of this by myself. I'll never be able to fit through the door."

Eva shook her head. Amelia took a few more chips from the bucket and Eva stole another teasing glance at the laptop and she saw something else. The position of the necklace. With all the jostling of the laptop, the necklace beside it had tumbled over itself, and the underneath of the smooth grey stone had been left facing upwards. The wiry metal casing which fastened it into the necklace was visible. The parts no one was supposed to see. *Which made the slot-like hole in the underbelly of the smooth grey stone far more interesting.* It was a little cutting, wide enough for nothing larger than a one-pound coin. Eva studied the stone discreetly. The hole didn't seem to have any obvious purpose in relation to the necklace. In fact, it didn't seem to have any purpose at all. But it did. The cut was neat and smooth and designed for a reason.

"What are you looking at?" said the girl, as she raised another chip to her mouth. There was a challenge in her eyes as much as a question.

This time there was no need to lie.

"I was just admiring your necklace. The one with the stone. You were wearing it the other day."

"Yes," said Amelia. She walked across the room and picked it up. "I only took it off because I wasn't sure if it went with this blouse." Eva watched the girl pick up the necklace. She rearranged it on the desk, and laid it face up, showing it the way it was meant to be displayed. Eva heard the lie in the girl's voice. The way she wore the denim shirt, neck unbuttoned exposing her throat, the stone would have looked perfect.

"It's a nice piece. I think it would go with anything," said Eva.

Jonathan grabbed a handful of hot chips and started munching. He seemed to pay no attention to Eva and Amelia's conversation. And from the look on his face, Eva couldn't be sure Dan was paying attention either.

Sebastian's awaited return with the fresh mayonnaise seemed to take an age. By the time the door knock came, Eva was certain that her impatience must have shown on her face. Amelia had been watching her in silence from the side of the room as she ate modest little pieces of fries while Parker took as many as he liked. Three loud raps sounded at the door to announce the mayo's arrival. The relief was palpable all round.

"At last," said Amelia.

Eva watched Amelia walk out of the room. She waited in hope for Jonathan to move as well, but the old man lingered by the chip bucket to steal a few more fries while his girlfriend was out of the picture. Eva couldn't wait any longer. Jonathan watched her as she picked up the necklace and turned the smooth stone over in her hand. She took a look the neat slot on the reverse side.

"What are you doing?" said Jonathan, chewing a chip. Eva ignored him. Parker turned to Dan.

"Well, what is she doing?" he asked. But Eva answered for herself.

"I like this necklace. The design fascinates me," said Eva. "Do you know anything about it?" She lifted the stone and ran her finger over the smooth surface. The hole in the back wasn't as smooth as it looked. The hole had been drilled and the drill had probably been dragged and wiggled around inside the rock until the gap was sufficiently large enough for the purpose. Eva's eyes tracked across to the mini-USB stick in the side of the white laptop. She didn't have the time to test her theory. Nor could she be so brazen with Jonathan watching. But by her estimates…

"I don't know anything about it at all," said Jonathan. It was hard to tell if he was lying, and his choice of words seemed too emphatic, but Eva nodded nonetheless. Outside, at the creak of the door, they heard some chatter. Then the chatter became a shout, then a shriek. Eva dropped the necklace to the table top. Parker hurried into the doorway, looked out, then reeled his head back in as Amelia was hurled back into the room. She spun on her heels and staggered inside, looking terrified. It was one of the first times Eva had seen the girl lose her arrogant cool. Eva stepped in front of the necklace and computer, to hide the evidence of her dabbling. In the next moment Cadson filled the doorway. He looked right and left at each of them, breathing hard after his climb up the iron steps. He was after something and it wasn't just Amelia. If the necklace was anything to do with it, Eva intended to hinder him anyway she could. Trouble was Cadson was holding a knife.

"There was a fool on the steps," said Cadson in a gruff voice. "Some idiot with a name badge on. Your idea?" He looked at Amelia, but the girl shook her head.

"It must have been one of Sebastian's shop staff," said Amelia.

"Sebastian? How many idiots have you got under your sway now?"

Amelia looked at Jonathan, as she subtly moved across the room. Eva saw she was trying to be careful, moving slowly to block the laptop and the necklace from view. But Eva already had it covered. Maybe it was Eva that she was worried about. She watched the girl appealing to Parker with her eyes, but Parker was by Cadson's side. If Parker had been a younger, fitter man, he might have been able to stop Cadson by knocking the knife from his hand. But Cadson didn't seem worried in the least, and from the look of Parker, he was staying put. Cadson pointed the knife at Amelia and she stopped moving. "You know what I want."

"You want something that doesn't exist..." said Amelia.

"Don't take me for a fool. I can't be stopped. Not by any of this lot, and this is far too important for me to ever back down. And as for you, old man..." Cadson swept his knife towards Parker. "I know you were involved."

"I don't know what you're talking about," said Parker. "I owe you some money, that's all. But we can come to an arrangement..." said Parker, hands held high.

"The money? The money you stole from me, you lying piece of—"

"*Stole?*" said Dan. He looked at Parker with a look of incredulity on his face.

Parker shook his head. "Please. Can we not do the whole *I'm-so-shocked* song and dance all over again. We had a little disagreement and Cadson here says I owe him money."

"No. You said you owe the man some money. But Cadson said you stole it!! Parker?!" said Dan.

Parker's glistening lip trembled with the tension. "Oh, I forget!" he blustered, with a shrug. "I'm not so good with the details these days."

"You're a joke, is what you are," said Cadson, "But you're still going to pay me. And you, Ammie dearest, are going to return what you took…"

Eva saw her eyes stay cool and blank. Even under such pressure, the girl was cool and unfazed. Eva realised they would have to watch her until the very end.

"I gave you a year of luxury," said Cadson. "Then you threw it in my face." Cadson stepped forward and offered an empty hand to receive whatever he was demanding. Amelia stepped to one side, intentionally bumping into Eva to push her away from the laptop. But Eva stood her ground. The two of them stood side by side, obscuring the console table and everything on it.

Jonathan blinked at Dan. The old man made an effort to mouth a few silent words. Dan frowned. He didn't understand any of it. But Cadson did.

"He can't help you, Parker. Because if he tries it, I'll hurt him bad," said Cadson. He smiled at Amelia. "And you know I will, don't you sweetheart?" His little eyes shone darkly. Amelia stayed steady and resolute as she leaned back towards the console table.

Dan stared at Parker, waiting to see if the old man would try to communicate with him again. But Cadson was close now, using the knife to force them back to the wall by the window overlooking Broadway. If Cadson kept coming, they would soon be within stabbing distance – all except Parker. They needed to distract him, to make Cadson think twice, because without a weapon, it was going to be near impossible to escape. But Parker's overtures had given Dan an idea. He nodded at Parker, once, and then again, more emphatically. Parker stared at Dan blankly, shrugging in ignorance. But Dan wasn't perturbed. He nodded at Parker again, mouthing something the old man couldn't understand. Parker frowned and flustered. Amelia looked at them, then Eva too. Cadson spun the knife towards Dan, who turned his face blank a moment too late – Cadson had already seen a hint of his attempt at communications, done with all the skill of the worst blagger in the classroom.

"You're up to something. You try anything and I'll stick this thing through you like a bloody kebab stick. She knows I will. She's seen what I can do."

Dan raised his hands in a surrender pose. "Okay. Okay…"

Cadson snorted in satisfaction. He relaxed his shoulders and loosened his neck, tilting his head one way then the other. "See. No one's going to help you, Ammie. You're in trouble. But I'll still let you off – but only if you hand it over now…"

Dan started again. He mouthed a few silent words across Cadson's shoulder while Parker continued to stare at him as if he was mad. Cadson tensed, ready to act. His arm started to move. In the end, the only word that mattered was the last one. "Now!" said Dan.

Cadson swung the blade at Dan's throat, and seeing him stay still, he turned sharply and quickly to defend himself from a suspected move by Parker. But as Dan had expected, the old man stayed by the wall, clueless, fearful, and frozen as if his feet had been glued down. Cadson blinked at the old man. As understanding dawned, Cadson started to turn again. But by then, it was too late.

Dan thrust two hands into the man's back, using all his weight. Cadson's legs were still off balance from his sudden turn. Cadson tried not to fall, but he swayed, and Dan leaned in and thundered his back with a hail of punches. He moved in close to Cadson's body, so the man couldn't turn to strike him with the knife. Cadson struggled, but he still couldn't turn. Smashing one blow into the side of the man's head, Dan followed up by stamping down on his Achilles heel. Dan's boot heel ground down and the man groaned out loud and sank down to his knees. Dan pushed him down to the floor and landed one foot hard on the flat of the blade. He kicked his other foot into Cadson's gut and the man rolled away in pain, letting go of the knife pressed under Dan's boot.

"That's it. Go. Let's get out of here!" said Dan. "Out!" He ducked down and grabbed the knife from the floor, then pulled Eva and Amelia past Cadson towards the hallway. Eva watched as Amelia snatched up the laptop, grabbing the stone necklace with it. Cadson watched them from the floor, his eyes hard, his face sweating from the pain. Dan pointed Cadson's knife towards his face.

"Parker. Get out of here now…" said Dan, his eyes fixed on Cadson.

"Um. Yes," said Parker. "Sorry about all this, Cadson. You know how it is…" Cadson growled as Parker followed Eva and Amelia out of the room.

"I'm going to stick you on a skewer, you old bastard," called Cadson in the old man's wake.

Dan shook his head. "No, you're not. Believe me. If getting rid of Jonathan Parker was that easy, someone would have done it a very long time ago. Nice to see you again, pal. But don't make a habit of it. You lost. Now go home and get over it." Dan backed out of the room, grabbing the door to close it behind him.

"You should be scared…" said Cadson. "You just messed with the wrong man," Cadson hissed in reply, spittle spraying from his angry mouth. "I'm getting it back. If you get in my way, you'll end up dead."

"Whatever you say," said Dan. "Thanks for the knife."

Dan winked and slammed the door. He ran out of the apartment to see Eva, Parker, and Amelia rushing headlong down the iron steps a couple of storeys below. Dan followed as fast as he could. When they reached solid ground, they looked up to see Cadson peering out from the top floor. A white door opened at ground level, and a man with a neatly trimmed goatee and a tanned face walked out. He looked at them in surprise.

"Amelia?" said the man.

"Sorry, Sebastian. Go to go," said Amelia, backing away with Eva.

"What's going on?"

"Thanks for the accommodation and everything…"

"Amelia!"

"Very kind of you," said Parker with a grin and a wave. Parker glanced down at the jar in Sebastian's hands. "And you can keep the mayonnaise thank you."

The man with the goatee put a hand on his hip and watched them rush down the alley towards the edge of Leigh Broadway.

Dan looked up and saw Cadson watching them, leaning over the black bars of the uppermost staircase. Their eyes met, and Dan felt the man's hatred bridging the distance. Cadson probably wanted him dead. But hey, so did a lot of people. These days, Dan was almost getting used to it. He moved on after the others.

"Where now?" said Amelia. Out on Broadway they made an eye-catching spectacle – a group of ill-matched, sweaty, nervy odd balls. An attractive young woman clutching a laptop to her chest, an old man in a snazzy suit, plus Eva and Dan. The sight turned heads in the nearby coffee shops, cafes, and boutiques.

Eva took it all in. Everyone was a potential witness – people who could tell Cadson where they had gone. Nowhere was safe.

"You'll have to come with us, Amelia."

"Come with you? Where?" said the girl with suspicion in her voice.

"Back to our office," said Eva.

The girl regarded Eva as if she was laying a trap. Eva tried to hold her irritation inside.

"You hired us to help you, Amelia. Now if you want that help, you'd better accept my offer."

"Or we could just leave them here?" said Dan, with a glint in his eye.

"No, we're coming!" said Parker. "We're definitely coming with you." He grabbed hold of Amelia's hand and drew her down the street with him.

They headed along Broadway, dodging between the posers, shoppers and drinkers as they went.

"But there's one more rule," said Eva.

"Not another one!" said Parker, wheezing as he went.

"From now on you're going to be scrupulously honest with us," said Eva, fixing Amelia and Parker with a hard look. "You've been lying and hiding the truth for long enough. Whatever you stole from Cadson – we need to know."

"I didn't steal anything," said Amelia.

"Lies, Amelia. Do you want our help? Do you?" said Eva, reducing her pace. Parker slowed for a breather, and Amelia stopped before Eva. She met Eva's eyes. Her face was a mask of resentment, but gradually, she gave in with a nod.

"Yes. For now," she said.

"Then the truth it is," said Eva.

Parker and Amelia looked at one another as they moved off again, heading past The Estuary pub and the closed down hotel. Dan snatched a look behind them, peering through the crowds as they hurried towards the car park. But Cadson was nowhere in sight.

Thirteen

"If you expect us to keep pulling you out of the fire, then you can't leave us in the dark," said Eva.

She pushed open the door of the office and walked in, while she continued the argument that had been simmering ever since Leigh Broadway. When she opened the door, she had been ready to greet Mark at the front desk. But Eva's eyes found his seat empty and his desk deserted. She winced, remembering the injury and the risks Mark had endured on their behalf. *And they hadn't even been to see him yet.* They were failing him all over again. If the kid didn't want to come back, who could blame him? When there was time, they would go and see him and make amends. *When there was time...* as if there ever was time enough for anything. Then Eva stopped moving. The door of the office was open – she hadn't needed to use her key. Mark was gone. The door should have been locked and shuttered. But the door had been open. Why was it open? A hint of panic set in as Eva looked around. Amelia, Parker, and Dan spilled into the office behind her, forcing Eva further inside.

"What's the matter?" said Jonathan.

Before she could answer, Joanne appeared at the back of the office in the kitchen doorway. She sipped at a coffee and looked at them from the back of the shop, her eyes taking in Amelia, a woman not much older than herself, before landing on old Jonathan. Eva watched Joanne trying to work out the dynamics. When she realised what they were, Eva guessed Joanne was going to be as impressed with Parker as she was. Not very.

"You're still here…?" said Eva.

"Yeah. I thought I couldn't leave you in the lurch just yet."

"But what about Mark?"

"He's with his mum. There isn't room for two alpha female nursemaids at his house, believe me."

"Ah," said Eva. Mark's mother was a friendly single mother, but Eva knew she was a helicopter mum. It was one of the reasons Eva had been glad to keep the woman at arm's length ever since he started work with them.

"Who's this?" said Amelia.

"A friend," said Eva.

"*And who's this?*" said Joanne, mimicking the thinly veiled disrespect emanating from Amelia and replying in kind.

Given half a chance, Eva saw Joanne and Amelia would likely be at each other's throats inside two minutes. It was another problem she didn't need. Eva decided to take the issue by the scruff of the neck.

"Amelia, this is Joanne. She's helping us with some things. We've had some issues here lately," said Eva.

Thankfully, Joanne refrained from passing comment.

"Joanne, this is Amelia. She is Jonathan's… business partner."

"Don't water it down," said Jonathan. "We're in love. Madly in love. That's the truth of it."

Joanne's eyes enlarged, and Joanne took a second look at the old man and the young woman with the long brown hair. A slight furrow appeared in Joanne's brow. Eva couldn't tell if it was the result of shock or disgust. It was probably both, she decided.

"Is he serious or just insane?" asked Joanne.

Amelia tutted and shook her head.

"He's serious," said Eva.

"Why is this any of *her* business?" said Amelia. "She doesn't have to know everything too, does she?"

Eva had taken enough. She walked further into the office, reaching the shelves of case files at the back. She pulled the flipchart-stand away from the shelves, set it upright, and kicked the feet into position.

"Please," said Eva. "We're way past the introductions here. Joanne works with us. She needs to know what's going on." Joanne raised her eyebrows and folded her arms. Eva caught her eye. "It's true," she said. "You're working with us... now, if you don't mind..." Eva picked up the thick black marker pen from her desk and flipped the chart to the next clean sheet.

Dan rested his backside on the edge of his desk. He folded his arms and looked at Jonathan and Amelia, where they stood at the front of the office.

"Close the door and lock it," said Dan.

Jonathan was the one to follow instructions. Amelia stayed where she was, looking around the office taking it all in. She clutched her laptop under her arm, pressing it to her chest. Her necklace was fastened back in place around her long neck. Eva took a breath and pointed the pen at Parker and Amelia.

"The fact is you've both drip-fed us the details of this case the whole way through," said Eva. "You've misled us, hidden information..."

"...lied to us, started a fire alarm at a dog track, and stolen money from us..." said Dan. "All that after supposedly hiring us for your case."

Parker scratched his head and looked at Amelia. He shook his head at Dan. "Was there any need to go into all that?" he said.

"Why? Because I should spare your feelings, or because Amelia isn't allowed to know what you're really like?" said Dan. "From where I'm standing I think you two already know each other pretty well. In fact, I think you two just might be made for one another."

Amelia shifted on her feet, giving off the aura of a teenage sulk.

"You're part of the problem too, Amelia," said Dan. "You've been using us to protect you from Cadson, and we don't even know what you've taken from him – or what this supposed investment is. As far as we know, you could be the villains in this whole caper."

"Come on!" said Parker. "You've seen Cadson in action. He's threatened to cut us to pieces twice since you've met him. Would you mark us as worse than him?!"

"Not worse, no," said Eva. "But that doesn't mean you're not up to something. This is where the lying stops, Jonathan. All of it. We're not getting in any deeper without knowing the full facts. I mean it."

"But you can't pull out now! Not when we're so close!" said Jonathan.

"No one said we were pulling out," said Dan. "Not yet."

The girl glared at them, then prodded Parker. "You said these people were trustworthy."

"Yes, yes, they are my dear. People like Eva and Dan are few and far between."

"Enough. Come clean, Jonathan, or we're out," said Dan.

"But, you don't understand. If we tell you, we won't be able to pay you," said Parker.

"Better to be out of pocket than end up in jail," said Dan.

"Jail? Who said anything about jail?" said Jonathan.

Amelia sidled close up to Jonathan and whispered into his ear. The old man nodded then Amelia pulled away.

"Okay. We'll come clean," said Parker. "But only if you commit to helping us see this through."

"We'll commit when we know what we're dealing with," said Eva.

"And I'm warning you, JP, my bullshitometer is in overdrive right now. You lie on this and we never speak again."

"A little harsh, maybe. But I take your point," said Parker.

"Okay then. From the top," said Dan. "Tell us about what's happening. And don't leave anything out."

"Where would you like me to start?"

"How about the beginning? Does Amelia here know about Thailand?" said Dan.

"Thailand?" said Amelia.

"I guess not," said Dan.

"Uh… don't make me go over all that, not here…" said Parker.

Dan looked at Eva. "I'm ready to quit this mess. Are you?"

"I'd be glad to," said Eva.

"Wait, wait! Don't be unfair. Give a man a chance. I'll tell you about Thailand if I must. But I should preface this first…" Parker turned to Amelia as he struggled along. "I came into a good deal of money. A family inheritance if you will. Dan here helped me get it back. After that, I decided it was time to spread my wings and live a little. So I went abroad to Thailand, the playground of the world, to sample its exotic delights. I was there for the best part of a year, and as one does, I made friends with the locals. And as a man who doesn't like to be lonely, I met someone. And for a while I thought I was in love. Oh, she was nothing like you, Amelia, my dear. Phee-lau was a charm, but you're a delight. My sweet rose."

Joanne made a face and looked away. Eva nodded at her discreetly.

"I don't like roses," said Amelia, with a hint of indifference.

"But you are a sweet and elegant flower, nonetheless," said Parker.

"Jonathan," said Dan. "Can we move this along?"

"Yes, yes. Don't rush me. Anyway, Phee-Lau was a lovely girl. But I didn't know how beholden she was to her family. The whole brief romance was a set-up. A trap. A trap designed to snare a foreign husband to drain his money dry. As soon as I saw it for what it was, I packed my bags and got out of there."

"And that's supposed to be the truth?" said Dan.

"It is the truth, your honour," said Parker.

"Jonathan, you promised to marry the girl then ran off without paying the dowry," said Eva.

"Exactly as I said," said Jonathan.

Amelia folded her arms. She looked more impatient than upset.

"And you've agreed to pay their family the dowry sum to clear your obligation," said Dan.

"Under duress, I might add."

"Whatever," said Dan.

"What about Cadson and Amelia," said Eva. "How did you end up involved with them?"

Parker turned to Amelia. "May I?"

"Just get it over with," said Amelia.

"Very well. I'm not sure Amelia here knows all the details, but I'll do my best to explain…"

"Sure you will," said Dan, adding an insistent nod.

"After my misadventures in Chang Mai, I was in something of a funk. A bit depressed, you might say. So unfortunately, I returned to old habits."

"You started drinking again?" said Dan.

"Oh no. I never stopped drinking in the first place," said Parker, indignantly. "I started gambling. But this time I told myself to stick to classier venues, so I could hold my head higher than before. I found a few decent gambling places which offered wagers on gentlemanly games, such as baccarat, and a little poker too."

"Gentlemen's games?" said Dan, doubtfully. "You said you'd given up the gambling altogether."

"Give me a minute to finish, why don't you?!" said Parker.

"One of these venues happened to be in Barking."

"Barking. You're spot on. That's classy alright," said Dan.

"It was better than it sounds," said Parker. "So, I spent some money to console myself. I played there for a few nights. I won big at first and enjoyed myself and thought my luck had changed. So I raised my stake the next night and I lost it. I lost everything I wagered."

"You lost everything? Again?!" said Dan.

The man's face flickered, his eyes turned towards Amelia.

"No. Not everything, obviously, otherwise I wouldn't have had enough to invest with Amelia here. But I lost a fair old chunk."

"Right," said Dan. He shook his head and pinched his brow. He looked at Eva. "He lost everything. Again."

"No," said Jonathan. "I'm not that dumb, you know. I was never going to stoop that low ever again. I swore it. So I did what I had to, and here I am. I'm a survivor, Dan."

"How, Jonathan?" said Eva. "You did what you had to. So… what did you do?"

Parker looked at Eva and blinked.

"Why is Cadson after you?" said Dan. "You just said you made the guy rich. I take it the Barking gambling den belonged to him…?"

"Yes. That was where I had the pleasure of seeing Amelia, on the first night, my winning night. The night I was lucky enough to catch her eye."

Amelia blinked. Her face remained blank and impassive.

"That night we talked about our hopes and dreams. And Amelia told me about her dream. The opportunity she had to make it big, to get her freedom, if only someone could help her make it happen."

"Rewind, JP. You forgot something. Why is Cadson after you? What did you do to him after you lost all that money?"

Parker's discomfort started to manifest in the awkward look on his face, the way his eyes turned downcast. He scratched his jaw, his mouth twitched, then he met their eyes.

"I happened on a slight flaw in the way his Barking operation stored the takings. The way they transport it from the table to the desk with the safe. The man they used for transporting the money is safe as houses, trustworthy and all that, but essentially he was an idiot. That's why Cadson uses him. He's the type who won't steal because he's not interested in money. But, I watched him, and I saw he wanted to talk to one of the glamorous young women who had come in at one of the tables on the second night. The poor fool could hardly take his eyes off her. So, I suppose I encouraged him. And then, like the kindly gentleman I am, I offered to keep my eyes on his job while he made his move. You may have noticed, Dan, I have a few grey hairs. More than a few, even. And some young people like to trust their elders. At least this young fool did. Unfortunately for him, the girl brushed him off, so I gave him his cash bag, and he got on with the job. He never noticed a thing," Parker smiled to Amelia at his side.

"You stole from him," said Eva, matter-of-factly.

"Sorry, my dear," said Parker, his eyes on Amelia.

"How much did you take, Parker?" said Dan.

"He took twenty thousand pounds," said Amelia.

Parker's eyes opened wide with shock. "What?! How do you know?"

"Come on, Jonny," said Amelia. "I'm not exactly stupid."

"But I told you I had the money to lay down on the investment."

"I saw what you made the first night, and I saw that you lost even more than that on the next night. You lost everything. I almost gave up on you then. But when I saw you with the cash bag, I realised you could do it."

"Do what?" said Eva.

"That he could play a part in whatever backhanded scam she was cooking up. See," said Dan. "They've even been lying to one another the whole way through. How sweet. It must be love."

"Then you knew I'd lost it all… and you didn't care about the fact I didn't have a penny to my name – even after I lost all that money right in front of you?"

Amelia shook her head.

"What mattered was what you did about it," said Amelia. "That took ingenuity. And it took guts."

"Stupid guts," said Dan. "The kind of guts JP has in spades. The kind that nearly got him killed last time round. And now you've got this Cadson guy chasing after you, threatening you again, just like the first time."

"Mr Bradley, thanks for your opinion and everything," said Amelia. "But we hired you to do a job, so now you've had your grand truth unveiling, why don't you quit playing judge and jury, and start doing what we're paying you for."

"In case you haven't noticed, Amelia" said Dan. "We've been hauling your arses out of the fire ever since we met, and we haven't seen a penny yet. Heck, this gig has cost us money. And as far as I recall, you didn't hire anyone. We work for him."

"Then you need your heads checked," muttered Joanne, from the kitchen doorway.

"I think you might be right," said Eva. "You stole twenty grand from Cadson? No wonder he's threatening to kill you."

"And he's threatening to kill you too, Dan, by the way," said Parker.

"Really? Me too? Great," said Dan.

Amelia looked around the walls and the windows of the office. "Are we safe here?" she said.

"Safe? Here? That's kind of a relative term," said Joanne.

"What does she mean by that?" said Amelia.

"It doesn't matter," said Dan. "You'll be safe enough from Cadson. He's not as tough as he thinks."

"Then let's get away from these windows and get on with the set-up. We're getting short of time if we want to make this thing happen. Where are we going?" said Amelia. She flicked her long hair over her shoulder, started walking, and pressed her hand on the door beside the kitchen at the back of the office – the door which led up to Eva and Dan's apartment. "Through here, right?"

"Hold on a second," said Eva.

The woman stopped and turned to face Eva.

"What now?" she said.

"It's your turn, Amelia," said Eva. "Your turn to confess."

"What is this? A Catholic church?"

"You've been holding out more than anyone else. And this entire job hangs on this so-called investment of yours."

"That's right," said Amelia. "So maybe I get started with the preparations before the window of opportunity shuts in our faces."

"Preparations? But using a stock trader website buy doesn't need any prep. It's a simple transaction. You choose your stock, click buy, and pay your fee. Job done."

Amelia glared at Eva and took her time to answer. "But an expert needs time to analyse the market. To pick the exact right moment to pull the trigger…"

"Really now? Warren Buffet. Have you heard of him?"

Amelia looked blank faced. She added a shrug.

Eva continued. "Warren Buffet, the billionaire stocks and shares investor. Warren Buffet says the stock market is simple. You just have to do the opposite of what all the sheep are doing. If they're selling up and the stock values are plunging, you buy then and ride the prices as they get higher. If the price is rising too high and all the sheep are jumping on board, sell. He says most people will just keep buying because they're greedy. And because they're sheep." As Eva spoke, she looked for any inkling of understanding on the young woman's face. The girl was inscrutable, but Eva couldn't see that much of what she'd said had gone in. "Warren Buffet. You've never heard of him? You with your super-computer brain," said Eva.

"What does it matter?" said Amelia.

"It matters that you're lying again. What *have* you got on that laptop, Amelia?"

"That's my business, not yours."

"What has this got to do with Basilica Holdings and very expensive art? And while you're at it, maybe you can tell us about the stone around your neck."

The young woman's eyes flashed with anger. "Basilica Holdings? Then you *did* sneak a look at my laptop. And the stone? The stone is just a stone. That's all there is to it. You want one, buy one. Or pick one up at the beach."

"Your bad attitude wore thin a very long time ago, Amelia," said Eva.

"Yeah. You should tell them to take a hike. Both of them," said Joanne.

"Tell that girl to shut up," said Amelia.

"No one tells me to shut up," said Joanne. She leaned out of the kitchen doorway and nodded at Eva and Dan. "These two are good at what they do. If you want them to help you, come clean. Otherwise stop messing around and get out of here."

Eva looked at Joanne, surprised at this defence from an unexpected quarter. She nodded in gratitude. Joanne shrugged and settled back by the kitchen door.

"Screw you," said Amelia.

"Sticks and stones, bitch," said Joanne.

Amelia raced towards Joanne, but Eva quickly stepped between them and blocked her way.

"Amelia, this stops now. No more attitude. No more lying. We have to know."

"And then? What happens if I tell you?" said Amelia, close up, looking into Eva's eyes.

"I don't know yet," said Eva. "Try me."

"I know what'll happen. You'll quit," said Amelia. She backed away from Eva as she spoke. "You'll tell us you won't help. And my only chance of getting Cadson back for what he did to me goes out of the window. There. Are you happy now? I don't have to tell you a word. You may as well quit. We'll find someone else. Jonathan…"

"Amelia," said Eva. "I said try me."

The girl sighed and looked Eva in the eye.

"What do you think, Jonny?"

"To be honest, I think we've got no choice."

"Fine," said Amelia. "If they really want to hear it, here it is…"

Amelia perched on the corner of Mark's empty desk and faced them all. Eva looked from the dull grey stone around her neck to the young woman's defiant brown eyes.

"Before I became Cadson's girlfriend, I worked for him for a time. Back then he seemed pretty cool. He looked the part, if you know what I mean. He was a rough, tough, rugged guy in a sharp suit. And I knew he had money. He didn't exactly bother to hide it. So when I saw all that cash flying around, and then he showed me his cloak and dagger casino operation, and then he gave me a ride in his Porsche, I'll admit it, my head was turned. Not long after that, he had me working in the casino. Counting the cash at first. Counting all those hundreds of thousands had my head turned even more. I was seeing two hundred big ones a week pass through my fingers. I had Cadson down for a millionaire on the up and I thought I was about to live the best life, that I was about to win, you know. He used that cash to seduce me. I know he did. And I happily went for it. And that's when the trouble started. Because dear old Cadson looks like one thing, but he's quite another. At first, when he was sweet on me, he spent his money like it was just what he did. He wooed me. He looked after me and gave me money to spend on myself. It was great. But that was the honeymoon period, and it didn't last long. By then I had keys to his apartment, and I had all but moved in with him. That was good for all of a week. Then he stopped coming home at night. At best he'd drift in about three nights a week. He wasn't talkative. He didn't make any effort with me, and the money dried up. There were no presents. No flowers. Nothing. Oh, he still had plenty of money. Just not for me. Two months in, I knew he was sleeping with the girl who replaced me in the casino. I was just the latest in a long line of stupid girls on the conveyor belt into his bed. But Cadson had made promises to me. Big promises about how he was going to look after me. About how life would be. When that started to go wrong – and I was stuck living with him – things went bad fast."

"Cadson made you promises? Promises like Jonathan made to a certain woman called Phee-Lau…?" said Dan.

"I don't care about that," said Amelia. "Cadson promised me the good life… I had sold myself on the idea too. I'd told people about where I was headed in life. I was going to fulfil my dreams… and then, everything crashed around me. I decided I wasn't going to let him get away with it. I 'd already sworn I was never going to be used like all those other girls. If anything I was going to be the one who did the using."

Joanne shook her head.

"I don't make any apologies for it," said Amelia, eying Joanne. "This is a cut-throat world. A girl has to look out for herself, or guys like Cadson will simply tear you apart."

"What happened, Amelia?" said Eva.

"Cadson started out as a kind man. A loveable rogue, yes, but still loveable all the same That's how it started but it didn't stay that way for long. He quickly turned cold on me. He gave me the cold shoulder, and then a little while later he started with the insults. One minute I was his queen, the next I was a slut. And worse. He threatened me. He hit me a few times, and that upset me, of course it did. No one had ever treated me like that. I hated him for it. And that hate festered. Even when he hit me, I reminded him of all those whispered promises. Then he got even more angry. He pushed me around, told me he wanted me to go. But I wouldn't go. I hated being hurt by him, but by then I wanted to see him suffer the way he made me suffer. I wanted to deny him the way he had denied me all the things he'd promised. Once he even used heavies from the casino to threaten me. But I still wouldn't give in. He kicked me out, but I broke back into his pad. Can you imagine that? He was beating the shit out of me, and I broke back into his place? But the crazy thing was he said he would forgive me. *He* had been the one knocking seven bells out of me, and here he was *forgiving me* for breaking a window! After all the threats, after all the hate, we found a strange kind of peace. It wasn't pleasant but it was peace. Looking back now I know it was the eye of the storm. But for a short time I was almost happy. Then he changed on me again. He said if I insisted on staying I had to do it on his terms."

"His terms?" said Dan, brow dipping over his eyes.

The girl looked away. "He was nice to me for a little while after we got back together. But I guess that was just to soften me up. It wasn't long after that he locked me up for the first time. He locked me in his bedroom. He kept me that way for days on end. Sometimes he'd even come home and try to get it on with me, but I nearly scratched his eyes out when he tried. He told me to go all over again, but by then I knew his pattern. He told me to leave for effect and I was furious and I said I wouldn't leave. He made me hate him worse than ever. Right after that, I heard him screwing that other casino bitch in the room next door. I started screaming and shouting so she would hear me in the middle of it all, but it only made them louder. She knew I was in there locked up like a prisoner and she didn't care. Right there, right then, I made a promise to myself that I was going to ruin him. I meant I was going to hit him where it hurt. I was going to take him to the cleaners. And I meant it. I've never been so certain about anything in my entire life. I wanted him burning the way I burned in that prison cell. I had to make it happen."

"How did you do intend to do that?" said Eva.

"By any means necessary. But I remembered what he whispered in my ear, back when he was still sweet on me. More than once he'd boasted about Basilica Holdings, boasted it was a cash cow that would last him forever. Like it was a magic fricking lamp, the answer to all his problems. I remembered that, and I decided Basilica was my way in. So then I had to turn it all around. It was awful at first. But I had to be smart and play the long game. So I started changing my attitude, outwardly, while inside I hated his guts. I used sweet talk. I asked him to come and see me. I played nice. I acted like his dream girl... little by little, it began to work. After a few weeks, he began to trust me again. I didn't want his trust. All I wanted was to bide my time and use it against him. I hated him during every single moment. I was smart. I watched him. I listened to his calls. I watched him on his computer, checked his search history, visited the sites he went on, took notes of what I found. It didn't take too long to piece it all together. Basilica Holdings is a massive art dealership. It buys art for companies and private interests all over the world. And it does so for a very healthy commission. But get this – and this is the part Cadson was wetting his pants over – Basilica Holdings kept a spreadsheet of their best regular clients. And on that spreadsheet was a list of their bank accounts, purchase card numbers, and security codes. Everything set up so that a new art purchase order could be set up and processed in a heartbeat. These art people trusted Basilica far too much. Basilica had everything they needed to rinse their clients for millions, and Basilica were complacent. Cadson knew someone on the inside. They told him about the data and he talked them into his idea over a couple of months, and then he sold this guy's colleagues on the idea too. They stole the magic spreadsheet and gave it to Cadson on the one proviso it wasn't to be used for a year or two – long after that data breach had died down and been swept under the carpet. The idea was that Cadson and his chums would be able to draw down various unobtrusive cash sums from those art buyers for years, decades even. If the sums were spread around the various clients, and they never over-targeted one buyer, Cadson was confident the scam wouldn't be uncovered for years. It sounded great. But to me it sounded too complex. A lot of thefts leave a bigger trail. I thought a single large cash hit should have been made on one main buyer. Hit them hard and get out of there. I never shared my idea with Cadson, because he didn't know I knew… but that's exactly what I intend to do. Use that data, use it once, and stay safe, and rich, and never be found again. The rest of the Basilica data would be useless after that. The fraud investigation would mean all the passwords would be changed. Cadson would lose out. But what would I care? I'd already be rich. Cadson would stew on that for the rest of his life. It'd be the perfect result all round."

"Correction – we'd already be rich. Both of us," said Jonathan.

"Of course," said Amelia, with a shrug. "The both of us," As if it went without saying that JP stood to benefit too.

"How did you ever get away from him?" said Eva.

"It wasn't so hard," said Amelia. "I'd spent a lot of time watching him - the way he worked, where he worked, all the places he went to after those secretive phone calls to his contacts at Basilica Holdings. From there I managed to work out where he'd stashed the data. All I had to do was wait until I knew for sure. Soon as I worked it out, I picked my moment, took the stone and ran. That was one of my greatest pleasures, wrecking his dream, proving that I had beaten him to it. Cadson thought he was so smart, hiding that usb in an ornamental stone amongst all those others. But in the end, it really wasn't smart at all. In fact, his hiding place only made it easier, because it meant he would have had to check through all those other stones just to be sure it was missing. That bought me enough time to get away, enough time to get out. From there I needed somewhere to lay low. I knew Sebastian would help me with a place to hide. But to make everything else work, I needed help."

"Help?" said Eva.

"This help," said Amelia, gesturing around her. "The temporary protection Jonny said you could provide... without that kind of help, my plan is a non-starter. I needed resources. Jonny had them. And I needed some security to keep him away while I set up the deal. I guess that's where you came in."

"And your plan - You're going to defraud a company for as much as you can get?" said Dan. "You were going to replace Cadson's fraud with your own?"

"I'm no villain, Mr Bradley. I was going to target a large conglomerate. People who wouldn't feel the loss."

"And that makes it alright?" said Eva.

"Hold on a minute," said Amelia. "I was going to target a company that buys art just to make itself look good. One of the pharmaceuticals would do nicely. Come on - they extort huge sums for vital medicines people need to stay alive, and they are insured to the hilt. They don't have a conscience. No one would lose out."

"It's a nice plan. And a decent revenge package. But that's not investment. That's theft, pure and simple," said Dan. "You don't need a down payment to steal money. So where does Parker's twenty grand come in?"

Parker's face crumpled. He looked at Amelia, speechless. His mouth hung open and silent.

"Sorry Jonny. The twenty k was my insurance policy."

"What do you mean exactly, by 'insurance', Amelia?"

"I mean that if everything went south, if my plan didn't come off, if Cadson stopped us, if he came after me, I needed another way out. After what I'd have done to him, Cadson wasn't going to stop coming for me until I was finished."

"Amelia?" said Parker.

The girl looked at him.

"Jonny – if the worst happened I needed a way out or I'd end up dead. That twenty would have helped me escape."

"And would you have escaped... alone?" said Parker.

"If I had to," said Amelia.

"Oh. I see," said Parker, crestfallen. The old man looked down at his fancy shoes.

"One woman wants a dowry, another woman wants your money for insurance," said Dan "Love is a risky business, JP."

"Isn't it, just?" said Parker, quietly.

"Hey…" said Amelia. The girl walked to the old man's side and gave him a playful punch in the arm. "Hold on. Running away wasn't the plan. I said it was the insurance. That's all."

"But you never told me about it," said Parker.

"And you never told me about Phee-Lau the Thai bride. And that twenty grand was never yours in the first place, Jonny."

"No, but…"

"Our plan isn't dead, Jonathan. Not until these two decide to walk away. Even then we could still find someone else to keep Cadson off our backs until the deal is done."

"It's getting a little late for that, I think," said Parker, his voice betraying a hint of sadness.

"It's not too late. It's not over yet."

"Yes… it's over," said Dan, looking at Eva. Eva nodded and let out a sigh.

"What do you mean it's over?" said Amelia.

"You hired us on a false premise," said Eva. "We were supposed to protect you from Cadson so you could complete your investment before he could get to you. An investment. But there never was any investment. You stole sensitive information from Cadson – which Cadson stole from Basilica Holdings."

"And you two are together under a false premise too," said Dan. "Look at you. None of this is what it first seemed."

"You're wrong," said Amelia. "No, this isn't an investment. But Cadson does want me out of the picture."

"He wants his data back to protect his own crime," said Eva. "That's what he's been after all along, only we didn't know for sure until now."

"But he can't have it! Besides, she's memorised it."

"That was what you told us at the start. That Amelia had a brain like a super-computer. But everything you need for the theft is on that laptop," said Eva.

"You think?" said Amelia with a smile. "It's not on there. Check if you like."

"I still know where it is."

"Where?"

"In your necklace – hidden inside that stone."

Amelia blinked, and her arrogance bled away. The young woman traced a hand up to the stone, her fingers sliding across its surface. She looked suddenly self-conscious and alone.

"How——?"

"It wasn't so hard in the end, Amelia. You left the necklace right beside the laptop when your friend Sebastian came to visit. I saw the slot cut into the stone. I saw the micro-USB drive stuck into the side of the laptop where you'd left it. They were about the same size. That's what Cadson wanted this whole time. The necklace containing the drive."

Amelia shook her head. "No. He wanted the stone. That's how he kept it, the data stick hidden in one plain stone in a glass dish full of stones on his mantelpiece at home. The necklace was something I came up with. My little in-joke at his expense. I knew if he ever saw me with one of those stones around my neck, he'd have worked it out in ten seconds flat. Oh, I'd have loved to have worn it in front of him, taunting him with it. After what I've told you about what he did to me, would you really want to stand in our way? Jonny could get a payday to turn his whole life around, and I would make enough to walk away from that scumbag for good…"

Eva remained impassive as Amelia spoke.

"How could you want to stop that?" said Amelia. She shook her head. "Shame on you people."

Jonathan shook his head. "No, Amelia. It's not about the USB, or that stone. He wants everything. He wants my money. But most of all he wants you, Amelia. You've already bested him, and he knows it. Cadson is worried you'll do it again."

The young woman shook her head and gave Parker a hint of a smile.

"He only cares about the money. He wants the data, and he'll stop at nothing to get it."

"But the data is in your head," said Parker.

"I can't store all that in my head. It's here, Jonathan. Miss Roberts is right. It's about what's inside this stone."

Parker groaned. "You're doubting yourself, Amelia. We don't need that stone. We can do without it. I know what you can do."

"No," said Amelia. "The memory stick is our way out of this."

Parker looked doubtful. He dragged a hand through his slicked grey hair and sighed with a shake of his weary head.

"Hang on," said Dan. "No one here can trust a word you say. You already took JP's twenty grand on false pretences. And if Parker wasn't so damn smitten then he wouldn't believe you at all. And you say shame on us?"

"Yes – shame on you!" said the girl. "You're practically helping Cadson to get away with everything- Everything he's about to do with Basilica Holdings, and everything he's done to me."

"Amelia... with all due respect. How can we even believe that anything you've told us is true?" said Eva.

The young woman looked at Joanne, then turned her eyes to Eva. When she spoke, her voice was slow and firm.

"You pushed me to tell you these things. Every word I said just now is true. But frankly, I don't give a damn what you think. I'm not here to win hearts and minds. I'm here to get a job done." The girl turned back to the door.

"Come on, Jonny. We've got work to do. They can't really stop us."

"What?" said Parker, looking up. "You want me to come with you?"

"Of course. We're partners."

The old man smiled. "But Amelia, I can't help thinking there's a much better way to do this. To achieve what we want without so much trouble from Cadson... or anybody else."

"There isn't, Jonny. Believe me. This is the only way," said Amelia, tapping the stone.

"Yes, you may be right there," said Parker doubtfully.

"Come on. There's no point in staying here, is there?" said Amelia. "It's plain to see that these friends of yours aren't going to help you at all."

"You're right on that score," said Dan, his face dark and angry.

Eva laid a hand on his chest to stop his flow.

"It's true. We can't help you," said Eva. "What you're proposing is an out and out crime. Which means we have an obligation to stop you."

"An obligation to stop us?" said Amelia. "I told you what that bastard did to me, and you're going to let him get away with it?!"

"Get away with it? No, not at all. You can still win here, Amelia. And Jonathan. You can still get what you want from this. So long as you're telling us the truth," said Eva.

"How exactly?" said Parker, with a snap of irritated frustration.

"Because Cadson wants that data so badly, I'm betting he'll be willing to do anything to get it. I'll bet he's so desperate, he's almost certain to make a mistake."

"You're underestimating the man," said Amelia. "I believed the same thing once, but I'll never make the same mistake again."

"Desperate?" said Jonathan, considering Eva's words. "Yes, he does seem desperate. Do you really think he'd make a mistake – enough to help us?"

Eva nodded. "I think so," she said.

"Whatever you're thinking, you're wrong, Miss Roberts. This isn't just about my revenge. This is about creating wealth. And a future. I need what's in this little stone. This is my only way out. I have to use it."

"No you don't," said Eva. "It's not your only way out. That's what Cadson needs. You're not tied to that stone Amelia, Cadson is. You have better options, believe me. You just can't see them right now."

"Better options, yes…" muttered Parker. Eva watched the old man thinking. He chewed his lip and looked away. Eva had to hope he was thinking what she was thinking, but there was never any telling with old Jonathan Parker. His thoughts were rarely exposed until he acted. And by then it was too late.

"He needs that stone badly," said Dan. "I heard him making assurances about it at the dog track. His people believe he still has it because that's what he told them. And he said he's going to do a test draw-down to prove it. Which puts him in a precarious position. As far as I see you're the one holding the aces."

"Then I need to play this hand before Cadson gets a chance to take it back," said Amelia.

"There'll be no fraud, Amelia. No grand theft," said Eva.

"But we have to get this man off our backs!" said Parker. "And we need that money too. Dan, you forced me to make financial promises to those Thai boys, and then I have to pay you as well."

"We'll find another way," said Eva.

Amelia blinked. "You're really going to blow the whistle on us, aren't you?"

"Only if you walk out of that door with that data stick" said Eva. "But if you let us, we can help you turn this whole thing around."

The girl looked at Jonathan, glum but defiant. There was a different kind of glint in Jonathan's eye, but no one could tell what it meant. The old man stayed silent.

"Then it looks like I don't have a choice. What did you ever see in these people, Jonny?" she said. "They've done nothing but let you down."

"They're smart people, Amelia," said Parker. "They don't always help in the right way, mind. But still, I think there's something in what Eva says. Something, yes…"

Eva studied Parker as he spoke, and watched as the old man drifted off into thought again. She didn't like it, but Eva had the merest hint of a plan. And if things went their way, there was even a slight chance her plan could work. But only a slim chance. Because success depended on being sure of the truth. And with a stack of lies like the ones they'd been fed since the start, it was likely they were building on the shakiest of foundations.

Jonathan nodded to himself as if he'd reached a decision…

and Amelia's eyes showed some speculation of her own.

"Would anyone like a coffee?" said Joanne. Eva found the girl studying her face. "Or a glass of something stronger maybe?"

It seemed the stress was showing already.

Fourteen

"I really don't see why this is necessary. I already know what's on that stick," said Amelia. Eva held her tongue. The four of them — Amelia, Parker, Eva, and Dan walked from the car park in the busy town centre and crossed the busy two-lane thoroughfare behind the high street. They passed the huddles of hobos and the street drinkers sitting around on the green of Warrior Square, swarthy characters who stared back at them as they swigged from their cans of super-strength lager. As they crossed the street, Dan turned his head and kept a watchful eye over their backs. Cadson would certainly be on the hunt, and Eva sensed Dan's thoughts were not entirely devoted to Cadson, either. There were plenty of reasons for Dan to be looking over his shoulder. Cadson was simply the latest in a long line.

"It's pointless arguing with them, Amelia, trust me on that score" said Parker, walking at the young woman's side. Out on the street they seemed an even less likely coupling. They looked like grandfather and granddaughter. Or perhaps care in the community outpatient and underpaid chaperone. The snazzy suits certainly weren't doing Parker any favours on that score.

"So why are we still cooperating with them?" said Amelia. "They're not helping us, are they? They're stopping us achieving what we set out for."

"Just wait, my dear. Let's see what happens. This little cloud will have a silver lining, I promise. You'll see."

"I think you're kidding yourself," muttered Amelia.

"Just trust me," said Parker.

The girl looked him in the eye and nodded as the old man held her gaze.

Eva glanced at Parker's face, then looked away before his eyes could find hers on him. She could tell Dan had been listening to them too. Eva exchanged a brief look with Dan as they walked.

"Look," said Eva. "We have to be on the same page, wouldn't you agree? That's the only reason we're doing this. We must have complete trust in what you're telling us."

"Yes. So we've come here because you still don't believe me," said Amelia.

Eva hesitated, and chose her words carefully. She slowed her walk as they got close to the door on the corner.

"Look. Adam Ferguson is our technical expert. This is for your safety as much as ours. He could check to see if there are any tripwires or hidden scripts or bugs in the data you obtained from Cadson. Not only that, he'll be able to see if there are any other files hidden behind it."

"You mean, such as files which I might have hidden from you and Jonathan? Is that what this is really about?"

Eva immediately dropped her pretence. The girl was smarter than she had realised. But Eva wasn't ashamed of being caught out. Amelia and Parker had lied to them so often, checking out the data stick for more lies was a sensible course of action to prevent yet more shocks.

"Partly, yes. But this is just a precaution, Amelia. Remember, you could learn something here too. We all could."

"Nice spin, Miss Roberts, but I'm not falling for it. Seems we're not the only people guilty of talking in half-truths."

Touché. Eva took the hit without complaint or reply. No matter how she spun it, they had come to check what the stick contained. If the data was what they had been told, then at least they had a baseline truth to work from. Everything else would be planned from there. Including a plan for how to deal with Cadson.

The hit the buzzer on the intercom by the glass door for Adam Ferguson IT, and Eva smiled at the fish-eye camera lens as Dan and the others crowded around her shoulders. It must have made for some unpleasant viewing at the other end.

There was an electric buzz before a voice came on the line. "Come in to my parlour," said Ferguson's nasal voice over the speaker, before a long buzz signalled to let them in. Eva opened the door and they climbed up a set of stairs where the carpet had been torn then secured with black and yellow hazard tape. The tape itself was peeling from the corners of the steps, adding a new hazard to prevent an old one. The intense simulated-chicken smell of hot flavoured noodles poured down the stairwell. One of Ferguson's favourite go-to meals.

As soon as they reached the top of the stairs, Eva looked around to find a reassuring mess of loose cabling spilling from spools of all colours, like plastic spaghetti, as well as the carcasses of old computers piled at angles on every spare surface. This was the outer room, where the filing cabinets stood like sentinels among the dead bodies of computers past. Eva led the way into the inner sanctum, where three laptops sat on the windowsill connected by long cables to a device on the floor. The mothership. The screens of the windowsill computers were docile, blue, and inactive. They looked like hospital patients safely dosed up to their eyeballs. And in the middle of the room, sitting beside a circular console piled with a jumble of tech, large and small, along with crumpled napkins, and more wire jumble was Adam Ferguson.

He pushed a set of goggles up onto his forehead. Then he laid his Hot Noodle pot aside. He was still chewing as he appraised them. Amelia squirmed. Despite her silence, the young woman's face conveyed a very loud 'Ugh'. Parker coughed into his fist and looked down the stairs behind him for the comfort of an escape. Adam Ferguson finished chewing his noodles and ran his fingers over the moustache above his beard.

"Well, Eva, this doesn't look like my long-awaited gourmet burger date," he said.

"No, I'm afraid not," said Eva, with a smile.

"So, this must mean another favour… Eva – come on. How many burgers do you want to buy me?"

"Shame it looks like you've just eaten," said Eva, nodding at the empty noodle pots littered around Ferguson's console.

"Noodles," he said, nodding at the pots. "All I get in life is noodles. Noodles in pots and noodles spilling out of these machines. I'm getting sick of noodles. You know, I might have to switch my diet to pastry slices if this goes on."

"Sounds like some kind of progress," said Dan.

Ferguson nodded thoughtfully and stroked his unkempt beard. "But you didn't come here to talk noodles. It seems you've brought me some new customers."

"Um, not quite," said Parker. "As it happens, Dan... so long as you don't mind, I was rather hoping I could take a moment's leave and get myself some fresh air?"

Dan looked at Parker and checked the look in his eyes. The office air was thick with chicken noodles, and Dan couldn't blame anyone for wanting out. But this wasn't anyone. This was Jonathan Parker. Dan clocked the obsequious look in his eye and didn't like it at all. But he guessed at worst, Parker wanted a cigarette. Or maybe a pint of beer from the sports bar establishment on the opposite corner of the street.

"You're leaving so soon?" said Adam.

"I'm afraid chicken noodles and computers aren't quite for me," said Parker.

Ferguson shrugged and leaned back on his chair. "You can't please all of the people all of the time."

"Okay, Jonathan," said Dan. "But don't be long. And don't let lost out there. And don't drink too much. Remember, Cadson is out there somewhere."

"How could I possibly forget?" said Parker. The old man shot Amelia a supportive glance. "Don't worry, I won't be long, Amelia. And I'll be careful."

Amelia folded her arms and looked away in protest – probably at being left alone.

Dan let himself enjoy a half-hearted smirk. Lately, the girl seemed more in need of Parker's protection than she imagined, but Parker still moved down the steps in a hurry. Dan guessed the old man must have seen a Happy Hour sign across the street.

"So, what is it this time, Eva?" said Ferguson, as the downstairs door slammed. "Don't tell me. You're being pursued by a crazed third-world dictator who's sent an army of assassins to hunt you down?"

"Adam," said Eva. "I think you watch far too much Webflix. No. This case is far more domestic than that."

"Shame. I was beginning to enjoy the challenging ones," said Ferguson. He folded his arms and reclined on his stool, eyes flicking between them while he waited for his brief.

Eva stretched an open palm towards Amelia. Reluctantly, the girl slipped off her necklace, and tapped the front of the stone until the little white memory stick dropped free into her palm.

"Now that's more like it," said Ferguson.

Eva took the USB and handed it to Ferguson.

"What have we got here?" he said.

"We need you to tell us what's on that stick. I know there's a spreadsheet on there, but we need to know if there's anything else. Anything hidden. Anything which looks cloak and dagger. Anything at all."

"And you said this was dull…" said Ferguson.

"I said domestic," said Eva. Ferguson smiled. He shifted in his chair, reaching down to plug the USB into the clunky, old-fashioned black tower computer by his knees. Then when he stopped and looked at Eva.

"This little stick doesn't contain malware, does it? I mean, my computer's not going to die on me or anything, but I'd prefer to save myself a little hassle if I can."

"That's what we're here to find out," said Eva.

"You're always such a tease," said Ferguson.

Dan raised an eyebrow and looked at Amelia, shaking his head by way of apology. Adam Ferguson inserted the stick into the USB port and tapped at his keyboard with lightning fast finger strokes. The screen in front of him burst into life, with a new white text box at its centre.

At the top left of the little box was a line of writing beside a tiny document icon.

"It looks like there's only one file on this baby. And I can tell you now, that there's nothing else. Nothing hidden, or corrupt. No malware or secret files."

"See? You wouldn't believe me, would you? I was telling the truth," said Amelia.

"There's always a first time," muttered Dan. Amelia shot him a scathing look.

"That's great, Adam," said Eva. "Now could you open that file and tell me what you see?" said Eva.

"Sure. Here goes…"

Ferguson clicked the icon and the spreadsheet popped open to fill the whole screen. The spreadsheet grid was filled with endless lines of names and numbers. Ferguson used his mouse to quickly scroll left then right before he scrolled back up to the top. After a moment, he swivelled around on his stool to face them. His placid expression betrayed a hint of intrigue. He folded his arms and looked at each of them in turn.

"If I didn't know better, I'd say that this file holds the names, bank details, passwords, and security codes of four hundred and seventy-five different people and or companies."

Amelia scowled and shook her head at the stained brown office carpet. Ferguson noted the gesture and carried on.

"The file was created two years ago, and has been regularly updated since then, until two months ago. A fact which tells me something in itself. If this data is genuine – all those names, accounts, card numbers, and pass codes – if they stack up – then this file is a crime waiting to happen. Or has already happened. Tell me. Is this real? Or is this some kind of dummy test file?"

"It's real, Adam," said Eva. She looked at Amelia, and the girl frowned. "Unless you have reason to tell us otherwise?" Amelia tutted and shook her head.

"Hmmmm," said Ferguson. "Basilica Holdings, huh?" He swivelled back toward the computer and typed again. A moment later the swish white and blue website Eva had visited before popped up on Ferguson's screen. The IT man clicked through a dozen web pages at typical blitzkrieg speed before he turned to face them again.

"Yep. I'd say this is the genuine article. This data holds a list of their clients, right? Clients who buy corporate art… expensive corporate art at that. And those numbers are almost certainly a list of payment credentials. An easy go-to list so Basilica can be paid as soon as they complete an art deal. Man, I wish I had clients who trusted me like that. Clients who would let me hold their payment details, so I could charge them whenever I billed them. That would make life so much easier. I'd get paid on time. In fact, I'd get paid! But the people in this file – these are very wealthy people, Eva. How in the world did you get hold of this?"

Eva turned to Amelia.

"My client came into possession of the file," said Eva. Amelia said nothing, but Ferguson made a cautious study of her face, until Amelia stared back, and he looked away.

"Interesting. It looks like this file stopped updating two months ago," said Ferguson. "May I hazard a guess?"

"Of course," said Eva.

"That's when this data was stolen, or more accurately speaking, copied. This spreadsheet is a tool for fraud. Has any fraud happened yet? And have Basilica called the police?"

"We don't think so," said Dan.

"It's possible Basilica might not even know their data has been stolen," said Eva.

"But they soon will," said Dan.

The girl sighed before she spoke up. "Basilica Holdings don't know," said Amelia. "Only Cadson's accomplices know anything about the file, and they work for Basilica. This was going to be an inside job."

"And they think this little stick is still held by the man who intended to carry out the fraud. Their agent, a man called Cadson," said Dan.

"This kind of information, the sheer value and scale of what is on that stick," said Ferguson. "Some criminals would kill to get their hands on this!" Ferguson's voice was charged with childish enthusiasm.

"That's right, Adam," said Eva. "They would." Ferguson blinked as he processed her words.

"Whoa!" said Ferguson. "You mean that someone is *actually* looking for this thing? As in, *someone bad?*" he said, as understanding dawned. He pulled the stick from the machine, wiped it clean of his fingerprints with a crumpled, yellow-stained napkin and left it on the desk.

Eva picked up the tiny USB from Ferguson's desk and looked Amelia in the eye. "Because you told us the truth," said Eva. She made a show of picking up the grey stone and raised the tiny white stick. "But only because of that."

"Of course I did," said Amelia, as Eva slid the little white stick into the slot and rolled the stone in her hand.

"Then maybe we can trust you with helping us make this right," she said.

Eva handed the necklace back to Amelia who quickly fastened it around her neck and set it in place. Eva watched the confidence and satisfaction return to the girl's face. She had her totem back. The girl clearly believed she was back in the game.

"If you had trusted me in the first place, we'd all have been paid, Parker would have got his money, and Cadson would have been finished. But as it stands, none of us get a thing…"

"Wait?" said Ferguson. "You were the one going to steal with that data?"

"No, not me," said Amelia. "I stole this from the man who stole it first."

"Come again?" said Ferguson. "And these are your clients?" he said, turning to Eva.

"That's exactly why we came to see you, Adam. To avoid a whole bunch of trouble."

Ferguson eyed Amelia with suspicion. "I'm not sure you're out of the woods just yet…" he said.

The intercom door buzzed loudly, breaking the spell, and they followed Adam's eye to a black and white screen which showed Parker's face distorted by the fish-eye lens. The lens made the old man looked like the BFG.

"As I was saying," said Ferguson. He buzzed the door open and Parker skipped up the stairs faster than anyone could have expected. There was a new light about his eyes, and a nervous twitching at the corners of his smiling lips. "That's better," said Parker. He clapped his hands together and rubbed them. "Amazing what a bit of sea air can do."

"What's with you?" said Dan. "Let me guess. The barman undercharged you."

"I'll have you know that I've not touched a drop," said the old man.

Dan sniffed the air.

"And you're telling the truth. Look out, Eva. I think this honesty lark might be catching. But Eva had already been at work studying Parker's body language, all sprightly and energetic. She saw Amelia had noticed it too. The young woman seemed intrigued, but found Eva looking at her and kept her mouth shut.

"So, then. How did it go? Any secret files?" said Parker.

"No. All that's been proved is that the data is genuine," said Amelia. "Which I could have told them at the beginning."

"Then it's mission accomplished. We know for sure there's nothing else going on," said Eva.

"Of course there isn't," said Parker.

Eva's eyes turned a fraction harder, but she offered Ferguson a smile.

"Thanks Adam. We'll make sure that USB ends up in the right hands, won't we?"

"Where is it, by the way, the USB? He's not keeping it, is he?" said Parker, nodding to Ferguson.

"Not on your life," said Ferguson. "I don't want anything like that hanging around, believe me."

Parker looked at Eva.

"I already gave it back," said Eva, quietly. Amelia nodded her head and tapped the stone around her neck.

"Splendid," said Parker. "So we're all done here, I take it? Good stuff. So, Eva, why don't we go back to your office and discuss this plan of yours?"

"I'm glad you're sounding so positive," said Eva.

"Yes, yes. Silver linings, as I say."

Eva stood up and adjusted her jacket in preparation to face the world outside. She hoped she had done enough to prevent further trouble. But even after Adam Ferguson's checks had been carried out, the lack of trust between them still lingered like a cloud. And Parker's strange behaviour wasn't making it any better. His nervy smile was starting to set her on edge. And from the look of it, Dan too. Dan led the way down the stairs, out into the street.

"I swear Adam's getting worse," said Dan. "You'd better take that guy for his cheeseburger before he starts devolving into some new noodle species."

"Where did you find him?" said Amelia, making a face.

"Hey" said Eva. "Adam's a friend. "And he was bang on about your file. He saw Cadson's people stole it two months ago. That's a long time to sit on a file like that."

Amelia reached for the stone around her neck and Eva's eyes followed the girl's hand as she toyed with it.

"Cadson and his friends intended to wait, remember?" she said. "They thought it was safer that way."

"Well," said Parker, "the long game certainly isn't for me. I'm far too long in the tooth for all that mucking around." There was an edge in his voice. It jarred Eva. She watched Parker gulp as his eyes stole furtive glances around the street. Dan must have felt it too. Eva watched him take a good long look at their surroundings, checking every face in the vicinity. When he was satisfied, he gave a nod.

"Okay. Let's go," said Dan. "Come on, Jonathan. What's the matter? You placed a bet and your horse came in? It's plain to see you've got ants in your pants."

"Horses? No. Not my cup of tea. Though I always did have a soft spot for the dogs."

"And you know what they say about old dogs, don't you Jonathan?"

"Dan? I don't know what you mean," said Parker.

Dan didn't bother to reply. Instead, he kept his eyes on the streets. They walked into the vast car park at the centre of town, which was busy with locals either heading to the ticket machines or back to their cars, and aimed for the middle section where they'd left the car. Eva and Amelia, Parker and Dan walked along two by two.

They reached the end of the car park's first square and turned right to follow a row of cars into the second vast square. For no discernible reason, Jonathan Parker's pace began to slow down. Amelia looked at him.

"You okay?" she said.

"Oh, Me? Fine. What about you, my dear?"

Amelia watched him, nodding slowly, as if she too was wondering what Parker wasn't telling her.

As Dan walked ahead, he looked out onto the side street of Victorian terraced houses which lined the car park on one side. Cars pulled out onto the one-way street which sucked them out into the hurly-burly of the rush towards the London bound A roads. Pedestrians hurried in to beat the expiry time on their parking tickets. There was nothing in particular to be worried about, but Dan paused, and Eva stopped. She watched him looked right and left down the main aisles of parked cars, checking every face he saw.

"What's the matter?" said Eva.

Dan's eyes flicked towards Parker's face. "Him," said Dan. He watched the old man's Adam's apple rise and fall on his scrawny chicken neck.

Before anyone could say another word, a voice sounded behind them. A gruff, arrogant voice.

"Turn around, but don't be hasty. Not too fast."

Dan blinked and recalled the darkness from a distant morning. He blocked the jarring image of the gunfire flash and stamped out the memory of the pain. As Dan turned to face the aggressor, his eyes passed over Jonathan. But the old man wouldn't meet his eyes. All four of them turned to find Cadson standing by one of the orange ticket machines which divided one car park square from the other. He was smiling and sharp-looking as ever, but for the stubble which covered most of his head. He looked a different man. The earlier tension seemed to be gone from his face. He looked cocksure and smarmy. Instead, it was Dan's turn to seethe. The anger swirled inside him, stirred the ache in his gut and bunched the muscles in his jaw. Cadson was holding a gun. A small gun, shiny as chrome. It was a prissy little weapon, not a man's gun. But he knew why Cadson had picked it. It would have been very easy to hide.

"How?" said Amelia. She stepped back, cowering towards the back of the group. Her eyes were bright and wide with fear. "How did you know where we were? Who told you?" Dan's narrow eyes flicked to Jonathan. They burned him so hard the old man's cheeks flushed.

"You mean you can't guess?" said Cadson. "Say thanks to grandpa over there. The old man sold you out to clear his debt. But you really shouldn't worry about it. This old man is the kind who'd put your kidneys on an eBay auction without you even knowing. But I don't mind any more. He's in the clear with me, at least."

"Parker, what the hell did you do now?" said Dan.

"What I had to do. That's all."

"How could you? You said you cared for me?!" said Amelia. "How could you do this? You know what he did to me."

"Amelia, my dear," said the old man, shaking his head. He stepped towards the girl as if he thought he might be able to appeal to her, but the scowl on her face stopped his approach dead. "But I did this to save the both of us, my dear. We don't need that damn stone… it's an encumbrance…" said Parker.

"Yeah. You're right on that score," said Cadson. He snapped his fingers. "It's a millstone around your neck. So take it off, Ammie. Take it off, then walk it over here and put it in my hand."

The girl's eyes were full of fire and bitter emotion. She stared at Parker as if her looks would be enough to finish him off. Cadson soon grew impatient. He snapped his fingers again.

"Do it now," snarled Cadson, as he looked left and right, checking for witnesses. There was no one nearby just yet. Cadson licked his lips. Dan stared at the man. He looked at the way he held the gun. There was a gentle quiver in his outstretched arm. Maybe the man had used a gun before, maybe he hadn't. But either way, he didn't look confident with it. In fact, Dan reckoned there was a fifty-fifty chance he wouldn't shoot. His body language didn't look convincing. Shooting in a busy public car park was a bad move. But even so, fifty-fifty wasn't great odds…

"Give it to him," said Eva.

"I can't. This is my last chance," said Amelia, touching the stone.

"Hey. You're right again," said Cadson. He jabbed the pistol at Amelia, but Dan took a lurching half-step forward and Cadson turned the gun on him.

"Don't give me an excuse, tough guy. I really don't like you at all."

"You're not in my top ten either," said Dan.

"Amelia, please…" said Parker. "Just do as he says – I'm telling you, there's another way."

Amelia blinked before she peeled the necklace away from her throat. She held it in her hands and stared at it, shaking her head. She stepped forward slowly, passing Dan's shoulder. Dan was focused on Cadson. Eva watched her the whole way, and the girl met her eyes.

"It's okay, Amelia. Let him have it. I don't think you have a choice," said Eva.

Amelia took one more step and dangled the necklace out in front of her. Cadson reached for it, his fingers raking past the fine necklace chain. His big hand reached past the necklace and he seized the girl's wrist. His fingers closed tight around her arm, and in one vicious move he dragged Amelia towards him. Cadson wrapped his arm around her throat and jammed the gun against her hip and looked around. He ripped the necklace from her hand.

The girl's eyes flashed with anger and reproach. She stared from Cadson to Parker.

"Say goodbye, Ammie. She's coming with me. Thanks for everything, old man. But stay away from my casinos. You're barred. And if you come near me ever again, I promise that I'll put you out of your misery. Understand?"

Dan snarled, his body was coiled, ready to go. But as Cadson started to withdraw, he kept the gun trained on them the whole time. Amelia struggled, but Cadson jabbed the gun hard against her hip and her resistance stopped. Her eyes took on a trance of fear.

"You've used up all your credit with me, Ammie. Don't push your luck…"

Dan followed them as they backed around the corner. Cadson eyed him as they backed away, then he reached back and opened the door of a sporty red Audi and shoved the girl down and out of sight into the back seat. As soon as Amelia was secure, Cadson moved fast. He walked around the car, with the gun over the roof, keeping Dan in his sights, before he ducked into the car, slammed the door, and started the engine. Dan started to run, but the Audi's tyres screeched as the car reversed, then the engine roared, and the car thundered away, sending a few pedestrians diving out of its way.

Dan shook his head and gritted his teeth. He watched as the Audi reached the dual carriageway and stormed into the local underpass at full speed, its engine noise echoing loudly as it disappeared. Shoulders locked and neck bunched, Dan spun around. His eyes locked onto Jonathan Parker. Eva saw the wild darkness in Dan's eyes and turned cold. As Dan surged towards Parker, Eva cut between them and laid a firm but gentle hand on Dan's chest. The old man shrank back and cowered.

"You tell us you love that girl? That is what you say, *right?* Then how come you just sold her out to the man who has been trying to get at her with a knife ever since we met her – today he brings out a gun! Parker! If we believe what she said, then guy kept her as a prisoner! And you gave him to her just like that! You hired us to help you protect her! Now you give her back to the very same man who wants to hurt her like that! What are you doing here? How many lies do you want to tell? Eh?!"

"That wasn't supposed to happen," said Parker, quietly. "You've got to believe me."

"Believe you? As if I could ever believe a word you say ever again!"

"It's true. I didn't want him to take her, not for a second. I didn't want her hurt."

"No? That's funny, because you called him here, didn't you? You told him where we were and put us all at risk."

"But this is your fault!" said Parker.

"My fault?!" shouted Dan. "Right. I suppose should have guessed it was my fault."

"It *is* your fault. You blocked our only possible chance of getting away from that scumbag. We had a way out - a way out together - but you took it from us. And you did too," said Parker, looking at Eva.

"You mean the Basilica data?" said Eva. "Your way out was criminal, Jonathan. But if you couldn't con your way out one way, you were prepared to con your way out another, so long as it got you off the hook. Damn the consequence for everyone else! You know, you might just have signed your girlfriend's death warrant."

Parker's eyes filled with a blur of tears. "No. That wasn't it at all. He double-crossed me. Surely you can see that?"

"Who knows what that guy is capable of. Who knows what he might do?" said Dan, "or you for that matter!"

"He was supposed to take the stone, that's all. He was supposed to take the necklace, take that USB drive and leave Amelia here with us! There was another way. She didn't see it. But I did…"

"Just goes to show you, Parker," said Dan. "These days you can't trust anyone. *Can you?*"

Dan turned and walked away, his hands balled into fists held stiffly at his side.

"But Dan… I didn't mean for this to happen. Honestly. I didn't mean for any of it…"

Dan turned and jabbed a finger at Parker. "I'm finished with listening to you. This case is closed. Permanently. If it costs me that terrible suit to get rid of you then so be it. Five hundred pounds is a bargain to be free of your rubbish for good. See you round, Jonathan. Enjoy the rest of your bitter, lonely life."

"Dan…" said Eva, with a hint of appeal. He heard her voice behind him, but kept walking on before he gave in and turned around. Dan looked at Eva and saw the appeal in her eyes. He frowned and shook his head, but the look remained. *Damn it.* Why did she always have to play the role of his conscience? While the old man hung his head in shame, Eva lingered by Parker's shoulder,

"Don't let him do a job on you, Eva. Don't you dare pity him. Not this time. After what he just did, he brought all of this on himself."

"Yes, I totally agree," said Eva. "But please come back here. Just for one minute. One minute, I promise."

Dan put his hands on his hips and ground his teeth. He walked back slowly, taking in long breaths just to stave off another wave of vitriol. He wanted to reach out and screw Parker up like a piece of junk mail. All the while, Eva's eyes implored him to be calm.

"You sold her out, Parker," said Dan, the fire waning in his words. "You sold us all out. You've got no loyalty to anyone, have you? Do you think your brother Devon could be proud of you after what you've done? I don't know how you can live with yourself."

"You're wrong, Dan. I care about that girl."

"Keep telling yourself. At least you got yourself out of hock. You can start again with the time you have left. But can she?"

"I'm sorry to break it to you, Jonathan, but you're not as free as you think," said Eva. Her eyes flicked to Dan. "And that debt certainly isn't cancelled."

"What?" said Dan. "What do you mean?"

"Why not?" said Parker. "He's just taken everything I ever had. He's got the data. We had a deal."

Eva shook her head. "No, Jonathan. That's what you thought, and that's what Cadson thinks. But the truth is he hasn't got what he came here for. In the end Cadson walked away with Amelia – but nothing else."

"What are you talking about?" said Parker. "I saw it with my own eyes."

"Amelia knew we wouldn't let her use the data on that memory stick," said Eva. "But the trouble was Amelia thought it was her only way out of this mess. I knew there was a chance she would run as soon as she got the data back from us, so I decided to keep hold of the data myself."

"What?" said Parker. Dan's eyes flickered from confusion to a dawning look of surprise.

"Ferguson gave it back to me. And I went to put the USB back in the stone, but I might just have missed the slot…"

"I swore I saw you put it back," said Dan, with a hint of a smile.

"It's called sleight of hand," said Eva, pulling the small white USB drive from her jacket pocket. "Which is something I think Jonathan knows all about."

Parker stared at the USB and trailed a hand down his face. "But Amelia will be in worse danger than ever. Cadson will be outraged. He'll kill us all!"

Dan shook his head. His eyes had a dark gleam in them as he looked at Parker. "No he won't. At worst, he'll come for us. And maybe he'll try and kill *you*. Heck, if I was him, I'd want to kill you. But Cadson needs that data more than anything else in the world. And look – we have it right here. Nice work, Eva… and as for you, Parker, you say you made a bad mistake. So prove it. Come on. If it's true, here's your chance. If there's a decent bone left in that selfish old body of yours, now's the time to let it show. This is where it counts. This isn't the audition, JP. This is it. The culmination of your life. That girl who you say you love. You owe it to her, too, don't you? So come on. How do you want this to go down?"

Parker wilted under the spark of challenge in Dan's dark eyes. The old man was speechless, his lips trembled as he floundered for a response. Parker without the power of speech? It was a rare thing indeed. Dan hoped it was a good thing.

"I'll take that as a yes," said Dan, "because this could be the last chance you've got."

Fifteen

"Before we do anything else, we'll have to go shopping,"
said Eva.

"Shopping?" said Parker "What? At a time like this?"

"Yes. And this time you're paying."

"What?!" said Parker.

"I take it you do have access to some money?" said Eva.

"A little, but not much. Can't you put it on my tab until after
we've done whatever the hell you propose to do?"

"No," said Eva. "You don't have a tab. The bank of Eva and
Dan is officially closed for business. This time you'll do the
shelling out."

"Oh, whatever," said Parker. "But this shopping had better
cost less than twenty quid, or I won't be able to do it."

"Twenty pounds? For what we need, I think that'll do
nicely," Eva smiled. But Jonathan Parker could manage no
more than a frown.

Parker begrudged spending the money. Of course, he did. But Eva refused to listen to his gripes and took the lilac note from his hand anyway. Even after she took it, Parker had insisted on going with her to the shop, to supervise whatever it was she intended to spend his money on, but Eva had refused point blank. Instead, while she went to Wilko's, Eva sent the old man out to smoke a cigarette at the top of the high street. When she had exactly what she needed, Eva handed Parker's last twenty-pound note to the cashier without a hint of remorse. In fact, she relished the experience. It felt good to finally get some money out of the old man, no matter how small the sum. After she was done, Eva found Parker pacing around the street like a grumpy old dog. She made a show of giving him all his change, all seven pounds and two shiny new pence. The old man glared at her as if she'd robbed his last meal. Eva carried on smiling. She knew better than that. Jonathan Parker was a true survivalist, a no-good wastrel with a chiseller's brain, the Bear Grylls of the urban gutter stuffed into a rich man's suit. Jonathan would never ever let himself starve. Come the apocalypse, it was going to be the cockroaches who needed to watch their backs.

"Well then, what did you buy?" He eyed Eva's small red Wilko's bag as if he believed he had X-ray vision.

"Never you mind. All you need to know is that if I'd bought it elsewhere, there wouldn't have been any change."

"Should I be grateful?" said Parker, stuffing what remained of his money back into his pockets.

"Yes, you should. You never do like parting with money. Not unless it's other peoples."

Parker shook his head. "I suppose you've got a point…" he said. "This plan you've got brewing. I suspect I know what it is, and I have to tell you, I don't like it. I don't like it at all."

"You don't know, Jonathan. You're just guessing. And you do know why I can't tell you anything about it, don't you?" said Eva.

Parker's eyes narrowed. He nodded and looked away.

"That's right," said Eva. "You'd leak it to Cadson as soon as I'd explained it to you."

"That's not true," said Parker. "And I didn't know Cadson was going to kidnap Amelia, I swear it. Look. When you and Dan forbade us to use that data, you made that USB stick worthless to us. But I knew it still had some value – to Cadson. When I contacted him it was with a view to getting something from a dead loss – to get our freedom back at least. Like I told Amelia, she's the one with the real value in this, not that data stick. All I wanted was Cadson to cancel my debt and let us go on our way. I figured it was the least he could do."

"And it was the least he did," said Eva. "The mistake you made was trusting Cadson above us."

"Don't rub it in, Eva. I've had enough of Dan giving me the treatment without you adding to it."

They walked away from Southend shopping centre precinct, heading past the big red brick cinema towards the supermarket where Eva had parked her Alfa Romeo. She felt the old man fretting at her side and sensed his burden. Maybe there was a hint of remorse there after all. But Eva had been suckered too many times to let Parker off the hook. She wasn't going to make that mistake again until the case was closed and the case fee was in the bank.

"And I don't see how I'm supposed to pay Phee-Lau's brothers now, either. Dan made me promise them. I've got a day left before that falls due then they'll want my head on a plate."

Phee-Lau– the Thai bride that never was. Eva shook her head as she remembered the trail of woe Parker had left in his wake.

"There's still time to turn things around, Jonathan."

"Turn things around? With your secret little plan? When he works out what you've done, Cadson will just as likely kill me on the spot. I knew Cadson was a gambling villain, I'd heard he'd hurt a few people, but I've never seen him with a shooter before."

"The least we need you to do is keep calm while we put this into action," said Eva. "Stay calm… can you do that?"

They walked through the automatic doors of the supermarket, passing the sandwich fridge and the tobacco kiosk, before they hooked a right to catch the escalator up to the rooftop car park.

"Calm? I don't think I've been calm since I arrived in your backyard. The best I felt was the night I'd had that win at Cadson's Barking Casino. There's nothing like it, Eva. Winning like that. It's the best feeling in the world. Better than any drug. Better than sex even…"

Eva winced and kept her eyes averted.

Parker noticed but shrugged and kept silent.

"If I'd only walked out of there and never gone back, none of this would have happened. I could have paid off Phee-Lau's family. I could have taken off and gone to another continent and never come back here begging for your help… and I never would have gotten so much cold shoulder from the both of you."

Gratitude wasn't a Parker speciality.

"But you didn't, Jonathan. Because that gambling high was an illusion, designed to lure you right back in until you lost every penny you had. Which is exactly what you did. The gambler's high is a false one. You know it is. It's pride before a fall."

Parker considered her words as Eva pressed the button on her key fob and opened the car doors of her gleaming red Alfa Giulietta.

"I suppose it is. But one good thing came out of it, at least." Eva started the engine and looked at the old man. He smiled at her.

"I met Amelia. And she's better than any gambling high." Eva glanced at Parker, intrigued. "I thought you said the gambling high was better than sex."

"This isn't just about sex, Eva. I love that girl."

"She's a third of your age, Jonathan."

"Must you bang on about that?" said Parker. "I didn't say it was conventional. Or easy. I know how I look to all of you, but I don't feel that old inside. She makes me feel young again."

"Excuse me for asking this question…" said Eva as she turned the car out of the bays of tightly packed hatchbacks.

"Go on," said Parker.

"Do you seriously think she likes you back? More than as an accomplice, I mean?"

"I know what it looks like, but she's young, Eva. She's playing the hard face like they all do. She cares for me. I mean it."

Eva shrugged and nodded.

"Okay. Then supposing she would ever want you back after what you just did… supposing she's telling the truth any more than you did, and that she genuinely does like you."

"I'm telling you, she does, you know."

"Fine. Supposing she doesn't dump you off as soon as she finds another meal ticket, or a twenty something with a six-pack and a fast car…"

Parker sighed. "Yes, yes, I get the picture."

"What then, Jonathan? What's your future together? What does that look like?"

"Eva. I don't like to think of the future. So please don't rob an old man of his present."

"Robbing?" said Eva, shaking her head with a smile. "I don't think I'm the one doing any robbing around here."

Parker looked down at the small plastic bag with Eva's purchase inside it.

"Oh, I don't know about that. Twelve pounds and ninety-eight pence feels like robbery to me."

"If this works, Jonathan, that little purchase is going to be the best money you ever spent."

"And if it doesn't?"

"Like you said. Let's stick with the present, shall we?" said Eva.

Parker narrowed his eyes and looked out on the streets of central Southend as the busy pavements whizzed past his window.

Sixteen

Dan walked into the office with a bundle of hot, delicious-smelling savoury food. Grease from the paninis had passed through the white paper bag and onto Dan's fingers. He tossed the paninis down onto Mark's front desk, once again shocked at the kid's absence. He felt a pang of regret at what had happened between them. And then he felt angry that he had been too busy to do anything about it. Mark deserved better than that. Much better. But Dan's mind had been wired with the problems of finding a man who didn't want to be found. And the threat which had hung over him and Eva all the more darkly ever since what had happened to Mark. And the way they described him – both Mark and Joanne, they made the man sound like an absolute beast. A monster, like Greg had described him and Proberty before him. That was all he had. For Dan he was a silhouette, a shadow, a set of demonic eyes above a dark car window. But not a man. Dan badly needed to find the figure behind the shadows, because the image was becoming more than he could deal with. He was becoming a legend. A terrible myth. Dan passed a finger over his rough unshaven chin as it occurred to him that the man was hiding deliberately. Was it possible he was using fear to create a legend, as if it was a strategy? The man was creating his own mythology, wasn't he? Turning himself into something more than he was, through use of intimidation and fear, hitting his victims when they weren't ready. That was his MO. *He was really just a bully.* Even so, the man had caused horrific damage, killed a man, and he had targeted the young employee they had sworn to protect. There was no way he could put it off any longer. He needed to call the kid and apologise.

Leaving his tuna melt aside, Dan sat at his own desk and took out his mobile. He scrolled past Malachy's name and winced as he remembered the encouragement and challenge Malachy had given him. He was the only one who could do something. *There was no one else.* And yet, all he had done was retreat into his work and let the bastard strike again. Was it out of fear? Or duty to the job? Dan was no longer sure. But the thought of fear seeping into his thinking made him feel soiled and weak. The bullet wound in his gut had already made him grow frail. It showed in how Geller had treated him. How Greg Saunders had looked at him like a lesser man. Yes, he had atrophied since the gunshot – atrophy was inevitable to a degree. He had been in hospital for weeks and then he'd needed to heal. But seeing his weakness reflected in the eyes of others was almost unbearable. From what Greg had said, Dan had also begun to wonder whether weakening him was part of the strategy. A grand plan to crush him like Proberty, step by step, a death by many cuts. Dan had to shake off all such thoughts as his call was answered.

"Mark? Kid? How are you?"

"Sorry to disappoint you. But this isn't Mark. This is his mother."

"Oh. Hi… how is he?"

"Come on. How do you think he is? Hurt. Upset. Suffering."

"Yeah, I'm… look… I'm really sorry about what happened."

"You're sorry?!" said his mother.

"Yeah, listen…"

"No. You listen," said the woman. "If you're going to let your office become such a bloody safety hazard that my son can have an accident like that in your kitchen, then your offices should be shut down. I've already told him, he should call ACAS and get the Health and Safety people onto you. And have you even called to see if he's okay? Nope. Not a word. Not a dicky bird. No wonder Mark doesn't want to go back. Not if this is how you treat your people. I've a good mind to hire a solicitor and take you to a tribunal."

Dan listened to the stream of angry words and tried to keep up. Little by little a faint smile crept onto Dan's face. He worked hard to prevent it leaking into his voice.

"Yes, Mark had an accident…" he ventured. "In the kitchen…"

"I know that already – no thanks to you. He told me about that rickety old coffee machine of yours bursting all over his hand, and told me how he slipped on that dodgy broken lino in your office kitchen."

"The, broken lino?" said Dan. There was old lino, tasteless black and white checked lino in that kitchen, but it wasn't damaged or torn.

"Yes. The broken lino. My son's hand looks like it's been melted. And the cut on his head from when he fell and struck it on the kitchen counter still hasn't healed."

"Yeah. He got a nasty cut out of that from what I heard… I'll have to have that lino fixed."

"Fixed? Your whole bloody kitchen needs to be condemned. Now, don't bother to call Mark again. He doesn't want to know. We'll consider our next steps, but I'm going to see someone about this. I promise you that."

"Okay. If you feel that's necessary."

"Necessary!" said the woman. "It's essential."

"Right. Well, good luck with all that. And please send Mark our best wishes. Tell him we miss him and wish him better. Okay?"

"I'll tell him you bothered to call, yes…"

"Thanks then."

Dan ended the call with a hasty thumbing of the red button and smiled at the kid's inventiveness. He sighed and leaned back in his chair, his stomach hurting as he stretched. His gut gurgled for food, and yet it was frequently a struggle to eat since his injury. Digestion didn't feel so good, and his appetite wasn't what it was. Remembering Geller's eyes and Saunders' comments about his withered body, he forced himself to stand up and grab his panini. He left Eva's inside the bag and stalked back across the office floor, thinking about his frailty, and about what he had to do. Cadson was a distraction, albeit a dangerous one who had to be dealt with. There was the girl to think of too. Amelia was a bad egg for sure, but she was young and didn't deserve whatever Cadson had in mind for her. Dan took a first oversized bite of the tuna melt, which should have been delicious. Instead he chomped on it like it was a mouthful of wet cardboard. More with determination than enthusiasm.

Behind him, the door creaked open and the bell chimed. Dan spun round to see Joanne breezing into the office.

"Oh. It's you," he said with his mouth full.

"Charming," said Joanne.

"Sorry," said Dan, swallowing too soon. "I've got a few things on my mind."

"Like the crazy old man and that cold little diva."

Dan nodded. "That's part of it."

"Or the brute who hurt Mark."

"He's another problem…" said Dan.

"He's a problem alright. And he's not going to go away by himself, is he?"

Joanne folded her arms and stood in the doorway. Dan chewed and watched her struggling on how to ask her next question, but he could feel what was coming.

"So, have you dealt with the old man and the diva, yet?" she said, walking into the office with a familiar, proprietary air. Ever since he'd known her, the girl had always been a little pushy, and a mite over-confident. But she did it with such style and aplomb. In truth, Dan admired the girl's spirit.

"The situation has just gotten a little more complicated."

"I don't like the sound of that," said Joanne. "Because I was hoping you'd be able to concentrate on tracking down the man who hurt Mark."

"I'm going to take care of that, don't you worry."

"But you said that already, so when are you going to do it? That menace is still out there, and he scared the living crap out of me, Dan… and he doesn't like you at all. You need to deal with this now or it's only going to get worse."

"Now you're sounding like Eva."

The girl made a half smile. "Do I?"

"Yes."

The girl nodded like she had taken it as a compliment. But she didn't bask in it. She met Dan's eye again, firmly.

"Please, you can't let this drift. Mark's still in pain, and he's frightened. He won't admit it, but I know he is."

"I tried to call Mark just now but his mother answered the call. Mark lied to her about what happened, didn't he?"

"Yes, he did," said Joanne. "To protect you and Eva. I know what that woman is like. If his mother ever found out what really happened in here, she would have screamed blue murder to everyone. You would have had police, press, and God knows who else in here – at the worst possible time. Make no mistake, Mark's done you a very big favour."

"I get that. He's saved us a bunch of trouble. Does that mean he might yet come back to us?"

Joanne looked away and shrugged. "I don't know. But I doubt it. If he never came back I'd support him in that. You're good people, but this work is dangerous."

"But you're here," said Dan, probing.

"You're good people. And this thing needs to be dealt with. I'm here to keep reminding you not to let this go unanswered."

"You didn't need to remind me, Joanne. It's a priority for me, I assure you."

The girl seemed to take heart from this.

"In that case, I'm here to help," said Joanne. "I know you're trying, Dan. I know you're hurting. I can see it. But this isn't just about you now."

"This was never ever just about me, Joanne. This bastard is hurting people I know. People from my past."

"And now he's hurting the people in your present."

"I know… but there's so much other crap going on right now."

"Then get it out of the way. Because I think I've got something you need to see."

Joanne opened her little handbag and pulled out a note. Dan saw it had been written on the cheap lined paper ripped from the pad on Mark's desk.

"There was a call while you were out. I wanted to let you know as soon as I could."

"A call? From who?"

"Two calls, in fact – but this is the one that matters." Joanne unfolded the note and slid it across the desk to Dan. He opened it up and read the big letters written in Joanne's neat bubble writing.

There was a time, a date, and the names of the callers. PC Dawson and PCSO Rawlins.

"I like these two," said Joanne. "Especially him. He's a good guy," she added.

Dan looked up at the girl's comment and saw Joanne's face had taken on a hint of blush, as if she had said too much. Dan looked back to the main message.

News on the BMW. Registered owner is one James Allen Cato of Hawthorn Lane, Loughton. Did a check on it. Found abandoned on the North Circular last night. Burnt out. Question - Any idea why? James Cato not found at address.

Dawson and Rawlins had brought home the goods again. Dan sent a mental thank you their way, as if they could hear his thoughts. "James Allen Cato?" said Dan

"Yes. I checked the spelling before I wrote it down. Does the name mean anything to you?" said Joanne, hopefully.

Dan narrowed his eyes and racked his brains. He wanted the name to mean something, and somewhere deep down, he felt it register, but it was a distant, foggy feeling which he couldn't bring to the surface.

"Did you Google the name?" said Dan.

Joanne shook her head. "I didn't think to. Should I have?"

"No. Nothing will probably come of a search like that. Not unless he wants to be found… Cato," said Dan. "I know that name… but I don't know how."

"You think he's the man who hurt Mark?"

"The car belongs to him… so it's the first genuine lead I've had. He's been so elusive. He paid a visit to all the others, face to face, but with me it's cat and mouse all the damn time."

"Dan – maybe he's scared of you. Have you thought about that?"

Dan frowned, confused.

"He's going in hard to throw you off your game. But it doesn't mean he's not scared."

"He went in so hard he almost killed me."

"And hard again on Mark – because you're still hunting him. He said the attack on Mark was a warning that you needed to back off. This guy is evil, Dan. He'll come back harder next time."

"I know. But I don't even know what he wants, and that's the thing bugging me more than anything else. Why is this scumbag going to all this effort? What for? Who is he trying to impress?"

"Does it matter? I thought the most important thing would be stopping him."

Dan nodded. "It does matters Knowing why will help me figure out how to stop him."

"Then find him. Get the truth from the horse's mouth. Then do everyone a favour and put this guy out of commission…"

Dan blinked at the girl, wondering what she meant. But he decided it better not to ask. She was emotional, that's all. She was young. "Please," she added.

Dan nodded and slid the note into his jeans pocket.

"You said there were two calls. So what was the other one?" he said, taking another bite from his panini.

"Oh, that was a call from Alice Perry, a reporter from The Record. She said you needed to phone her back. She used the word pronto – can you believe that?"

"Yeah, I can believe that," said Dan, forcing a smile as his stomach tingled. "These newshounds, eh?"

The door chimed again as Eva and Parker walked into the office. "Did you get it?" said Dan.

"Yes," said Eva, raising the little plastic Wilko bag. "It's in here."

"And Parker paid?"

"Yes. And he resented every penny of it," said Eva.

"Jonathan, you're predictable to the end," said Dan.

Eva gave Joanne a nod of greeting.

"Then let's get this over with," said Dan. He pushed his seat back and stood up. "There are other matters which need my attention."

"Matters more important than saving Amelia?" said Parker, insulted.

"Hey. The only reason she needs saving in the first place is because you sold her out. You should be grateful, JP. Here comes your chance to make amends."

"My chance? You're the one cooking up some ridiculous bloody plan…"

"Plan? What plan?" said Joanne.

"The plan to haul Parker's bony backside out of the crap once again," said Dan. "You do know Cadson's number, don't you, Jonathan?"

"Um…"

"Of course, you do. You called him to arrange the last set-up. So call him. Tell him that his little stone's empty and we've got his magic data stick, just in case he hasn't managed to work it out yet."

"Oh, he'll have worked it out alright. He's probably looking for me now."

"Then call him and fix a meeting. It's time we got your sweetheart back – it's time Cadson got what he really wanted."

Eva smiled, and Joanne shook her head. Parker looked sheepish as he delved a shaking hand into his pocket to retrieve his phone. Dan smiled too. But his was only skin deep. He felt the thrill of the chase, felt Eva's enthusiasm for turning the case against Cadson just when he thought he had won. But Dan couldn't help the thoughts churning deeper inside. He felt impatient to move on and face what he had to face. *James Alan Cato, if that's who he was.* The man who was trying to turn himself into a legend. And the more he thought about it, the more Dan realised the man was thinking like a boxer. The bastard had created his own pre-match hype. He had amplified his strengths by exploiting the weaknesses of others. He'd used gimmicks such as hiding and ambushing others to make himself seem monstrous. Hiding in the dark. The implied threat to Eva in the drive-by outside Proberty's small, dilapidated home. The puppet-master managing of Proberty's fears, and now doing the same to Greg Saunders. Dan would have to work hard to stop the puppeteering having an impact on him – but he feared it had already begun. Dan grimaced and drew a mental line in the sand. Of course, this monster wasn't just hype. Hype was fake, but this was real. One man was dead, and countless others had been hurt. Cato… or whatever his name was had taken this far enough.

Dan was determined to find the man.

And when he found him, he was going to crack him open so he could understand the man's motive. And then he was going to crack him some more – this time until he was good and satisfied. Until the deep poisonous anger inside him was thoroughly purged – and the fear was gone.

"Dan?" said Eva. Her voice snapped him back to the present. He looked up to see her watching him as Parker's call was connected. Nearby, Joanne was watching him too. Dan nodded, conveying a silent message. He was going to deal with it. It was going to be okay. Yeah... *Keep telling yourself Danny boy...* Dan turned his attention to Parker on the phone.

"Is that Cadson?" said Parker. "Good... well, about that stone of yours, you know the one... Yes, I know, but hang on a minute. I said hang on... it appears there's been something of a misunderstanding. Oh. Then you've noticed, have you?"

Parker pulled the phone away from his ear as a torrent of shouted abuse poured down the phone line. The raw noise was audible to everyone in the office.

"JP?" said Dan. "Do you want this girl back or what?" said Dan.

The old man nodded. "Of course," he said.

"Then now is the time to be strong," said Dan.

Parker nodded. Putting on a fortified, manly face, Parker put the phone back to his ear.

"Now listen here, Cadson," he said, resolutely. "You weren't supposed to take Amelia. That wasn't the deal. No. No. No, you listen to me. If you want that damn USB thingamajig then you can jolly well meet us, and we'll give it to you. Yes, we'll give it to you. So long as you give Amelia to us. Yes, you give her back to us. And let me be clear, Cadson. There's no way on God's green earth you'll get that stick any other way. Are we clear?"

Parker pulled the phone away as another wave of shouting poured down the line.

"He wants to know where we should meet?"

Dan and Eva looked at one another. Then Dan remembered a place. An isolated place with open space, remote but accessible. A place where it was almost safe for such a confrontation. A place not far from where he'd been shot himself.

"Tell him 9pm tonight. Shoeburyness. By the end of the beach huts – on the beach. If he wants that USB stick back, he'll be there."

Parker visibly gulped before he put the phone back to his big, drooping ear. He repeated Dan's instructions verbatim, before his call was finally cut dead.

"He's going to kill us all," said Parker. "You know that, don't you?" said Parker.

"No. He's only going to try to kill you," said Dan.

"But he can't hurt us. Not if he wants to get his hands on this…" Eva pulled the small white micro USB from her pocket. "Cadson needs this more anything else in the world,"

***

A nine o'clock meeting gave Dan a few hours to kill, which was good. Aside from everything else Alice Perry had been gnawing at him like a maggot chewing its way into an apple. She needed dealing with. And if not dealing with, then at least putting back in her box. He made an excuse of needing a break from the office. Joanne had gone to see Mark. Parker was edgy, and in his current anxious state, Dan knew Eva wouldn't mind if he left her alone for a while. She was still cutting him slack, because she knew what was consuming him. It didn't make Dan feel any better for knowing that he was meeting Perry in secret – although only to make the problem go away.

He parked the Egomobile on the seafront and walked along between the big new hotels, the tall blue aquarium and the crazy golf by the beach before turning into the tea rooms. The place was all bunting, polka dots and shabby-chic furniture. Not exactly his kind of place. It wasn't Eva's style either, but the location was perfect. Easy to get to. Off the radar, and not frequented by anyone he knew. At least not usually.

Dan strode in off the street and was satisfied to find the tea rooms mostly empty. By late afternoon the mumsy crowd and the students had taken their fill of tea and cake. The only people left were a couple of slow-eating OAPs and some young mothers with cranky kids, doing their best to keep it together while shoving cake in their children's faces. It was ideal noise cover for a difficult conversation. Seated three tables back, with a smug smile was Alice Perry. She had a fine china cup of tea before her, set just beneath her cleavage like it had been staged that way. The girl smiled at him, lifted her cup and sipped. Was the gesture supposed to look sexy? Dan couldn't figure her out. He walked in and took the seat opposite her, nodding at the guy behind the counter as he settled in.

"When I said take me for a drink," said Perry, "this wasn't exactly what I had in mind. But it'll do – for now."

"This is a meeting, Alice, not a date."

"Good. Then you still owe me a proper drink."

"What is this about? Seriously?" said Dan. "You're not telling me that you're all out of negative, sensational stories at that rag of yours?"

"Not exactly, no," said the girl. "Come on, settle down. Order yourself a drink. You're going to be here a little while."

"Oh. Am I?"

The girl nodded. "Yes, you are. There's no point meeting at all unless we're really going to talk about things. About you. About your cases. Your past…"

The way she said it, the word 'past' seemed loaded. And it was. Dan was able to think of a score of unpleasant things he'd done or been involved with across the years without bothering to consult his memory. The flashes of the past rose up in him like the seething of a witch's cauldron. Thankfully he was skilled at suppressing them. It was time for a poker face. The only face to present to a girl like Perry. "What are you thinking of specifically, Alice? You're still after the Ricardo Burton case?"

"Oh no," said Perry. "You don't get off that easily. That ship has long since sailed. I've heard talk about a third inquiry – and after Jason Reith was arrested for the Croyde Crew murders, a few of the nationals are saying Reith could be in the frame for the Burton murder too. Who would have thought ladies' man Jay Ray would have been a race hate killer…?"

"These days people rarely surprise me," said Dan.

"I think I could," said Perry. She didn't add further comment, but her eyes stayed fixed on Dan's.

Dan shrugged and batted it away.

"I wasn't interested in those people. We were there working the Croyde case and we uncovered more than we bargained for, end of story. If Jay Ray killed Ricardo Burton, then I'll be glad if he finally gets time for it. The Burton family deserve some justice."

"Justice brought by you, Dan," said the girl with a hint of admiration. "Well done, but the story is already out there. It's got no juice left for me." She turned her head and raised her hand, appealing for service from the counter. One of the waiting staff came to the table. The waiter smiled.

"More tea, please. And make it a large cup for him."

The young man nodded deferentially before he walked away.

"So, you're pissed off I didn't give you that story on a plate?" said Dan. "Is that what we're here for? I've been pretty busy you know."

"Pissed off?" The girl made a side-to-side gesture with her head. "Maybe. You could have given me something back when it would have made for an exclusive. Especially with the Novichok angle. Chemical weapon poisonings have got plenty of mileage. But that's not the reason for this little meeting. You promised me an article, Dan. In fact, you promised me two, and you haven't delivered either one. That's just poor form, Mr Bradley. And I happen to know that's not like you at all... so... I'm prepared to give you one more chance."

A faint sneer crossed Dan's face.

"Not like me at all? How would you know who I am or what I'm like? If you knew me, you wouldn't be trying to blackmail me."

"Blackmail?! Come on, please. This is a tea room. This is hardly thumb screws. I thought we were having a drink and a chat."

The young waiter brought Dan a tea in a fine china cup. Dan left it on the table and continued to look at Alice.

"But I do know you, Dan," she said, leaning over her cup and resting her face on her hands. The girl had almond-shaped eyes and a cherubic face with big soft looking lips. Not altogether undesirable. Quite attractive really, but the attitude killed the effect of her face. That bosom kept calling to his eyes, but Dan refused to glance. Instead he surrendered to looking in Alice Perry's eyes. It was the safest option of the two.

"You think you know me. How? From the libellous crap your predecessor used to write about me?"

"Almost. There was an overlap between us, remember? I worked alongside Gemma for a good while before I took over her job."

"I remember. You jumped into her shoes while her body was still warm, Alice."

The girl's face flickered at the bitter accusation. But her smile returned all too soon.

"I worked with Gemma for six months before she had her downfall. Because that was what it was. A downfall. A true fall from grace. She was the editor's favourite hack, until her sudden decline… a decline I could easily link to you."

"Or maybe it was linked to you pushing her out of her job, so you could take her place…"

"Nice try. But if Gemma had been at the top of her game, undistracted, there was no way she would have ever let that happen. And why wasn't she at the top of her game? Because of you."

"Fake news, Alice."

"No. I was a witness, Dan. I saw her work calendar then and I've seen it since. I saw her notes. She was a journo, Dan. She made copious notes, even when she didn't have to. You met with her more than once. I know you did. You met her alone. You took her for a drink. You even went to a hotel with her... a hotel, Dan. Together. Alone."

"That was for a job, damn it!" snapped Dan. "We were in the middle of a dangerous case. She forced me to take her with me."

"Forced you? To a hotel? Dan, Dan, Dan. I'm young but I wasn't born yesterday, and I've been worldly wise a long time. Gemma fancied you rotten, and you had your little fling..."

Dan growled. His eyes flared, and he looked around. "I'm telling you that's not true. You're taking two and two and making seven here, Alice. Just because you've seen a few random notes doesn't mean that I ever had an affair with Gemma Cassidy."

"An affair? That was your word, Dan, I didn't say it," said Alice, as if he had confessed. "Tell me. Does Eva know?"

"Eva knows I've been loyal. She knew all about Gemma. So, yes, she knows – now leave it there. You're way out of line. Way, way out of line."

"No, I'm not. I'm right on target, Dan. You see, Gemma Cassidy got involved with some very bad people not long after that. Then she ended up dead. And I'm wondering whether you let that happen... or whether you engineered it... so that all history of your fling could be wiped out."

Dan gripped the table, his knuckles turning white.

"Or... whether you simply made a mistake."

"Mistake? Gemma made the worst mistake of all. Let me tell you about it. Gemma Cassidy got involved with a ruthless bastard, so she could chase a story as close as she could get. That man was a killer."

"Oh? Because for a second there, I thought you were describing yourself. A little harsh. Because I don't think you're a bastard, Dan. Far from it. Do you see what I'm getting at here, Dan?"

"Apart from me?"

The girl laughed, then cut it dead.

"Not you. Just at what's around you. Trouble, intrigue, danger, whatever you want to call it. It follows you around like a cloud. You're a story in waiting, Dan, and I want a piece of that action."

Alice blinked at him, smiled and let her words sink in.

"A piece of what action?"

"Oh, I didn't mean..." said Alice. She looked almost flustered for a moment, but her smile returned too soon to be believable. "But seeing what happened with Gemma... if you think it would help grease the cogs of our working relationship, I'd be more than willing to, you know, break a few personal boundaries..."

The girl trailed a hand beyond her teacup towards Dan's half of the table. He looked at the invitation of her painted nails waiting for him to respond, but left her hand empty, exactly where it was.

"Nothing happened with Gemma."

"You kissed her, Dan. I know that much. The rest isn't in Gemma's notes, but the rest goes without saying." Dan saw the hand still waiting for him. He drew back away from it and folded his arms.

"What do you want, Alice?"

"To be your number one press contact. And more than that, I want you to give me stories. Insights. Exclusives. Stories follow you, Dan. You could have given me that Burton exclusive, but you didn't. Or the Novichok thing, but you didn't. You owe me, Dan. And the way I see it, I have the negotiating collateral to make it happen."

"Make what happen?" said Dan.

The girl peeled a lock of hair away from her eyes and tucked it behind her ear. She beamed at him. "To make you call me with news, as you get it. As you make it happen."

"You want a hotline? Is that it? Come on, get real."

"Dan, I know about Gemma. I know you had a hand in her downfall, maybe even in her death…" She waited, watching Dan's eyes for a response. His eyes drifted to the memory of finding the woman's body on the floor of a building high above the high street. An awful bloody scene, in every sense of the word. Alice saw his haunted look and nodded.

"See…? You can't walk away from that."

"Dangerous games are what got Gemma killed, Alice," said Dan.

"Hang on. *Is that a threat?*"

"No. It's a fact, pure and simple. I wasn't the one who killed her. But she kept playing Russian roulette with the wrong people. You really don't want to start copying her methods. I mean it, sincerely."

Perry's face flickered again. "Sincerely…" she said. But she covered her feelings with a smile.

"Dan. Let's talk turkey. You had a thing for Gemma. Fact. You kissed her. Fact. You took her to a hotel. Fact. Your partner doesn't know the whole story…" she said, pausing to read Dan's eyes. Perry nodded. "Fact. You're already print-worthy right there. I could make a decent story out of that with your profile alone."

"There. Right there, Alice. You're crossing the line," said Dan.

"But we don't have to go that route, do we?" The girl's open hand slid across the table and pushed Dan's cup towards him.

"Tea has soothing properties, so they say," she said.

Dan ignored the tea.

"The alternative is we build a relationship based on trust. You pass me the odd story, oh, let's say once a month. Keep it nice and easy. We meet and chat. That's how it'll work."

"And that's it?"

"That's it," she said.

"That's it," said Dan, finally. "And what about this dumb profile piece you want to do?"

"So long as you deliver, you can forget about that. That was just leveraging to get us to this point," said Perry. Her eyes glinted at him.

"We meet once a month?" said Dan.

"Or, as often as you like…" she said.

Dan shook his head.

"Was that a no? I could always go back and write the other piece I mentioned."

"It wasn't a no, Alice. It was an expression of disbelief at how low you people will go for a by-line."

"So, it's a yes, then?"

"For now. To keep you off my back, it's a yes. But you're wrong, Alice. Wrong about Gemma. Wrong about every part of it."

"But not about the kiss… or the hotel?" said Alice.

Dan turned quiet.

"Let's meet again, eh?" she said. "Next time, we'll make it friendly. And you can buy me that drink. You know, I'm looking forward to getting to know the real Dan Bradley."

"He's sitting in front of you right now, Alice."

"No. I mean the one Gemma knew…" The girl's eyes sparkled at him as she sipped her tea, then Alice Perry stood up, plucked a business card from her handbag, and scribbled a note on the back with a biro.

"My work number's on the front. But that's my home number on the back. Like I said, we may as well make this friendly. I know you're not averse to making friends."

"Alice…"

"I'll be waiting. Enjoy your cuppa."

She put her handbag over her shoulder and turned out through the door onto the seaside street. Dan's eyes followed the sway of her hips, before he realised himself and ground his teeth. The girl turned and looked through the window as she passed by and caught him watching. She smiled, and Dan caught the last hint of a wink on the girl's pretty, vicious little face just before she disappeared.

"Damn it!" said Dan. He smashed the pad of his fist onto the table and the teacups bounced into the air, sending a slop of tea across the table. The waiter stopped cleaning the counter and blinked at Dan. The big woman who owned the tea room emerged from the kitchen, put her hands on her hips and scanned the café for trouble, but Dan was quiet, keeping his anger in check. Alice Perry. In plenty of new and interesting ways, she had already become far worse than Gemma Cassidy. And with hardly a redeeming feature in sight.

"It was only a kiss…" muttered Dan under his breath. A kiss that should have never happened, and now it had come back to haunt him in the shape of Alice Perry. As sirens went, Perry was to be avoided at all costs. *Especially now.*

Shame she was the one with all the aces.

Seventeen

They rocked up at Shoebury at five to nine, not far from Uncle Ron's café. The long beach was virtually empty, give or take the odd straggler. The evenings were getting longer now, but the breeze which had been light and airy by day was turning into something more rabid. The kite-surfers must have known about the wind in advance, and the boys with the expensive coloured kites were no bigger than ants on the distant estuary waters. They raced one another and cut shapes along the waters, their wide arcing kites rocking and bowing in the air above. Kitesurfing. It wasn't a sport for Dan, although they were often fascinating to watch. But not tonight. Tonight, Dan's mind was charged with a thousand different feelings. Some were the memories he was busy trying to block – dark and shocking. Proberty hanging from a rope. A stolen kiss with a dead woman – a kiss which should never have happened. A bright blast in the darkness which knocked him flat on the nearby street. Alice Perry's confident eyes, the appeal of her cleavage and a cup of unwanted tea. Life was becoming messier than Dan felt able to deal with, yet he couldn't let any of them down. He knew Eva didn't exactly depend on him. Dan wasn't stupid enough to believe that. But she needed him almost as much as he needed her, he was sure of that. And then there were Joanne and the kid to think of. It was too much pressure. And now this… the beach at nine pm… Parker's latest poisoned chalice.

Dan stalked up the concrete slope by the last of the beach huts. At the top of the rough cobbles he stared down at the sand and shingle beach and saw the tide was further out than he had expected. The beach looked vast. But beyond the shingle the sand turned to endless brown silt. Thames mud which would suck your boot off before you could pull your foot back out.

"Are they here yet?" called Parker from lower down. Dan looked back at the old man. He looked puny and pathetic from high above, like the incredible shrinking man. Dan supposed a lot of that was down to his nerves. His voice was quaking, and anxiety was pouring off him in waves.

"Stay strong, JP. You're going to do the right thing tonight, okay? The right thing. I know you can do it."

"I said is she here, yet?!" he snapped.

Dan shook his head. "Not yet. But then, we're early." Dan looked right and left. On the right he looked out over the roofs of the beach huts and couldn't help seeing the navy-blue-gloss Victorian shelter – where the gunman had parked his car and switched off the headlights six weeks back. He looked past the blue shelter to the cars' headlights streaming down the seafront towards them, already glowing brightly in the fading daylight. But the light was still good enough for their purposes. On the left were the wide undulating greens, ponds and concrete relics of the old MoD area. It was an open space now, for the use of walkers. There were no more explosions. No more drills. And plenty of hills and dips to hide in. The truth was that Cadson could have been watching them from anywhere.

"So," said Parker. "Are you going to tell me the details of your grand plan now? Or do I have to walk in blind?"

Dan didn't need to ask Eva for the answer to that one. A Parker who knew too much was a risk.

"Blind," said Dan, saving Eva the bother.

Parker sniffed and trudged up the slope towards the beach, resigned to his fate. "Blind it is then…"

Eva, Dan, and Parker walked down the slope on the other side, until their feet crunched on the shingle. They stood on the beach as the sun stretched their shadows long behind them, cutting dark diagonals across the shingle. They looked around, watching the silhouetted dog walkers and the joggers in the distance, willing them not to come close.

"Okay. You can hear it," said Eva, looking at Jonathan. "We insist on a trade. Cadson won't want to do it. But he'll see he must, so he'll agree to it. When Dan has a hand on Amelia, he can have the USB stick. But not a moment before. Are we clear?"

Parker nodded, but he looked jittery. Eva took out her phone and glanced at the screen.

"It's nine. They should be here," she said.

"What? I don't get it," said Parker. "Where is he? Maybe he's planning to shoot us from behind the wall, and then he can come and do whatever the hell he wants…"

Dan's eyes tracked along the low concrete wall. His heart lurched. *A trap? A shooting?* It was a thought Dan hadn't considered, and it took him a moment before he realised it was absurd. Cadson wasn't a sharp-shooter. He didn't look confident with a gun. Besides, the pistol he had was no better than a peashooter. And with the plans he had for the Basilica Holdings data, he really wouldn't want the extra police attention.

"You know what to do," said Eva. Dan nodded.

"Here," she said, handing him the white micro USB and Dan flipped it over between his fingers.

"All this fuss, just for this dumb little thing."

"That dumb little thing," said Parker, "was the key to my life until you two ruined everything."

"Can you hear the violins?" said Dan cupping his ear, smiling. Parker shook his head.

Eva looked at Dan and dabbed a hand on his shoulder.

"Damn. I left something in the car," said Eva. "I'll be quick as I can."

Dan looked at Eva, his voice even. "You forgot? Then you better hurry."

"Oh dear. Your secret little purchase," said Parker. "Forgotten it have you? Best laid plans and all that. You had better hurry. If Cadson's coming he'll be here any second."

Dan nodded in agreement. "Whatever you do now, Eva, make sure you're not seen."

Eva sighed and nodded. "I'll be quick."

"Be safe," said Dan.

Eva skipped up the concrete slope towards the beach huts and disappeared between them towards the green behind. The moment she was gone, Dan's eyes tracked along the line of the beach huts. He saw movement in the middle distance, people moving along by the wall. Two figures close together. At first it looked like a romantic walk in the early evening. Then Dan saw it for what it was. They were close together, but they walked stiffly and the closer they got, the more awkward they looked. One man, shaven-headed, his arm hugging his girlfriend close and tight to his chest. The shaven-headed man looked their way, and even from a distance, Dan felt Cadson's eyes on them.

"It's them," said Parker.

"This is your moment, Parker. Your time. Whatever you do next is going to stay with you for the rest of your days, so make sure you make the right call…"

"I hope so," whispered Parker, shivering.

Dan looked towards the beach huts. Eva had crossed Cadson's path without knowing. There was a chance he had seen her. But the man was still a way off, and the light was quickly fading. Dan could only hope she'd gotten away with it. If not, they were all exposed, and all the components of the plan were not yet in place. If Cadson had seen her, the whole plan would soon go up in smoke. Dan watched, tense, unable to do a thing but stand on the beach beside the most unreliable man he had ever known. Cadson watched them the whole way.

He didn't bother with the cobbled slope down to the beach, just stepped over the wall, pushing Amelia before him. The girl stumbled and almost fell, and Parker lurched forward as if he intended to run to meet her, but they were still a good way off. Dan laid a hand on the old man's bony shoulder and pulled him back.

"Stay cool, JP. She's okay. Now keep your head…"

The old man shrugged off his hand as Cadson continued to force the girl forward until they stepped over the nearest wooden sand-break. The light was still strong enough to make out the distress on the girl's face. The anger in her dark eyes. And Dan caught a fractional glint of light sparkling on the weapon in Cadson's hand. Cadson saw Dan's eyes on the gun. Dan read a fighter's confidence in his eyes. They were getting near now. He saw the fear on Amelia's face and felt the energy in Cadson.

"You rotten old lying bastard," said Cadson. "You dangled a carrot, and then took it away. By rights I should shoot you and leave you for the seagulls. They've got more honour than you have."

"You handed me over to him – and kept the USB stick!" said Amelia. Her voice shook with indignation, it was half way between a scream and a roar of anger.

"No, my dear, I didn't. I gave it to him to save us both, but Cadson double-crossed me. We couldn't use the data, so I thought we could strike a deal and get him off our backs. He wasn't supposed to take you. He was supposed to leave you alone – with me."

"What?!" said the girl. Cadson smiled and let her talk. He looked amused as she shouted. "You didn't even ask me! You just did it! And look what happened. Now we've got nothing."

"Not true," said Cadson. "The old man has still got the data. But he wants you more, the idiot. Where is it then, eh? Where's that data stick?"

"He's got it," said Parker, nodding toward Dan. Cadson and Amelia turned their eyes to Dan and Cadson raised his weapon. The little silver gun blinked at him reflecting red light from the sinking sun.

"Does this silly old codger really think she'll go for someone like him?" said Cadson.

Dan swallowed, looked at the gun, looked at Cadson and nodded. "I think he does."

Dan looked from Cadson's eyes to Amelia. The rogue and the babe. They looked a good couple. He was handsome in a villainous way. The kind women tended to call 'a bit of rough'. Amelia was slender, attractive, and as devious as they came. He saw Cadson's point. She was far more Cadson's type than an ancient old man like Jonathan Parker's.

"Then the old boy's gone senile. This one is only out for what she can get. And what's he got now? Besides wrinkles and a very lairy suit? If he had anything worth having, she'd have taken it off him in a heartbeat."

"Yeah. And you're a real charmer with a heart of gold," said Dan.

"Hey. I'm telling it like it is."

The girl struggled in his hands. "Shut your mouth. You don't know me. You never did."

"No," said Cadson. "I had the measure of you alright. You were a gold digger. But then it turned out you were a thief as well."

"Don't talk to her like that," said Parker. "That girl is a million times what you are," said Parker. The old man's face shook with emotion. Dan was shocked.

"Well, will you listen to that. The old geezer's gone all romantic hero on us. Tell you what, Gramps, if your third-rate minder gives me back my data stick, you can have her. But I'm warning you, if she performs for you like she did for me, you should go and book your burial plot now. You won't last the night. Know what I mean?"

Cadson gave Parker a wink and the old man turned dark red. Amelia struggled again, and one arm got loose. She turned and slapped Cadson hard in the face. The rogue winced in anger. He snatched her long hair and yanked it down hard, forcing the girl to cry out in pain. Parker sprang forward and Cadson turned the gun on him. Amelia's face was pressed down towards the sand, but she sought Parker from the corner of her eyes. They were wide and wild.

"Jonny... don't do it, he'll kill you!"

"She's right. Don't push it, old man. Back off and I'll let you keep breathing. You there, Minder," said Cadson, calling to Dan. Dan felt the USB small and warm in the centre of his palm. He hung his fists loose and low by his hips and tried to keep his breath calm and even. He focused on Cadson's eyes, looking for the thing he looked for in the eyes of every opponent he'd ever faced. One crucial weakness. The way in. A chink in the armour. Cadson was arrogant. He was overconfident. They were weaknesses, yes, but Dan the man was still deadly...

"You've got the stick or what?" said Cadson.

Conscious of Eva's absence, Dan needed to play for time. Every moment's delay was precious. He needed her safe – and he needed her help too. Dan stayed quiet.

"Where is it?"

Dan nodded and raised his hand. He opened his palm and showed the small white stick pressed against his palm. Cadson's eyes lit up. A smile broke across his face. There was his weakness. His need for the stick, his greed. Dan glanced to the low concrete wall – just a momentary glance, hunting for Eva. She wasn't there, so he looked away. Cadson didn't seem to notice. Cadson shifted so he held Amelia with the gun tight against her hip. He reached out his spare hand towards Dan and beckoned him to come closer. "Hand it over, then we can all go home and get on with our lives. Come on. Don't mess me around."

Dan looked deep into Cadson's eyes. Beneath the excitement and the grin, he saw a dark, mean edge. But he felt it more than he saw it. Dan recognised it. The darkness in the man didn't bode well. Dan stood his ground and shook his head. They stood on the shingle beach where it sloped down towards the water, before it gave way to the smoother, finer wet sand and the line of black seaweed. Cadson had all the aces. There was no more than ten or maybe twelve feet between them and Cadson had the advantage of height and a gun to boot. The USB stick was all they had.

"I came here for that data, and you're going to give it to me now," said Cadson.

"It's a swap, Cadson. A swap, remember," said Dan.

Dan looked into Amelia's eyes, and saw the quiet panic in her wide black pupils. Dan offered her a faint nod of reassurance, but until she was free Dan knew it meant nothing.

"A swap, then," said Cadson. Dan watched the glint in Cadson's eyes, the mean and calculating grin. The man was planning something. But until the move was made, there was nothing Dan could do apart from limiting the risks.

"I'm going to pass it to you. Okay? I'll pass it into your hand, and when I do, I'm taking the girl from you. If you don't let her go, I won't release the USB. Are we clear?"

"Clear enough," said Cadson.

Dan stared into the man's eyes, wondering how he would play it. He swallowed on a dry throat. Cadson was revealing nothing, so Dan had to play it straight, and be swift enough to react to whatever came next. He looked past Amelia, beyond Cadson's shoulder and saw a shadow passing between the beach huts. It was Eva, small and distant on the pavement side of the beach. Time. Dan needed to play for time. And he needed to keep Cadson busy enough to forget that Eva was missing from their number. Eva was a way off, with the beach yet to be navigated, and the shingle beach was loud under foot.

Cadson beckoned Dan closer. Dan nodded once and stepped forward, the sand and gravel crunching under his foot. He stretched both hands out ahead of him, one presenting the tiny white micro-USB, the other reaching for Amelia's hand. The girl stretched her arm towards him, but Cadson yanked her back.

"First I get the stick!" he said.

"No. The same time, Cadson. The same time or it's no deal." Dan took another step forward and blinked at the gun gleaming in the man's hand. The sunlight was fading now, the sky beginning to turn a shade of magenta in the evening twilight.

Now the gun was as close as Amelia's hand. The closer Dan got, the more dangerous the gun became. Small guns weren't reliable for aim or power. A shot from one of them was often survivable, though most people didn't know it. But up close, the odds of survival dropped to almost nothing. Dan's heart pounded hard in his chest and he felt the sweat slick on his lip.

He switched his eyes from Cadson to Amelia.

"Here. Take my hand," said Dan. He leaned forward and wrapped his hands around Amelia's wrist and gripped it tight as he planted the memory stick into Cadson's palm. In Cadson's moment of triumph, his grip on the girl weakened enough for Dan to pull her clear of him. She stumbled with him down the steep shingle beach.

"You okay?" said Dan.

She nodded, but the panic was still evident in her eyes.

"Better now," she said, quickly, before she moved alongside Parker. Cadson kept the gun on them as he turned the little USB in his fingers.

"How could you do that to me?" said Amelia. Her voice was as sad as it was angry.

"It's not like you think, Amelia. I promise. He wasn't supposed to take you – only the stick."

Dan watched Cadson roll the USB in his fingers. The man was thinking about his next move. Dan felt it, saw it in his eyes. The decision making. The calculating of risks. So here it came. Crunch time. In the background, Eva swung a leg over the concrete wall and stepped quietly onto the beach. Dan returned his full focus to Cadson in the foreground. He fidgeted with the USB stick. Then he raised the gun again. Dan blinked his eyes shut and shook his head.

"He's not lying," said Cadson. "The old man here promised to give me back my USB drive. Which makes me glad I took you as well as the necklace, because he tried to con me. If I hadn't taken you, Ammie, who knows where you'd both be by now? But unfortunately, I think we've reached the end of the line. You shouldn't even know about this stick. None of you. This thing was supposed to be a secret."

"That was your own stupid fault," said Amelia.

Cadson shrugged. "Either way, it's too risky to have you around. With you out there, hating me, harbouring a grudge – well, I doubt you'd ever let me do what needs to be done. You'd rather blow the whistle than let me get away with this…" Cadson lifted the USB, held pinched between his finger and thumb. Cadson glanced at it oddly for a moment. Dan narrowed his eyes.

"That's not true," said Parker. "We won't tell a soul."

"I can't rely on any of that, especially from you. So, start walking. All of you. Back away, down towards the sea."

Dan looked at Eva, picking her way across the shingle beach. Parker must have seen her, Amelia too – it would have been impossible not to see Eva's quiet approach but none of them said a word. Eva stepped down cautiously, holding something down by her side, shaded by the failing light.

"But the tide is miles out, Cadson," said Dan. "You want us to walk all that way? You'll get your suit all muddy."

Cadson grinned. He kept the gun on Dan, as he fidgeted and flipped the memory stick between his fingers. His grin wavered again, his eyes glazed in a moment's thought before he put on his battle-face once more.

"No. I don't need you to go all the way. Just far enough. You can do some of the walking for me. The sea can come and finish the job later."

Dan raised his hands and backed away, walking down the wide slope towards the first hints of the slick silty mud. "You're going to kill us then?" said Dan.

"Sorry, pal. It wasn't exactly part of the plan. But I'm learning to be flexible on these things."

Dan moved back slowly. Parker edged back with him, Amelia following suit at the old man's side. They took a few more steps and Dan's boots began to sink into the watery sand, before Cadson stopped moving. They all stopped moving. Dan watched Cadson's face fall. The hand which had been fidgeting with the USB stilled. Further back, halfway along the beach, with a strained look on her face, Eva stopped her advance. Cadson kept the gun on them as he raised the USB in front of his eyes. He ran his index finger over the back of the smooth plastic surface of the miniature device and lifted it close to his face, then squinted at the stick and rolled it over between his fingers.

"Hang on a second…" said Cadson. His face drifting from suspicion to hard-eyed shock.

Cadson's finger traced a dipping line across the white plastic surface of the stick. He traced it again, his eyes flickering with doubt. But the dented line was there, no doubt about it. He lifted it close to his eyes until the indentation had caught the light. Where there should have been only a blank, smooth surface, a generic manufacturer's name had been left machine pressed into plastic. Shock turned to rage.

Cadson's eyes flared. He bared his teeth and howled.

"This isn't my stick. Where the hell is it! I'll kill you where you stand, all of you, one at a time, unless you hand it over now! Where is it?"

"It's okay," said Dan. "Don't shoot. Just give me one more chance, okay? It was worth a try, don't you think?"

"Worth a chance?!" sneered Cadson. "Hand it over. Now."

Eva was moving again, quickly now. Cadson was wild, incensed. The gun shook in his hand. Dan stepped forward, staring at the gun barrel the whole time, willing the man not to shoot. He dipped his hand into his pocket and licked his lips, then took his time as he rummaged in his jeans pocket, seemingly looking for something. One long moment later Dan smiled. He pulled his hand free and waved his empty palm at Cadson.

Cadson stared at Dan's loose empty fingers and his eyes flared.

"Give it to me now!" said Cadson.

"Sorry, pal. I can't give you what I haven't got."

Cadson roared and lifted the gun, aiming at Dan's face. On the beach behind him, Eva broke into a run. The shingle crunched loudly under her feet, and Cadson started to move, his eyes turning away from Dan. Cadson wheeled around, his gun seeking a new target, just as Eva got close enough to strike. She lifted the hidden weapon from her hip and swiped it up and sideways across the man's cheek as he turned to find her. The head of the rubber mallet crashed through Cadson's face, sending him down to the gravel with a groan of pain. Dan blinked at the mallet hanging from Eva's hand, and she shrugged.

"It was cheap," she said. "And Parker was buying."

"It worked," said Dan, before he dropped down hard on top of Cadson, landing a knee in the centre of his chest, drawing a fresh roar of pain. Dan pinned the man down and twisted his hand back around his wrist until Cadson was forced to release the gun. Dan pulled the pistol free and held the gun down against the man's cheek.

Parker raced across the sand and planted a shiny patent leather winkle-picker into Cadson's gut. Cadson groaned again and tried to roll away, but Dan pressed the gun hard into his face.

"Doesn't feel nice when the gun's on you, eh?"

"How?" said Amelia. She picked up the USB from the sand by Cadson and looked at it in the light. "You swapped the USB sticks?" said the girl, in amusement and disbelief.

"Yes," said Eva. "We bought a lookalike replacement," she said, as she raised the mallet in her hand. "Shame the USB didn't hold up under scrutiny."

"But it did the job," said Dan. "Just like that mallet." He nodded down at the black-headed mallet hanging loosely in Eva's grip.

"Another gift courtesy of Parker's last twenty-pound note," said Eva, with a smile.

"You should have bought a claw hammer," said Parker.

"I wanted to stop the man, not kill him, Jonathan," said Eva. "Besides, I didn't think your budget would stretch past two ninety-nine."

"And where is the real memory stick, Miss Roberts?" said Amelia, with a fresh glint in her eye.

"Oh. That's already been taken care of," said Eva.

The girl looked at Eva with a flash of doubt in her eyes. Eva nodded until the girl saw she was telling the truth.

Eva shook her head. "The police have it."

The hope faded from Amelia's eyes once more. The girl folded her arms and turned to face the sea. The wind picked at her hair.

"Don't worry," said Parker, drawing close to her side. "I've still got some money. The twenty grand remember?"

"Oh, I'm not worried," said Amelia. "I'm sure we'll survive... somehow."

"When I get out of this, I'm going to come and kill all of you," called Cadson from his prone position on the beach.

"That's enough," said Dan. He bent over and smashed a punch through Cadson's jaw, knocking the man unconscious, then stood up and shook out the pain from his hand.

"By the way, Parker," said Dan. "You haven't got twenty grand. You're still paying those Thai boys, just like we agreed."

"And then you're paying us too," said Eva.

"Paying you? Are you serious?" said Parker. "You confiscated our only means of making any money! You want paying after ruining the only chance we had?"

"Let me remind you, we just saved your sorry arse several times over, Jonathan. And we kept your man Cadson at bay, just like the doctor ordered," said Dan. "And you owe me some money for that appalling suit."

Parker shook his head. "Do you want me back in the gutter? Is that it?"

Amelia slipped an arm around Parker's narrow shoulders. She turned him to face her, leaving her fingers resting on his face. The old man was stunned to silence.

"Jonny? It doesn't matter. Pay them."

"What? But what about our plans…?"

Dan and Eva watched and listened, in quiet surprise.

The girl looked the old man in the eyes and planted a kiss on the Parker's cheek. Dan arched his eyebrows and looked away.

"Ahem," said Eva, coughing into her hand.

"I thought I'd seen it all," muttered Dan.

"You have now," whispered Eva.

The girl looked at them, appealing for their attention.

"He'll pay," said Amelia, finally. "Just give us until tomorrow."

"Does that translate as *just give you long enough to run away?*" said Dan.

Amelia shook her head. "You've doubted us for long enough. Just put us to the test."

"Been there, done that," said Dan.

"Then test us just one more time," said Amelia. "What have you got to lose?"

Dan and Eva shared a glance.

"One more time?" said Eva. "What have we got to lose?" She nodded at Amelia, and the girl nodded back in thanks.

Dan sighed and shook his head. "There goes our fee," he muttered, before he bent down to haul Cadson up over his shoulder. As he lifted the big man, Dan's stomach muscles protested, and he half-dropped the man's inert body back down to the sand. Not long ago, lifting a man like Cadson wouldn't have been an issue. Now it was an ordeal. As Dan reached down a second time, Cadson's suit jacket splayed open and Dan's eyes found the edge of a neat brown leather wallet poking over the top of his inside jacket pocket. Dan stared. He picked out the wallet, opened it and smiled as he ran his thumb over the smooth edge of a stack of twenties.

"Good news, Eva," said Dan. "Cadson here just volunteered to cover our fees for the case."

Dan pulled the cash free and slid the empty wallet back into Cadson's suit.

"Do you think that's wise?" said Eva.

Dan looked at Parker and Amelia, who seemed lost in their own private world. A world Dan didn't want to know about. "I think it's necessary," said Dan. "Besides, where he's going, he's not going to need any money for a long time."

Eva didn't protest. She shrugged her shoulders. With one final heave, Dan fought through the pain to heave Cadson up over his shoulder. Then Eva and Dan, Parker and Amelia trudged up the beach two by two, four slow-moving silhouettes with the wide mudflats shining brightly behind them in the late evening sun. Dan struggled for the entire walk, grim-faced at the atrophied, worn state of his fragile body. It wasn't supposed to be like this. He had never been like this. And the thought made him feel almost as alarmed as the one which followed. He would soon have to face a stronger man. A brutal man. The monster with a boxer's battered face. Someone far tougher than Cadson.

James Allen Cato – if that was his name. Cato… or whoever he was, had scythed him down with a bullet. A man so brutal that he beat poor Carl Proberty as he was hung. Dan reached the wall and dumped Cadson's body down onto the top, then he stuck his hands on his hips, and dragged in deep and desperate breaths.

"Are you okay?" said Eva, touching his arm. Dan nodded, but couldn't speak as he gasped for air and forced the pain out of his mind. As he recovered, Dan's eyes turned to the old man and his girl.

Parker was grinning from ear to ear. Arm in arm with a girl so young and stunning that she made him look like a museum exhibit, and Parker smiled on. Dan shook his head. It was an unbelievable sight, but it looked true all the same. Parker had been telling the truth. *They were a couple.* They were the oddest couple Dan had ever seen. From the corner of his eye, Parker saw Dan struggling and haggard from his exertion, taking in gulps of air with a wide-open mouth.

"It's old age," said Parker with a wink and an airy smile. "Don't worry, sunshine," he said, patting Dan on the shoulder. "It happens to us all."

And as the happy couple stepped over the wall to reach the pavement by the beach huts, Dan grimaced even more. From the corner of his eye, Dan saw Eva coming to give him some moral support. He knew Eva meant well, but Dan wasn't in the mood for pity. He looked at her and shrugged. "We got paid," he said, sniffing, and wiping his face with the back of his arm. "That's what counts, right?"

"It helps," said Eva, pulling up short.

"Then let's get this over with," he said. Dan stepped over the wall, and heaved Cadson back onto his shoulders. They headed towards the car. Eva watched Dan struggle on, a look of concern etched on her face.

Eighteen

It had been a few long days since Mark's absence had begun, and although they hadn't expected it, Joanne had taken to filling his shoes for two or three hours each day. The girl appeared at their office in smart work attire – very likely the same duds she wore for her part-time job at the Civic Centre. Sometimes Joanne appeared in the morning, other days she showed up unannounced for a couple of hours in the afternoon. Neither of them questioned her about it, but they always used it as an opportunity to ask after Mark's wellbeing. And on that score Joanne was happy to oblige. The answer was generally the same. *Mark was the same. He was healing, but still shaken up.* Dan could almost feel Joanne's eyes on him as she spoke. He didn't need to ask why she had taken to helping in the office. He knew the reason well enough already. Joanne was there to remind him of the promise he had made – the promise to make things right. Joanne was there to make sure he delivered. She didn't need to use words. Being there was enough. But at least she helped by fielding a few calls and making the odd cup of coffee. In truth, Joanne was becoming a natural fit behind the office front desk. Dan didn't say it out loud but if the kid wasn't going to come back, then maybe they already had someone to take up his mantle. Joanne knew the rough and the smooth, and from what Dan saw, she could handle both with relative ease.

He was considering the girl's potential worth to the operation as he counted the lilac twenties he'd plucked from Cadson's wallet. He laid the last note down on his desk, nodding as he counted eleven hundred and forty in his head. Okay, the sum was a way short of the fee they'd originally agreed with Parker, but it was still decent money, and it would have to do. Relying on Jonathan Parker had always been a gamble, one which had never been likely to pay off. When the office door chimed, and Joanne's voice sounded surprised, Dan's spell was broken. He stopped counting the cash and looked up in shock.

"Look who it is. Beauty and the beast," said Joanne, grinning. She looked from Dan to Eva. "I thought you said they weren't coming back."

"Then it looks like we were wrong," said Dan. Hastily, he shoved the stack of notes into his desk then locked the drawer and slipped the key into his jeans pocket before it could gravitate to Jonathan's hands. The door creaked fully open, and Amelia led the way, with a relaxed looking Parker following her in. The moody look had departed from Amelia's young face, replaced by a subtle smile. Instead of the denim shirt dress she wore a flimsy, bright summer dress printed with seagulls and pineapples. Quirky and colourful, it was designed for a far warmer climate than Southend-on-Sea. Meanwhile, Parker was on a dress-down day. His sleeves were rolled up to reveal thin tanned arms with liver spots and far too much silver hair. But at least the suits were gone. The old man looked happy too. In fact, almost too happy. Experience had shown that when Jonathan Parker looked this happy, it was generally at someone else's expense. Without realising what he was doing, Dan double-checked that the desk drawer was still locked.

"Jonathan. Amelia," said Eva. "Nice of you to drop by."

"I told you we'd be back," said Amelia. "You didn't believe us, did you?"

Eva smiled and tilted her head.

"No. They didn't believe us. Still, who can blame them, eh? We came to say goodbye," said Jonathan.

"Goodbye?" said Dan. "What about paying off those Thai boys? You've not told them we're going to pay them off instead, have you?"

Jonathan tutted. "No, no, no. Phee-Lau's brothers are all dealt with. They're probably on a plane back to Chang Mai as we speak. That is, if they ever intended to give Phee-Lau that money in the first place."

Dan looked at Amelia for verification. "It's true," she said. "That debt has been paid off."

The girl seemed to be telling the truth. Dan frowned in confusion.

"Eva, did you give the police the real USB stick when you gave them Cadson?" said Parker.

Parker's careful choice of phrase made Dan and Eva exchange a glance before they spoke.

"Why do you ask?" said Eva.

"Just wondering, that's all," said the old man.

"We did. We gave it to PC Dawson and PCSO Rawlins, so it's gone for good. I think Cadson and his contacts at Basilica Holdings are going to be in very serious trouble for some time to come."

"Interesting," said Amelia.

"Interesting why?" said Eva. Joanne drew up beside Eva and folded her arms, as if she was thinking the same thing. Dan looked at them. Joanne and Eva, the cynical detectives. They were cut from the same cloth, those two.

"Interesting because your police contacts can't have acted very quickly on what you gave them," said Amelia.

Dan frowned, wondering at her meaning, and the old man beamed. Before they could ask another question, Amelia took an envelope from her handbag and laid it on Eva's desk.

"Here. I believe this will cover the fee Jonny agreed with you. And I've added a little more to reimburse you for that suit," she added, looking at Dan.

"You're blasting the last of your money to settle your debts?" said Dan. "Respect, Jonathan. I never knew you had it in you," said Dan. "First you faced down Cadson and kept your cool, and now you're settling your debts. I've got to say, I'm shocked. You're going up in my estimation."

Parker gave him a crumpled smile "That's nice to hear, but all the same, it's not entirely true," said Jonathan.

"What do you mean *not entirely true*?" said Dan. "Jonathan?"

Eva regarded Amelia with a cool and intuitive eye. Eva smiled at the girl, and Amelia gave her a subtle nod, confirming what she had already guessed.

"Just don't tell us where this money came from, because I think it's best we don't know," said Eva.

"I think that's a very good idea," said Jonathan, nodding.

"But if I *were* to hazard a guess," said Eva. "I'd say this money of yours must be down to that super-computer memory of yours – the one Jonathan rhapsodised about when we first met."

Amelia's eyes twinkled, and she suppressed a smile.

"You remembered some of the payment details from that data stick. You had access to the information long enough I suppose."

"You don't want me to answer that, do you?" said Amelia.

"Maybe not," said Eva.

"Then let's just say I didn't remember everything. Only one specific line of data…"

"Such as the pharmaceutical giant you were targeting"

"You could assume that," said Amelia, with a smile.

"She did it!" said Dan. "Hey. Forgive me for asking, Amelia. But let's assume you hit one of those firms… that would make you pretty rich right now."

"You could assume that," said Amelia.

"So, assuming all of that…" said Dan, looking from Amelia to Parker with an inquisitive gaze. "What would be next for a girl like you?"

Amelia looked at Jonathan standing by her side. She looped her arm back through his and moved close.

"Do you mean '*what's next for us?*'"

Dan raised an eyebrow and said nothing more.

Parker grinned. "The world is our oyster, Danny boy. Sometimes, even things that seem too good to be true are still true nonetheless. I paid you what I owe you. Amelia and I are together. And now we're off to enjoy the best that the world has to offer."

"But that money. And where you got it from…" said Dan.

"Small print, dear boy, small print. Never read the small print. My life has been a lot more fun since I gave up reading the small print. Life's too short for that. Keep the money. You've earned it. Now, my dear, I think it's time we went before our friends ask any more questions, don't you?"

"Sounds like a plan," said Amelia.

The odd happy couple made their goodbyes, and left them with a long, fond wave. There was something deeply final about it. The time Parker took to wave, and the poignant look in the old man's eyes. For the first time, Dan felt like he would miss the man. He stood up and walked to Eva's desk, and he picked up Amelia's plain white envelope. He opened the unsealed flap. "Let's see if this is money or an IOU..." He pulled out a thick stack of more crisp lilac beauties, two of them bound in paper bank bindings with a £1000 printed on each.

"Well, what do you know?" said Dan. "We actually got paid."

"Those two still make me feel icky," said Joanne. "Think of the age difference. She's only a year or so older than me, gotta be. I'd never date a man that old and wrinkled."

"No. You prefer the younger ones," said Dan.

"Younger than you, that's for sure," said Joanne.

"Touché," said Eva, with a smile. "Now make yourself useful, will you, Dan?"

Dan frowned and raised an eyebrow. Eva picked up two empty red mugs from the desk and handed them to Dan.

"Milk no sugar," said Eva.

"I'm the same," said Joanne.

"You can say that again," said Dan. And as he walked to the kitchen, he made a point of walking just as slowly as he could. Resistance might have been futile, he mused, but he was going to resist all the same. For as long as he lived.

Nineteen

Dan slept fitfully. No matter which way he shifted, the pain in his guts seemed to move with him. Changing his sleeping position seemed only to alter the degree of pain – from steady, brain-thumping ache, to sharp, nerve-shredding agony. Dan blinked his eyes open and looked at the ceiling as he remembered hauling Cadson's unconscious body up the last steep slope of beach, the pain growing worse all the time. He remembered his determination to reach the beach wall before his body gave out. Well, he was paying for it now. He'd done himself a mischief and he would have to hope he didn't need another surgical procedure to fix whatever damage he'd done. Unable to accept such a steep and rapid decline he had forced his body to do what it used to do. Fool. And it wasn't only his gut which was in trouble, either. He was weak. The enforced lay-off from the gym and weeks of recovery had caused him to lose body mass and with it, strength. He recalled Greg Saunders' pitying looks and comments. Geller's too. Malachy hadn't mentioned his obvious decline, but maybe that was from kindness. Or because Malachy needed to believe that someone could help him, and no matter what state he was in, Dan Bradley was his best bet.

He reached for Eva, her breathing quiet and slow with sleep. He was tempted to touch her soft, pale freckled skin, for a mite of comfort, but he drew his hand away. It was selfish to wake her now. Just because he was struggling didn't mean she had to suffer too. Instead, Dan stood up and walked to the chest of drawers, his gut forcing him to hunch over to limit the pain. He pulled the drawer open and found a half-used strip of ibuprofen tucked in with his socks and boxer shorts. He used ibuprofen because they were supposed to reduce the muscle inflammation as well as stop the pain. In the old days, Vitamin I had been one of his favourite tricks to recover after a fight, or to help him through a long training run. Back then it was a trick. But these days Vitamin I was becoming a daily essential.

I wasn't good enough.

It wasn't supposed to be like this.

The thought rebounded through his mind time and again. Dan swallowed the pills dry, three of them – a dose of two like it said on the packet and one for luck. He grabbed his jeans and T-shirt and walked out of the room. Car headlights streaked through his slatted bedroom blinds and swept across the ceiling, one set then another, as the never-ending traffic passed. Dan ignored the wash of headlights and continued into the pitch-black hallway then turned to walk down the steps towards the office. It was almost four am. Far too early to get up without suffering an all-day weariness, and yet too late to stay stewing in bed. As the door to the apartment swung shut behind him, and Dan was swallowed into the blackness of the stairwell, a new wash of headlights struck the top floor ceiling once. But this time the reflected light didn't wash past and disappear. The bright light clung to the ceiling and slowed to a halt. And once it had settled, the lights blinked out to darkness, and the engine noise died. A car door clunked shut outside, and Dan didn't hear it. He walked out into the cool office, looking out on the safe metal shell of the shutters that protected the outer windows. The pinprick of green emergency lighting barely picked out the shapes of the office desks, chairs and computers. On instinct, Dan turned for the back kitchen, reached around the door and flicked on the light, heading for the coffee machine.

A shadow loomed and blocked the light through the gap in the front shutter. Dan added a third scoop of Italian blend into the filter before he heard the scraping sound coming from outside. His eyes opened wide and he froze, a chill feeling spreading across the back of his neck. The sound was close, metal on metal, something like the sound of a metal bar being dragged along the floor. Dan angled his head and looked towards the ceiling, listening more keenly. His breath froze in his lungs, and his heartrate started to pick up. Southend was a town that never slept. There were people of all kinds who might be up making noises at 4 am... Dan listed a few other reasons to stay calm, but it didn't work. *What the hell could have made a noise like that so close to home?* And another problem. The noise was so close he couldn't yet discern whether it had come from the backyard, or out front. He was still foggy from his lack of sleep. Dan waited, breathed, and heard no more. He dropped the rest of the coffee into the machine and he pressed down the lid.

SZZZCCHHHHHUFFFFFFD. There! Damn it. There it was again, loud and clear. Dan stared towards the front of the shop, looking towards the metal shell of the roller shutters through the glass. He blinked at them. He was safe enough from intruders, but he resented the fearfulness in is body. He hated it. He had never been dominated by fear. But he could feel the battle raging inside and fear was gaining the ascendency. Raw fear. He swallowed and shook his head as the coffee machine began to gurgle. Proberty's large fearful eyes filled his mind one moment, and then he saw Proberty's dead eyes the next. Saunders. Malachy. They were all afraid, but he refused to join them. Dan gritted his teeth and walked out across the cold office, ignoring the pain in his stomach, walking forward quickly as though hurrying could save him from the fear. It was bravado, designed to impress only himself. When he saw a flash of movement through the small rectangular gap halfway up the shutter door Dan stopped and stared. Movement, black in the blackness. Then a glint of something shining. Then an eye. An almost reptilian eye. The eye flicked left and right as it peered into the office, before it landed on Dan standing in the dark. Dan stared back and knew who it belonged to. There could be no doubt. He turned cold but refused to cower. Wasn't this what he wanted? To face the man? To know what he was up against. Yeah, but right then, it didn't feel like it.

"You're messing with the wrong man," called Dan, out loud. The eye stayed where it was, fixed right on him. His words sounded pathetic. Hollow.

"I mean it," said Dan.

The eye disappeared and was replaced by a flash of light reflecting from a metal surface. A gun?! Dan turned away from the door and launched towards his desk in the back-right corner. He yanked the drawer open, pulled away the paper covering he'd stuffed over the top of it, and pulled Cadson's sad little pocket pistol free. It was no match for the gun which had ripped his innards apart, but it was something. He ducked behind the desk and waited, waiting for the hole in the shuttering to be filled by a gun barrel. But the gun barrel didn't appear. He waited on. The metal shuttering rocked in the frame and Dan jolted upright in shock. The metal rocked and creaked, and he watched it bump and concertina upwards – the section which covered the door was being forced upward. A light started to blink on the alarm device mounted on the wall, but the alarm was old and needed fixing. And it offered no protection against a killer. Dan stepped towards the door. He was naked but for his boxer shorts, T-shirt, and the pathetic little pistol but he had to face the man. He knew it. There was no way around it. As the shutter rocked and was shunted up in the frame, Dan went to meet his fate. He slid the bolt on the door, shaking. He took a deep breath and jolted back as the shutter leapt up a half foot.

"This stops now," said Dan. He nodded to himself and returned to the door. He slid the last bolt back and flicked the snib off the latch. The shutter leapt up again, and Dan saw the shaft of the metal bar being used to lever the shutter higher still. Dan blinked at the man's shining black boots and solid looking legs. He took one more breath and pulled the door open, as a set of thick fingers reached beneath the shutter and yanked it high. Dan pushed Cadson's short barrelled pistol out into the darkness.

He found he was aiming it into the face of his enemy. Rough-skinned, pale, ugly as hell, with eyes so pale they could have been white, the man could have been carved in rock – desolate features set around two eyes which burned at him and mocked him in the same instant. Yes, he was scarred. He had face of a fighter. Dan recalled the outline of the man who'd shot him in the stomach, his silhouette picked out in the flash. It was him. *It was him.*

In the face of the gun, the man held his metal bar low by his ankles. Dan watched the man's arm twitch as he thought about striking him. He was weighing up his chances.

"Try it, and I'll end this now," said Dan. "I'll stick a bullet in that big head of yours. Hell, I know you deserve it."

The man nodded, as if thinking it over.

"Yeah," he said, his voice as gruff and raw as the scraping of the metal shutter ever was. "You could do that. But then you'd go to prison. And then you'd never know why. And you… you're an investigator, aren't you? At least that's what you're supposed to be, anyway. I guess it must have made up for the fact you couldn't hack it in the ring."

"*Who the fuck are you?*" said Dan.

"Heh. That's more like it."

Dan slid his finger tighter around the trigger.

"I mean it. You bastard… you killed Carl Proberty. For what? To show someone a lesson? Who are you trying to hurt here?"

"All of you. But some worse than others," he said. His mouth twitched into an ugly smile.

"I don't even know who you are. I'm nobody to you. I'm nobody to anyone," said Dan.

"That's not strictly true. But you won't be anybody soon."

Dan felt the threat. He got it. But he wasn't going to react. Not yet.

"You're hitting them all. Proberty, Saunders, all of Malachy's boys. Why?"

"You're getting closer. Which is funny. Because look at you, you're not going to be able to do a damn thing about it. You're finished… and you know it. Don't you?"

Dan pointed the gun closer to the man's face. Anger twisted into the fear filling Dan's body. He was worried he was going to pull the trigger. But the man didn't blink. The wind tugged at a coke can and dragged it noisily into the gutter behind them.

"You're a better actor than Carl Proberty, and Greg Saunders never even tried to hide it. But I can smell the fear on you, Bradley. I can see it in your eyes. At least you'll make it more fun than the others. Because at least you'll try. But it's going to end the same way."

"It ends with you being taken out," said Dan. "I don't know who you are… why you're doing any of this. Care to enlighten me?" He jabbed the gun at the man. The big guy stared at it and shook his head.

"Come on. Why don't you tell me why you shot me in the guts, eh? Why don't you tell me?"

"I don't have to tell you shit, pee-wee. But you can have this for free. It's high time all debts were paid."

"Debts?"

The man nodded and blinked at Dan, his pale eyes full of mirth.

"What debts?"

"No more questions," said the man.

"I'll be the judge of that" said Dan, fighting the cold on his skin and the weakness inside. "Because right now I feel like you owe me pretty big…" he pressed the gun closer. "Maybe I should collect. What do you say?"

"Don't kid yourself, Bradley. Don't believe your own hype. You're just another one in the tally. You're going down like all the rest. It'll end for you like it did for Proberty. And the harder you fight, the worse it gets – not just for you, but for everyone. The people you know. The people you care about. Maybe you should think about that before you start threatening me with that gun."

Dan reached out and pressed the gun against the brute's forehead. He was bigger than Dan, wider too. But a gun was a gun, even a stupid pistol like Cadson's could kill.

"At this range, you're dead."

"Maybe," said the man.

"What do you mean, maybe?!" said Dan.

"Then again, maybe not," the man swept his hand towards the gun and knocked Dan's hand away. Dan stumbled back, and the big metal bar swept up. Dan saw the metal rise and dodged as the bar swept the air in front of his jaw. He sucked in a breath and tried to aim the gun again. This time the man batted it clean away with the bar. The pistol arced up into the air and landed with a thud on the carpet behind him.

"Who are you?" roared Dan. "Why are you doing this?"

The man looked at him and dropped the bar to the pavement with a loud clank.

"I'm going to wipe them out. I've made you weak, little man. Now you can either accept the fact, and stand aside, and maybe I'll go easy on you. But if not, it doesn't end pretty. Not for you, not for any of the people you know. Not for that pretty little redhead you keep upstairs…"

Dan's eyes filled with fire. "Cato. Your name is James Cato."

"So you think," said the man, grinning. He turned away from Dan and walked towards the kerb.

"You don't frighten me. I won't back down. I won't do what Carl Proberty did. Or Greg Saunders. I'm here to stay and I'm coming for you."

The man turned around and looked him in the eye.

"Face it. Talk is all you're good for, Bradley."

Dan growled and ran out into the street, fists raised as he neared the big man's back. The man snorted and spun on his feet, raising his big arms high over his head to block the punches. Dan launched a wild volley of angry blows into the man's arms. The man twisted left and right to block every strike. Dan simply couldn't get couldn't get past them. Then he saw the man's pale eyes peer above his fists. *Finally, a way in.* Dan launched a punch, but before it could connect, a massive blow connected with his chin. His head rocked back on his shoulders and he slammed back down onto the ground. The big man shrugged and pointed down at him.

"That's the last time I go easy on you. Your bluff has been called, Bradley. Now back off and shut up before you get stepped on harder than the rest. The gloves are off. You heard."

Dan's head spun as the words filled his ears. He looked up and the shape of the man in the suit blurred back into focus as he turned away shaking his head in derision. As Dan sat up he gripped his chin and watched the man get into his car. He started the engine and slid the window down, then the man stared out at Dan and smiled as he pulled the car out into the street and bade him goodbye with a dismissive wave. "I'll be seeing you, Bradley. You get to decide how that goes."

The car pulled away with a roar. Still reeling, Dan stumbled back into the shop and shut the door. The apartment door beside the kitchen opened and Eva appeared, her red hair wild and messed up with sleep. But her eyes were wide and clear.

"What was that?"

Dan sniffed and dabbed his bleeding lip. "This has to end, Eva. This bastard has to go down."

"It was him?"

Dan nodded. "And he just declared war…"

Dan picked up Cadson's gun and hid it back in the drawer. Eva didn't comment. She reached for Dan as he moved past her, but he ignored her hands. Dan moved past her and ran up the steps towards their apartment.

"Dan…?" said Eva. She continued to watch until the door eclipsed him from sight. Eva paced around the office in shock and saw the ruined shutter by the front door. She looked out at the smooth metal bar on the pavement. Seconds later, Dan's feet thudded down the stairs behind her. He emerged from the door wearing black tracksuit bottoms, trainers, and a dark hooded sweatshirt.

"Dan? What the hell are you doing?"

"He's exploiting my weakness, Eva. He's trying to crush me from the inside out, just like he did with Proberty and Greg."

"Your weakness? He shot you in the stomach!"

Dan nodded. "But I can't let him win. I can't. Mark and Joanne are depending om me. Old Ed Malachy is depending on me."

"I'm depending on you, Dan. I want you to stay alive. Dan! Are you listening to me?"

Dan nodded but carried on heading for the door. "I still have to do this, Eva.

"Do what? Where are you going?" she said, as Dan opened the door.

"I'm going to the gym. Back to the boxing club."

"It's the middle of the night!"

"It's early, but I've still got keys, Eva. And if I'm going to have a chance of facing this guy down then I'll need to get my strength back. I have to get in shape. I can't wait another second. Every moment I wait, he wins."

"Calm down, you're just in shock. We can talk about it in the morning. We'll deal with this together."

"Sorry, Eva. I have to do this part by myself."

"Dan!"

He turned out onto the street and headed off with his kitbag over his shoulder, then turned right heading for the old Southchurch Boys Club. Dan hadn't trained properly in a year. He had been bedridden for a fortnight a few weeks back. His body had been patched and stitched back together on a wing and a prayer, and now he was going to risk it all. But Eva saw there was no stopping him. Exasperated, she knew there would be no sleep either. She turned for the kitchen, swearing under her breath, and went to the coffee percolator to finish making the coffee Dan had started. It was going to be a very long day.

"It'll be okay," she said. She said it again as she sipped the black concoction and locked the office door.

Epilogue

Dan turned the key in the old rusted lock. He had to try twice before the key finally snagged the tumblers and forced the door open. The squeal of the door hinge echoed into the cold darkness within. Dan was nervous to be back, but the adrenaline still coursed through his body and kept him walking. He reached for the light switch and watched it flick on, filling the stinking concrete shack with an electric buzz. The light hurt his eyes. Dan blinked a few times and looked around at the walls. The old fight posters mingled with a few new ones pasted over the top. Cheap and nasty looking notices, fight posters never changed. The Boys Club was the same as when he'd last seen it. The same old skipping ropes hanging up on the wall. The same fetid dirt everywhere he looked. Yeah... it felt like home. And yet he felt as nervous as when he first set foot in a boxing gym all those years ago. Because this time it mattered so much more. He didn't know if it would work, but with whatever strength he had left, Dan was determined he was going to give it his all. He looked at the torn, taped punch bags. He looked at the empty ring. Dan dropped his kitbag and headed for the whip-like leather skipping ropes hanging from the wall. It started here. It always started here. Hard work. Determination. And pain. He didn't have a choice.

It was the only way he knew.

And it was the only way out.

To fight.

To win.

To kill... or be killed.

There was no other choice.

To be continued…

Thank you for reading The Stone Girl

Can I ask a favour? If you enjoyed this book would you please post a review to let other readers know? Just a couple of sentences would go a very long way. Thank you - I really appreciate your help!

If you would like to access more great free novels, entire boxed sets, novellas and short stories, then you are cordially invited to join the Readers' Group at SolomonCarter.net. It's totally free to join. Once you're in I'll send you links to lots of cool stuff, I won't ever spam you, and you can quickly and easily unsubscribe at any time.

Harder They Fall
Bradley and Roberts series 5
Thrilling adventures featuring Eva Roberts & Dan Bradley, private detectives

1. Harder They Fall
2. The Stone Girl
3. Harvest of Blood
4. Last Man Standing (coming soon!)

More books from Solomon Carter

The Long Time Dying Series
Bradley and Roberts series 1
The first thrilling adventures featuring Eva Roberts & Dan Bradley, private detectives

Series list - in reading order
1. Out with A Bang
2. One Mile Deep
3. Long Time Dying
4. Never Back Down
5. Crossing The Line
6. Divide and Rule
7. Better The Devil
8. On Borrowed Time
9. The Dirty Game
10. Only Live Once
11. Behind the Mask
12. The Dark Tide
13. Lucky For Some

Luck & Judgment
Bradley and Roberts series 2
Thrilling adventures featuring Eva Roberts & Dan Bradley, private detectives
1. Luck & Judgment
2. Truth Be Damned
3. The Sharp End
4. Don't Go Gently

London Calling
Bradley and Roberts series 3
Thrilling adventures featuring Eva Roberts & Dan Bradley, private detectives
1. Rite to Silence
2. London Calling

3. Promise to Pay
4. The Pressure Zone

The Final Trick
Bradley and Roberts series 4

Thrilling adventures featuring Eva Roberts & Dan Bradley, private detectives

1. The Final Trick
2. Taste of Death
3. The Danger Room
4. Killers and Kings

The Darkest Lies
DI Hogarth series 1

A gripping detective crime mystery series featuring DI Hogarth and DS Palmer

1. The Darkest Lies
2. The Darkest Grave
3. The Darkest Deed
4. The Darkest Truth

Also, look out for **The Last Line** conspiracy thriller series, featuring Eva, Dan, Jenna and Harry as *The Company,* the Roberts and Bradley short read casebooks, **Flesh and Blood, Rack and Ruin** and **Two Wrongs**, plus **Black and Gold**, the vigilante justice series, featuring Simon 'The Man in the Mask' with Jess. All series cross-over and each comes with a free lead-in book. For more information or to access any of these free books, simply join the free Readers' Group at SolomonCarter.net

THE STONE GIRL

Harder They Fall Private Investigator Crime Thriller Series
Book 2

First published in Great Britain in 2018 by Great Leap

Copyright © Solomon Carter 2018

Solomon Carter has asserted his moral right under the
Copyright, Designs and Patents Act 1988, to be identified as
the author of this work.

This book is a work of fiction and except in the case of
historical fact, any resemblance to actual persons living or
dead, is purely coincidental.

Printed in Dunstable, United Kingdom